THE
UNTIMELY
RESURRECTION OF
JOHN ALEXANDER
MACNEIL

THE
UNTIMELY
RESURRECTION OF
JOHN ALEXANDER
MACNEIL

A NOVEL

LESLEY CHOYCE

Roseway Publishing
an imprint of Fernwood Publishing
Halifax & Winnipeg

Development editing: Fazeela Jiwa
Copyediting: Kristen Darch
Text design: Brenda Conroy
Cover design: Tania Craan
Printed and bound in Canada

Published by Roseway Publishing
an imprint of Fernwood Publishing
2970 Oxford Street, Halifax, Nova Scotia, B3L 2W4
and 748 Broadway Avenue, Winnipeg, Manitoba, R3G 0X3
www.fernwoodpublishing.ca/roseway

Fernwood Publishing Company Limited gratefully acknowledges the
financial support of the Government of Canada through the Canada Book
Fund and the Canada Council for the Arts. We acknowledge the Province of
Manitoba for support through the Manitoba Publishers Marketing Assistance
Program and the Book Publishing Tax Credit. We acknowledge the Nova
Scotia Department of Communities, Culture and Heritage for support
through the Publishers Assistance Fund.

Library and Archives Canada Cataloguing in Publication

Title: The untimely resurrection of John Alexander MacNeil: a novel
/ Lesley Choyce.
Names: Choyce, Lesley, 1951- author.
Identifiers: Canadiana (print) 20230461026 | Canadiana (ebook) 20230461042
| ISBN 9781773636399 (softcover) | ISBN 9781773636474 (EPUB)
Subjects: LCGFT: Novels.
Classification: LCC PS8555.H668 U58 2023 | DDC C813/.54—dc23

For Angela Parker-Brown (1972–2023)

PROLOGUE

IT PROBABLY WON'T SURPRISE YOU when I tell you that Death and I were sitting down at the kitchen table face to face for some time before one of us decided to speak. And it was he who spoke first.

"I suppose you are wondering why I'm here," Death said.

"Not in the slightest," I answered.

"I like to think timing is everything," he continued, ignoring my intended lack of interest.

"Well, I like to think you don't know a whit about timing. In fact, experience tells me you have a very poor sense of judgement when it comes to that area of expertise."

"And why would you say that?"

"Many years of watching good folks come to their final chapter just when the going gets good."

His mouth twisted into a crooked smile. "And when does the going get good?"

"Somewhere around eighty," I said. "Thereabouts."

"Thereabouts? Really?"

"Really."

It was an odd conversation, I'll grant you that. But the good news was my impertinence was enough to discourage the arrogant son of a bitch. He scraped his chair back and walked out the door into the harsh, windy morning, leaving the door to flap in the breeze.

CHAPTER 1

IT WAS IN THE MIDDLE of the dark night before that I stopped breathing. I was always a man with a loud snore according to my long-departed wife, Eva, and that particular night it must have ceased midsnore. Mick Gillis once told me that on a quiet night in the valley here, if the hoot owls were not too lively, he could hear me from all the way down at his place. I had even set up a digital recording machine that Sheila had bestowed upon me one dreary Christmas and digitally recorded more than an hour of my vocal activity while I slept. I turned the recording over to Angus Phylo, a young performance artist friend of Emily's from Halifax so that he could turn it into what he called sound poetry.

You see, the snoring is so loud and vigorous that it sometimes wakes me up. But waking up wasn't exactly on the agenda quite yet, you see. Death was.

So, to take you back to that frightening dark night, you should know that I was alone (as always), fast asleep with my snoring serenading the room when my breathing stopped. Since I was not at all awake, nor had I any intention of waking and dealing with the sad loneliness of the night, I lay there in a state of perplexity as to why my lungs had ceased to cooperate in the usual way.

And it was then that my heart stopped. I felt the final thud that sounded in my own skull like wet cement poured down on granite bedrock. And like many, I suppose, my somnambulant brain was in rebellion with the inevitable. *No. Not like this.*

Suffice it to say, I was at that point in my life, in many minds at least, beyond my expiry date. Well beyond it in fact, in so many of the petty minds and opinionated thoughts of our little town of Inverary, here on the shores of the Gulf of St. Lawrence on the blessed island of Cape Breton.

But, as noted, I, like so many, was not ready for the inevitable conclusion of my life story. You must keep in mind that my heart had been keeping up a steady tattoo for ninety years. What could possibly stop it now? Perhaps we all say that. Perhaps. Despite all evidence to the contrary, deep down we all believe we will never die until we actually do.

In my mind's eye, I had opted for immortality. Such an ego, you might say. Here is some old fart living in a rundown farmhouse in Deepvale, Nowhere Cape Breton, out hither and yon beyond a burgh of even the slightest importance on the so-called world stage, purporting to be immortal. Don't get me wrong. It is only a myth to live by. We absorb into our mental pores so many half-truths, balderdash, bullshit baloney, codswallop, hokum, poppycock, twaddle, mumbo jumbo, mindless malarkey, rubbish and lies in a lifetime, so why not hang on to a few ridiculous myths of our own making?

It may come as a surprise to you that so much would go through an old man's head upon his death on a random night in what would turn out to be a very fretful year.

But there it is.

I am sure some quantum physics egghead at Dalhousie University would explain that time is this elastic band, a veritable eternity that we the living choose to parcel up into little tidy packages so that we can live our ordinary lives in what we think is the proper order. And if that is true, then once you give up on exercising your lungs and your heart stops, you may well look forward to having a universe of endlessness to ponder whatever it is you care to ponder.

But that would be a hell of a lot of pondering. At first, I myself was mostly just surprised at what was happening. And curious, of course. Most of us, I suppose, fight the inevitable for as long as we can. Then, eventually, fatigue sets in and we drop into the river and float down into the sea.

But I've always been a fighter.

Why fight the inevitability of your own predestined death? you might ask. Hadn't an old cranky geezer like myself already lived longer than most any person in town? The only two I knew to be older were a couple of old women down at the Allan J. MacEachen Retirement Home. Florence Bonnie Halpern and Eleanor Pryde. Both over a hundred, sparring daily, and crabbing about the food and the hired help. Florence, or Flossie as I knew her, was her own version of a New Age (or Old Age, really) guru and Eleanor was a dyed-in-the-wool Bible thumper. Aside from those two beauties, I was the oldest. So that made me the oldest male in Inverary. Which, if you think about it, should have given me a privileged status. But that would never happen. To many, I'd always been a bit of a buffoon, heroic in my own buffoonery, but not an elder worthy of a second's thought.

Still, what was it in me that would deny death its dignified duties?

Sheer cussedness, as my own father would say, a phrase he often used in reference to an old mule that he kept for plowing up the field where he planted his beloved cucumber crop. Sheer cussedness, that would be me. Maybe that implacable mule was my real mentor when I was a child.

Let me return to the moment eternity came knocking. Tapped me on the chest and interrupted my breath, my beating heart.

Yes, there was a voice in my head. Because, if you must know, there is always a voice in my head. "That's the voice of the universe," Florence Bonnie would say. But Flossie was wrong. The voice was my own. Does that make me God? I doubt it. Does that make me the cooing voice of Mother Nature herself? Fat fool's chance of that.

No, it was just the cold clear voice of the cantankerous old man up on the hill. Me. John Alexander MacNeil, son of Alexander James MacNeil who was the mean-spirited son of Alexander Robert MacNeil and so on and so forth.

And that voice was announcing to the greater forces of the known and unknown universe that, not only was I not ready to die and get stuffed into that godawful black suit Eva bought me half a century ago, but I was *not going* to die. It was as simple as that.

My body had been more or less good to me all these years and I provided it with as much pleasure (within reason) that it was requesting and now I had a damn prerogative to take my stationary heart and demand that it continue to beat.

Which it did after I screamed at it with all my inner silent strength and a considerable amount of ragged-ass determination. You have to realize it was my big showtime moment to rebel against the natural nature of things. So I gave it all my all.

I'm sure you would like me to report that there was a tunnel and light at the end where Eva and brother Lauchie and all those others stood beckoning me to join them in paradise. But, as far as I could see in my desperate straits, there was none of that horseshit.

Instead, there was the master of ceremonies himself, Death incarnate. I could not see him. Not then anywhere, but I could sense that he was there. I believe I could smell him. I'm sure he had been stalking me before but had considered me to be too much trouble to take on. Now, on this pivotal twenty-first century night, the darkest of the dark, he saw an old old man beneath several layers of blankets, his body weary to the bone, his mind weak and vulnerable, all alone and as helpless as a frail old geezer could be. *Why not just take him out now?*

But, as you can see, I refused to let it play out that way.

So I stared down deep into the abyss of darkness, reached down into my own chest with my mind and commanded my heart to pick up where it left off. To get off its lazy ass and go back to work.

Now an old man's heart is not really all that accustomed to

taking marching orders from the brain, if you catch my drift. I mean, it was working on its own for all those years, its own captain with no other body part really trying to boss it around. And now this.

My heart must have realized that the request was perfectly in line with its own desire, so it slammed back into action and pushed off the hands of death that had so callously squeezed it into submission.

My lungs immediately realized that the vacation was over. No retirement and pension yet. They joined in the battle and decided that the delivery of oxygen, nitrogen and a variety of inert gases to the old fart lying flat on his back in the bed was in order.

And with that I woke up.

And no, don't go telling me it was just a dream.

Because the evidence was clear. By the time the light filtered in through the window and I stumbled out of bed coughing and cursing, there was that bastard sitting all smug and unwanted at the kitchen table.

CHAPTER 2

WELL, THE UNWANTED VISITOR GOT up from the kitchen table and walked out the door, leaving it wide open to swing in the early morning breeze coming off the Gulf of St. Lawrence and prompting the old rooster I'd named Jack and two of the laying hens to prance into the kitchen and start pecking at scraps on the old linoleum floor.

I made myself a cup of tea and tried to pretend that the whole shebang — dying, then returning to life in the middle of the night and then rising from bed to find Mr. Death or whoever that bastard was, sitting right in my house — had been the product of that possibly dodgy fish supper I ate too close to bedtime.

I had to admit to the chickens that it threw me. I was clearly off my game and maybe off my rocker.

But at least I was not dead.

In fact, I was now convinced that I had truly died and come back. Lazarus of the Maritimes. And I wanted to know who or what had provided the round-trip ticket to hell and back. If there was going to be a genuine resurrection in my old house, I wanted a fair explanation. And this insult of being presented with a seemingly flesh and blood man claiming to be the mastermind of all human endings, well, that deserved some serious cogitation as well.

But sitting on me arse thinking about it wasn't going to work. I needed some good solid advice and maybe that's why Florence Bonnie Henderson had come to mind. She was one of the very few people around who was older than me and she'd always been smarter than any of us. If the old Ford truck was willing to start, I'd drive into Inverary and pump Flossie with a hundred questions.

Well, the damn battery was dead on the truck, and I admitted to the old beast that it was better *it* had the dead battery and not me. So I had to charge it up, shoo the chickens out of my kitchen and feed them, feeling proud of myself for staring down Death and watching him walk out my kitchen door. But this fleeting and foolish moment of glory was immediately followed by a bout of feeling sorry for myself — an old man living alone whose wife had died so long ago.

All that worrying and whining took up most of the morning while I had the truck battery charging with the old five-amp charger. By then it was time for another cup of tea.

At that point, the truck engine blessedly cranked over and something about the dashboard reminded me that I no longer had a driver's licence, but I'd been driving without one for so long that, like so many other things these days, it didn't seem to matter. Driving down the old rutted lane, I noticed how much the forest had encroached on the laneway with such little traffic. And I must say, I was feeling a little light-headed in a good way. What I mean is that I was in a fairly good mood and excellent frame of mind for a man who might have been labelled deceased by a medical examiner at one minute and revived the next. For some reason, the chicken salad sandwich had convinced me to stop feeling sorry for myself. Or maybe it was that second cup of tea.

Anyway you cracked it, for a ninety-year-old wanker, I reckoned I was in mighty good form. Or so I told myself. And looking forward to a visit to the Allan J. MacEachern Retirement Home on the Green Park Wellness Campus. Mind you, there was no green park anywhere near there and it was not really a campus like you'd see at a Halifax university. And to be honest, there weren't a lot of well people to be found there. The so-called "retirement home" was a goddamn nursing home for frig's sakes. A hellhole for the heaven bound, as Florence said about the place because of the overly religious, self-righteous pricks she had to put up with.

As I pulled into the parking lot, I congratulated myself on having remembered the route here and having negotiated every turn and having stopped at every stop sign — of which there were not many.

When I turned off the engine of the truck, it almost felt like the old Ford was thanking me. Battery charged, a trip to town — what could possibly make an old pickup happier than that? Only thing I could think of would be a bale or two of hay in the back and maybe some class A gravel for the driveway but that just wasn't on the agenda today.

Millie at the front desk knew me, of course. "Mr. MacNeil. Finally decided to give up the lonely life of a bachelor and join in some social fun here at Green Park?"

"Even if I won the 6/49, I wouldn't entertain the idea this millennium or the next," I replied.

"Pity you think so little of our community," she said, but smiled so sweetly I wanted to pinch her check. "What brings you to town then?"

"I was hoping to have a chinwag with Florence Bonnie if I might."

"She wants us all to call her Flossie."

"I know that. Flossie then. Where can I find her?"

"Flossie would be in the Big Room. Today's Wednesday and social hour so you are just in time for the festivities." Each Wednesday they had a themed social event. Florence — Flossie — had explained all that to me before. "And what might the theme be today, Millie?"

"You're in luck. This afternoon it's Siesta Fiesta."

"Sounds thrilling," I said. "Okay if I just pop in?"

"Please do."

The Big Room lived up to its name. Big. High ceilings, a view out over the dunes and the blue, blue waters of the Gulf. The old fools of Allan J. MacEachen at Green Park were in various locations, some in wheelchairs, some reclining on sofas, some having a good afternoon nap in a row of La-Z-Boy chairs. The event was living up to its name. A few of the old wieners wore Mexican hats and everyone had a colourful shirt that looked like it had found its way to Frenchys from someplace tropical.

And everyone had a strange-looking drink in front of them. The sleepers as well as the socializers. I spotted Flossie on her lonesome by the big wall of windows. One of those drinks with a tiny umbrella in a funny-shaped glass was balanced on the arm of her chair.

I weaved my way as carefully as I could around the wheelchairs. "Florence, hello."

She smiled when she looked up from studying the cuticles of her nails. "John Alex. Damn."

"How are things?"

"Things? Well, according to the news, the world is going to hell in a hand job. Me, I'm as blissful as a baboon with a baby. And damn it, man, call me Flossie."

"Flossie then. When you were a teenager, you always wanted me to call you by your formal name. You wanted to be Florence Nightingale if I recall correctly."

"When I was a teenager, you were just what, a tiny thing? Still in diapers maybe. I could be wrong."

"Well, diapers no, I don't think so. But you were my babysitter."

"That I was. My God, I can still remember having to give you a bath. You must have really liked to be out rolling in the dirt. You'd get so dirty."

I actually recalled that I did like rolling around in the dirt when I was little. I don't exactly know why. It was so long ago, but vivid in my memory. And yet here I was reminiscing about childhood days with a woman who was ten years my senior.

"As I recall, your bath was a big galvanized tub and I had to light the cook stove and heat up the well water. Then set you in it.

A lot of work it was. But Florence Nightingale wanted to get the job done."

"I'm embarrassed to remember it all."

"You well should be. Allowing a girl like me to undress you and put you in the tub as you complained to high heaven. Jesus, John Alex, you had about the smallest penis I would ever see in this long lifetime."

"Well, I was only little. That's not fair."

"It was about the size and shape of a champagne cork. Not that any of us had ever seen a real champagne cork back then."

"Well, thanks for the memory."

"Well that explains it then. Can I get you a drink?"

"What are you drinking?"

"They claim it's a margarita. But I don't know. Whatever it is, they've measured the alcohol into it with an eyedropper."

"I'll pass then."

"Suit yourself." She raised her plastic glass and someone in a white uniform appeared with a pitcher and poured her another modest dollop of the stuff.

"I've come to ask for your insight into what happened last night while I was asleep and then a follow-up event that happened this morning."

Now I had her full attention. "I'm listening."

So I explained about dying and coming back. And then I paused, uncertain if I should even tell her about the guest.

"Go on, John Alex. Don't stop there."

"Well, then this man, this person, this, I don't know, apparition appeared at my breakfast table. He claimed — well, sort of claimed — to be Death."

"Like Death — like a single entity, appearing to be a human being?"

"He seemed very much flesh and blood to me."

"Go on. What did he look like?"

I wasn't exactly sure how to describe him. "Well, kind of like Mel Gibson and Russell Crowe mushed together."

"Russell Crowe and Mel Gibson. You mean like a gladiator rolled in with William Wallace."

"Somewhat. But dressed in modern clothes. Suit and tie kind of thing. A bit baggy but executive-looking. Or maybe looking like someone from the government."

"So let me get this straight. You say you died in your sleep, and it wasn't just a dream. You pulled yourself back from this so-called abyss, you woke up and had breakfast with this businessman who claimed to be the Grim Reaper?"

I nodded that she pretty much had it right.

So I guess I should explain why I was telling this to Florence Flossie Bonnie Henderson.

Two reasons, I guess. She was the oldest citizen in Inverary. I'd known her apparently since I was six with my minuscule penis and she was also the brightest and smartest of anyone on the island of Cape Breton. Flossie had grown up here and gone off to Montreal for her first degree at McGill, then moved on to Columbia University in New York City where she finished a PhD in Philosophy. She stayed on for decades to teach several generations of young Americans about ethics and the nature of reality.

"Then what exactly is your question, John Alex?"

"My question, I guess is, do you think these things are true? Or am I crazy as a loon?"

"John Alex, you've always been — well, not exactly crazy — but an independent thinker. Ever since you were that little boy rolling in the dirt. Why look for validation now?"

"But these two events seemed so real. You've studied these things — the nature of reality. So tell me what you think."

She took another sip of her drink and set it aside. "I think that you are not the first person to come back from death. Nor the first to encounter Death as a corporeal being. Literature is full of such encounters. As are medieval paintings and Ingmar Bergman films."

"But that was all art. Not real life."

"Art is often more accurate than real life. Fiction is often more truthful than facts."

I'd heard her speak like that before and it was a bit over my head.

"My roommate, Mrs. Pryde, would probably say you were visited by the devil but she believes any old thing it says in the Bible."

"You don't think it was the devil, do you?"

"Well, the devil is our own creation. If we believe in him, he exists. I doubt that your Russell Crowe-slash-Mel Gibson visitor was the devil. But there is corporeal evidence of demonic beings amongst us. Consider the American. They had been looking for a proper devil for many years and finally invented him in the form a Donald Trump whom they elected president and cheered on as he tried to destroy the nation."

"My visitor did not look like the American president. Or any American president."

"That's comfort to my ears. Still, you had your visit. And rest assured that, in nearly every culture of the world, there is a personified version of death. If you had more Irish in you, it might have been a banshee who visited you. A female of course. She could have even seduced you."

"I think I would be too old for that."

"Never say never. If you were a Bible thumper like Eleanor Pryde, you might have been graced with the Four Horsemen of the Apocalypse and then have to clean up after their damn horses tromped around your kitchen and shit all over the place. I could go on, but you get my point. You may not recall this, but I consider myself a student of phenomenology and we phenomenologists believe that direct awareness is the basis for truth."

"Now you're over my head again."

"What you believe to be real is real ... or at least might as well be real. So your Mr. Death was most certainly there. And just for the record, let me remind you that the appearance of Death as a corporeal being is not always negative. His job may well be to separate the body from the soul. According to eastern religions, that may be a good thing that we all would want. Assuming we have a soul. I myself am a skeptic."

"I don't know where I stand on that one but I'm pretty sure I don't want my body to be separated from my soul."

"Well," Flossie said, "some days I wish I could do just that. I'm old, young man, and finally feeling my age. And I have also recently been delivered some discouraging information."

"I'm sorry to hear that. What did you find out?"

"That new doctor came to see me and did some tests. Turns out I have ALS. Amyotrophic lateral sclerosis. Deterioration of the muscles. I was gripping your hand as hard as I could. Eventually I'll have a tough time swallowing or breathing. Can't say how long. The doctor said that it's bloody rare for anyone my age to come down with it. He says I might have cancer as well."

"Jesus, Flossie, I'm sorry."

She let go of my hand and waved it in the air, then used both hands to lift her drink. "Let's not dwell on it. What am I going to do? Start complaining life is cruel to me … at my age? Cheers." She took a long gulp of her margarita.

Flossie seemed almost amused now. "Ah, John Alex, you've made this afternoon, the Siesta Fiesta, so much more interesting. How I miss discussing the nature of reality with my students back at Columbia. But tell me this. Eva used to visit you long after she died, did she not?"

"She did. And I continued to set a place for her at our table long after her body was put in the ground."

"And why did you do that?"

I couldn't bring myself to answer but I could tell from the look on Flossie's face that I didn't need to.

"The Scots and the Welsh used to see black dogs come to lead souls into the world's beyond."

"No black dogs. I didn't see any black dogs. But the chickens came right into the house as soon as the unwanted guest had vacated."

"Ah, chickens. Well, that means you will have good luck."

But I knew she was only making that up.

"John Alex, I surmise you are not ready to die. Perhaps Death was just tempting you. I too have been tempted. Not quite like you but look around us here. Is this not one version of a living death? A purgatory, of sorts. I am probably more curious than the next person as to the adventure to come. Well, I use the word adventure. But the academic in me, the one wielding Occam's razor, wants to say simply, this is it. When it's done, it's done."

That really wasn't what I wanted to hear.

"Don't give me that look, John Alex. Remember, I used to give you a bath when your penis was only the size of a wine cork. I know you have lived a long and noble life and your life living alone is probably what brought dark company to your door. Should he appear again, perhaps you should listen to what he has to say."

"He was a bit annoying to be honest. A sharp sarcastic bugger."

"Why would you expect anything different? Be open to what might happen next. I fear we are about to embark on a much darker time in this plane of existence than what has come before. A kind of Dark Age, if you will. Maybe your visitor has made a courtesy call — selected you among the millions — to give fair warning. What was it Emily Dickinson wrote: 'Because I could not stop for Death, he kindly stopped for me'?

"Or you think of it this way, as Epicurus did. He said something like, 'If I am, then death is not. And if death is, then I am not.' But I must say, I find that dualistic mode of thought does not well suit the age we live in."

"You have my head swimming. Then why is it, Flossie, that you and I live on while so many others have passed on?"

"I hate to get all Socratic on you, but I can only answer with another question that has been troubling us philosophers since we've been able to reason. And that's this: why is there something instead of nothing?"

I looked around at the others in the room — the men asleep on the reclining chairs, the grey-haired women drooped over in wheelchairs. A few chatty old dolls sipping watered-down drinks. And Flossie, the fetching Florence Nightingale of my most youthful years, tending to my scrapes and bruises and even giving me a bath. The creases in her kind and wise face told a story of their own. Her mind was as sharp as ever, housed in the now-frail body of a century-old woman.

She had been of immense assistance to me with that conversation, even though I remained as curious and confused as ever.

A nurse walked in and rang a handheld bell, much like a schoolteacher in my distant youth who used it to call us in from the playground where we wrestled each other to the ground with regularity. "Siesta Fiesta is over folks," she announced. "Back to your rooms for a rest before dinnertime."

CHAPTER 3

IT WAS A RARE BRIGHT and windless afternoon when I walked out of the MacEachen home, shielding my eyes from the sun. Would I have been overly surprised if a pair of angels had appeared before me as I squinted into the light? Possibly not. I knew I had unfinished business of my own back home. Would that worrisome man still be lurking somewhere around the farm in broad daylight? Would he perhaps be looking for a convenient second chance to take me down?

It seemed likely to me that he would. He had struck me as the persistent type, a being who does not take failure lightly. But I for one wasn't ready for another stare-down with the bastard. I was pretty sure he would be back at a most inconvenient time for me. Besides, I was out in the world. I was looking for reassurance that I was still alive and not in some purgatory and imagining all this. Despite all that had come before in my life, I was a big fan of concrete reality. Despite the coaching from Professor Henderson, I just wasn't sure of where you were supposed to draw the line between what is real and everything else.

I guess I could have gone to the medical clinic and had a check-up, but they'd been wrong about my health so many times that it seemed pointless. Back when I'd fought off silicosis, they had me scheduled for death a dozen times. But I refused to accept it. Then the heart issues and a couple of false heart attacks. Stubbornness kept me going, as always.

Stubbornness and something else that no one could ever nail down. A fire burning within, still so strong that it would not be put out. Love was part of it, I knew. I was still a married man, in love with his wife even though she'd been gone for so many years. And whenever Eva appeared to me in my many dreams, she'd say over and over, "Not yet, John Alex. Not yet."

It felt good walking around town. But not as familiar as the old days. Things kept changing. I walked into the new Shopper's Drug Mart thinking that maybe I needed some vitamins. I'd read somewhere that a lack of Vitamin B could give you hallucinations. Or maybe it was Vitamin D. Sure, my diet wasn't as good as it used to be. And if I was going to keep warding off death, maybe I needed some vitamins. Or something.

But once I was in the aisle with all those little plastic jars of vitamin pills, I grew confused and weary and settled for a chewable multivitamin with a picture of Fred Flintstone on the label. I opened the cap with great difficulty right there and popped a couple. Tasted like the penny candy we kids used to buy at the old hardware store. Yes, they sold candy in the hardware store in those days.

I put the container in my shirt pocket not really meaning to steal it. I've been called many things. But never a thief.

That's when I spied the blood pressure machine sitting all lonesome in the corner. A perfect way to test that I was still mortal. I sat down before it. My reflection looked back at me from the video screen. What I saw was an old man, of course, not a corpse. An old man who had not shaved for a couple of weeks. I put on my glasses and leaned forward to read the instructions. Okay, put your arm into the proper place. Done. Push the button.

The contraption squeezed my arm and I nearly panicked but my reactions were so slow that by the time the news got to my brain that I had been apprehended by a machine, it was already letting up on its grip. I could still feel my own pulse in my arm.

Then the machine spoke out loud, "130 over 90. Moderately high." And a smiley face appeared on the monitor.

So there.

I popped a couple more of the chewable Flintstone vitamins in celebration. Moderately high didn't sound all that bad. That's when I noticed a young man in a white coat hovering behind me. I could see his reflection like a ghost in the now-blank computer screen.

"Everything all right?" he asked.

I turned to get a good look at him. "Why do you ask?"

"Well, you're sitting at the blood pressure machine. I just thought you might be worried about something."

"Of course. I'm always worried about something. Aren't you?"

He seemed baffled that I threw it back at him. I studied his face. He looked to be twelve. Maybe thirteen. "Who are you?" I asked. I know there was unintended harshness in my voice. I've tried to correct that many times but have given up. Young people are always crabbing at me about something because of my age. And I don't like it.

"I'm the pharmacist," he said. "Just trying to be helpful. Blood pressure okay?"

"Yes." I said. "The machine has given me a clean bill of health."

"That's most excellent," he said. He touched a couple of buttons on the machine and my numbers popped up. "130 over 90. Perhaps a tad high but good stats for someone your age."

I hated the phrase "someone your age" as much as if he had slapped me in the face. "How do you know how old I am?"

"I don't," he said defensively. "Look, I'll leave you alone. I was just trying to be helpful. Just be sure to pay for the Flintstones before you leave."

I'd forgotten about the vitamins in my shirt pocket already. "Indeed," I said, now slightly embarrassed.

As he was walking away, I asked him, "You got a name?"

He paused and turned back, pointed to the name on his lapel. "Bradley," he said. "Bradley Rasmussen, but you can call me Brad."

"You're not from around here, are you?"

"No. I'm from Ontario."

"Ontario?" I know it sounded more like an insult than a mere fact when it came out of my mouth, but again I couldn't help myself.

"What brings you to these parts, Bradley?" Suddenly I was the curious old bastard making small talk with the local pill pusher.

"Work," he said. "Why else?"

"Been here long?"

"Two months."

"Whaddaya think?"

"Think about what?"

"About here."

"I like it here."

"And why is that?"

"Everything seems more ... um ... authentic."

"Authentic?"

"Yes."

"You think this is the real thing?"

"Yes, I do."

I must have had a stunned look on my face. Others had mentioned this particular look over the last decade or so. I assume I am not the only old geezer who wore such a look. Once you hit that certain age, you're baffled by many things. I figured I was baffled by at least forty percent of everything I encountered.

He reached toward me with his hand and took the vitamins right out of my pocket. I was ready to clock the little bugger. He turned smartly, walked off toward his cash register at the prescription counter and did something at his computer. Then returned to me and put the vitamins back in my shirt pocket. "On the house," he said. "Drop back in if you need anything else."

I was about to walk out of there and be happy about the free vitamins but, aside from my morning encounter with you know who, I hadn't had much in the way of what you'd call social interaction. So I must have just sat there by that damned machine looking more than a little stunned.

"Are you okay?" Bradley asked.

"Well, that's a pretty big question and it's up for debate."

"I'm listening."

"Well, Brad, it's just that you don't know me and you're acting unusually, well, friendly."

"And that's strange?"

"Well, yes." After my morning with Mr. D, I was beginning to worry that I might have more supernatural encounters. And this was starting to feel like one. "So what's your angle?" I asked.

"No angle. New here, like I said. Trying to make myself useful."

"Why?" I now realized I was being a nosey old son of a bitch.

Bradley took a pen out of his white coat pocket and clicked it on and off a couple of times. "Well, if you must know, you remind me of my grandfather."

"Oh. Okay, I get it."

"He died."

"Of course."

"And then my father died. And then my dog died."

"Ouch." I scratched at my significant hair growth on the right side of my face. This is what old men do when they are concentrating on a stranger's hard luck story. "And then you moved here?"

"Not right away. My wife left me after that."

"Did you deserve it?"

"Maybe."

"It still sucks."

"It does."

I was afraid to ask more, lest the list go on. "Well, I'm sorry to hear of your difficulties in marital affairs. But you're young. You have your whole life ahead of you." Which wasn't exactly true but from my vantage point, he was very young and could regroup easily. "Maybe you'll meet a girl here." Girl, I'd been told was the absolutely wrong word to use nowadays for any female over seventeen.

"I think I might have found one."

"That's good. I hope it works out."

"Me too."

"Well, look, Bradley Rasmussen, you've been through a rough patch. I can see that. And you are obviously a kind person, at least kind to an old codger who reminds you of your grandfather. How'd he die?"

"Tractor accident."

"Farmer?"

"Yep."

"Sad way to go."

"I miss him. And my father too."

And he didn't have to add the dog, but I took that for granted. And maybe even the departing wife still grieved him, but I didn't want to go there. I was thinking about my own losses. "We lose a hell of a lot of things we love in this old life." *This old life?* Folksy. Very folksy. "Listen, I'll buy you a beer sometime and we can commiserate."

"I'd like that," Bradley said. "Now I better stop wasting your time and get back to work."

"Thanks for the vitamins."

"It was a pleasure."

Bradley Rasmussen turned and walked back to his perch behind the prescription counter.

An alarm of some kind beeped loudly when I walked out. Must have had something to do with the Flintstones and the fact I didn't pay for them. But I pretended not to hear it and no one came after me.

One of the privileges of aging.

CHAPTER 4

AFTER THAT I FORGOT WHAT else I had come to town for. I was pretty sure I needed something from the hardware store but decided to let it go and trucked myself on back to Deepvale.

Lunch was out of a can — corned beef sliced thick and tucked between two pieces of homemade brown bread with Dijon mustard. It was Eva who had introduced me to Dijon mustard. We went through quite of a bit of it back when she was alive. I couldn't taste the damn stuff without still tearing up a bit over the loss of her — and that was decades ago.

I half expected to see my unwanted visitor show up at lunch, but he didn't. Dinner also came and went and he was nowhere to be seen. So I was coming to the conclusion that maybe the whole thing was some wacked delusion. *He* was probably a delusion. Simplest explanation. Only it didn't feel that way. He had seemed to be very much flesh and blood.

Well, the sun set on what seemed like a day way too short to even call a day — but that was pretty common now. The only way to really stretch out time, I discovered, was to get good and bored. This, I felt, was one of the myriad ironies of life. If you are having fun or if something is downright exciting, time speeds up so that it wants to cheat you of the good stuff. But if you are bored out of your gourd, you could slow it right down to a crawl. Bloody hell.

I thought there was a good chance I might die that night, thinking the previous night was maybe just a dress rehearsal for the real curtain call. Just before drifting off to never-never land, I accepted this possibility with a stoic skepticism — if that is the right term.

But I didn't die. I woke up a couple of times from a dream

about dying but they were both just dreams. I was pretty sure the other thing was the real McCoy. By 5:00 a.m. I was ready for some morning coffee, concluding that maybe Death had come for me again, tried to take me, but found me to be such a tough old bird that he decided to move on to someone easier. Maybe someone down at Green Park — plenty of easy targets there. Or someone like Bradley's farmer grandpa or his father.

I fried some of the leftover corned beef with some brown eggs from my hens for breakfast and studied the dust motes drifting in the sunlight like it was a micro ballet. I listened to the CBC news about some kind of new flu in China. There was more trouble in the Middle East, a so-called political scandal in Canada that was not even newsworthy compared to what was going on in the States. And what else? Inflation. Job losses. Taxes. A candy store in Sydney robbed. Some fool driving his truck off the Causeway. And something about cryptocurrency which made no sense to me at all.

The world was going to hell in a hand job as Flossie had surmised. Maybe better not to listen to the damn CBC.

I left the door unlocked in case anyone should come to visit and I didn't hear them at the door. That included the unexpected visitor. My point being, I decided not to be afraid of him — whoever *he* was. Maybe it was a prank. I mean, who would expect Death to look like a mashup of a couple Hollywood actors?

I made a small plan in my head to befriend this Bradley person from Ontario. He was clearly in need of a friend — a surrogate grandfather or something. Most folks from Ontario who had moved here with some fool notion in their head that this was paradise were delusional in their own way. Maybe I could discuss my death and rebirth with him and get an Ontario pharmacist's opinion on it all.

One of my favourite pastimes since I turned ninety, I must admit, was napping. I had learned that here was a hobby for which you did not have to study at length, read any how-to books, or

look up on the damn internet to figure out. If they included napping in the Olympics, I would say, I could possibly win a gold
medal. Finally, here was something I was good at.

When I awoke from my nap, however, I heard someone washing
dishes in the kitchen. I lay there in a post-sleep haze thinking, yes,
the damned bugger has returned. And if I could have remembered
where my baseball bat was, I would have retrieved it immediately.

So I wiped the sleep out of my eyes and shuffled like an old
man into my kitchen. Instead of finding Death washing my dirty
dishes, it was Father Walenga.

"Ah. John Alex. I saw you were napping, so I wanted to make
myself useful."

Ever since Father Walenga had arrived from Cameroon to
become the local priest, he had been trying to make himself useful.
"Father, you don't need to do my dishes."

"Don't need to but want to," he said. "Back home, I always
helped my mother with her chores. Ever since I was a little boy."

"Well, I'm sorry about the mold on those pots. Been meaning
to do something about it but —"

"Not to worry," he said, cutting me off. "No need to apologize
about mold. God created mold just like he created you and me.
We're all in this together."

It was just like Father Walenga to put a positive spin on just
about everything under the sun. Having known the cleric for so
many years, I had begun to see how he had merged his somewhat
pantheistic religion from Cameroon with Christianity so that anything he considered "natural" was worthy of praise. He'd preached
a sermon once on algae and I came away feeling uplifted about
the green scum on my duck pond. He was that kind of a spiritual
leader.

"John Alex, let me put the kettle on for tea. I came to visit
because we have not spoken in over a month."

"Has it been that long?"

"Yes. I have you logged into my Outlook calendar. And this morning the computer-generated voice on my Mac said, "Father Walenga, you should visit John Alex today."

"Your computer told you to do that?"

"Yes, she did."

"And here you are washing moldy pots and boiling water for tea."

"I believe it is all part of God's plan."

Well, if anyone other than Father Walenga said that phrase, I may have punched them in the nose. But the good Father was a most gentle soul — at least when he was not defending old growth forests or protecting the diminishing habitats of spring peepers.

"Well, now that you're here, I do have something I want to talk to you about."

"Anything. Anything at all, John Alex. I am all ears."

So, as he poured the tea, I told him that I was fairly sure I had actually died in my sleep, that my heart had stopped and, after that, I willed myself back to life. "What do you make of that, Father Walenga?" I asked, feeling a little embarrassed about such a question.

He studied the steam from his teacup for a full minute and then tapped my hand. "It sounds like what you had was a near death experience. An NDE as they say now. It is not as rare as one might expect."

"Well, it's a hell of a lot rarer than I would expect."

"This I understand. Perhaps you were not ready to die."

"Whoever is?"

"I have known several of my own parishioners who were. Why are you so certain that it was not just a vivid dream?"

"Well, you see I woke up and had this guest in the morning." So I spilled the beans about the stranger and how he looked like those two movie actors.

Father Walenga just smiled. "Perhaps someone really was there but it was someone who was fooling you. Are you sure that it was not perhaps Mr. Gibson or Mr. Crowe. Mrs. Eleanor Pryde told me she saw Steven Spielberg in the IGA not long ago."

"No, I'm fairly certain this was not an actor, but then I suppose anything is possible."

"That's right, John Alex. Anything is possible. Back home in my country we have a love for things we cannot explain, while here in your country, the inexplicable can be troubling."

"So you suggest I simply accept this coming-back-from-the-dead event and that this person, this manifestation, was real."

"If it seemed real to you, why does it matter if it would be real to the next person?"

"I think I can see your point. But what do I make of this? Am I supposed to change my life in some way?"

"If you have come back from the dead and had a conversation with Death himself, I would consider yourself a very privileged person. As a boy, I nearly drowned once in the Makombe River. It was a very muddy river with a swift current and the rainwaters had swollen the river and swept me far from my home. I kept sinking underwater and coming up but finally I was too weak to struggle to the surface and, in my mind, I saw a very large spider."

"A spider?"

"Yes, we had very large spiders in our area. And the spider spoke to me and told me to reach my arm up high and wait for help. And so I did this. And suddenly a very strong woman with powerful arms pulled me out of the muddy water and threw me on the bank of the river. I looked into the eyes of this woman and thought I was looking into the eyes of a lion, and I fell unconscious. When I awoke, it was nearly dark and there was no one there. Until a very large spider crawled across my face and spoke to me. It said, 'I have saved you because there are many things in your life you must do yet. And now you must do them.'"

"The spider saved you?"

"Yes, well, the spider must have spoken to the woman with the eyes of a lion. Spiders are very powerful spirits. Even the Bible says that the spider is found in king's palaces. And then the very helpful spider, he told me to become a Christian so I could go to an island I had never heard of and tell people to protect the trees and to be kind to everyone and every living thing."

"And that's how you ended up in Cape Breton?"

"More or less. And John Alex, I must tell you that this spider, this *anansi,* is considered to be highly deadly. He was my version of death and he saved me."

"We call that irony," I said.

"I call it a miracle. But it was *my* miracle and I only tell you because of what you told me. So now you must make of it what you will."

"Well, thanks for the heads-up. You always seem to make more sense than the priests who came before you."

"Yes, I have heard that before. And that is why I had to leave home so many years ago and come to your island. I love it here, but I do miss my home. And the spiders do not speak to me here."

"It's true. They are very shy and quiet. But I can't say they have ever come to my assistance in a pinch."

"Of course not. Perhaps you have not needed it. Has *anyone* truly done you harm, John Alex?"

Well, yes. I did not want to speak it out loud. But death had taken away Eva so many years ago. And now he was coming for me. "I do have a list and not all can be forgiven," I said.

"Forgive and you will be forgiven. And now I must go. Peace be with you."

"And you."

CHAPTER 5

AS I WAS WALKING FATHER Walenga to his ancient Saab, he told me that maybe I should see a doctor, just in case something was really wrong with me. However, the nosey citizens of Inverary had been saying that very thing to me for several decades now. And, for the most part, I tried to avoid any dealings with the medical profession. He said that the town had a new doctor and that he was very modern and knowledgeable about many diseases none of us has ever heard of. This probably just meant he was good with the internet which seemed to be everyone's tool for self-diagnosis, financial advice, relationships, self-esteem, and even sex.

Not that I would have anything to do with it in this life.

* * *

The ensuing days slipped by as they do without the aid of internet advice on chicken raising, diet or visions of death personified.

But then there was this.

I woke up one morning and didn't know who I was.

The surroundings were familiar, but I didn't know my name. I thought I should maybe call someone on the phone but couldn't think of any names to call. I had some faces in my head. Eva among them. But she had been gone so many years now and her wonderful ghostly appearances had ceased as soon as the baby — her namesake, Evie — was born. Eva was wherever she was and I would not bother her for help.

But my two dependable feet still found the floor. One. Two. So I got up and walked outside. The smell of the salt air drifting up from the coast was comforting. The dew sparkled on the branches of the old maple trees. The overgrown field where I once grew an acre of corn, tomatoes, cucumbers and potatoes had gone back to the wild.

It felt good to be alive, even though I did not know who I was.

My old rooster, Jack, came out of the barn to see what I was up to and I explained my current situation. He saw that I had no corn for him, so he turned to go back into the barn with the hens who seemed to be sleeping in on this fine morning. I walked back into my house feeling baffled but thinking that possibly this was the new normal. Had I lost a large portion of my memory overnight? Was it a stroke?

Worse yet, it occurred to me, given the events of the past week, that I was now actually dead. I put some water in the kettle to boil and ponder this possibility. Ever since Eva had died so long ago, I had read a great deal about death and the afterlife. There were so many conflicting opinions and no real facts concerning where you go when you are gone. And, as the kettle boiled and whistled, it seemed to affirm that, if I was dead, you could still make tea in the afterlife. So I poured the water into the red ceramic teapot that Eva had herself brought into our marriage and waited for it to steep.

And that's when I had to pee very badly.

You'd think that this is a fairly common situation for a man in his nineties upon waking on any given morning but this was different. Taking a good long whizz, it dawned on me that I most certainly must be alive. I studied what was down in the toilet bowl and, I admit, I even poked a finger into the yellow liquid that had spent the night in my bladder.

And that was that, I said to myself, as I washed my hands. I was most certainly alive and peeing. So I went back to my tea.

Still not having a name to attach to myself, I toasted a slice of raisin bread and buttered it. All routine, all familiar. But why no name?

That's when I remembered that my name was on my old mailbox far down at the end of my driveway. Not that the old mailbox served any purpose other than collecting weekly flyers from

Canadian Tire and the IGA. But it would be easier to solve the current dilemma than anything else I could think of.

Besides it was a grand morning for a walk.

The rains had rutted the driveway but made everything look so fresh and renewed. Birds were singing overhead and, halfway there, I forgot why I was walking down my driveway. This might have caused another person to panic but not me.

Memory loss opens the mind to any number of charming possibilities. Perhaps someone of my age can say this and thus I am saying it now. After all, why am I here? is one of the great ponderous questions of all time, is it not? Shakespeare among a myriad of poets and philosophers spilled great quantities of ink over it. Why should I not take my small stab at establishing an answer?

But by the time I'd run it through the mill of my muddled mind in several versions, I was already at the road and there it was: J.A. MacNeil.

J.A.? MacNeil sounded familiar. Yes, I heard the voice of a classmate from grade three yelling something at me from the distant past. *MacNeil, you silly asshole, zip up your pants.* It was the young scoundrel, Larkin Trask. Larkin had grown up to be a fish plant owner in North Sydney and had made a fortune selling small fish to the Japanese while paying the lowest wages possible to his workers and cheating fishermen as best he could. He was a millionaire when he died and had received honorary degrees from both Dalhousie and St. FX for his accomplishments. He was dead, of course, as were most all my other classmates from the old Inverary District School. And it seemed ever so odd that it was his voice I could hear in my head.

I studied the J and the A a bit more closely and recalled that it was Eva who had painted those letters on the mailbox. This brought a tear to my eye, of course, and then I remembered tracing over those letters with a paint brush as they began to fade over the years. And that was enough to bring back her voice. *John Alex, I will always love you.*

Powerful words. *Always. Love.*

And the man she had loved had a name. My name. John Alex. John Alexander MacNeil.

I opened the old metal mailbox and, sure enough, it was stuffed with flyers from the last three weeks at least. But there was a hand-written note as well. Written in an elegant cursive hand as if with an old-style ink pen were the words *We will meet again.* Unsigned.

Prank, I told John Alex. A kid's prank. Like the old days.

Well, mission accomplished. What does a name really matter anyway?

I decided to do some more reading about memory loss and wondered if I could cultivate a selective process whereby I could remove bad memories and keep the good ones.

Bad memories, go. Good memories, stay.

But no.

Sad memories are keepers. Sadness has shaped my life as much as the happy times. Loss is a consistent theme as you get older and older. Those you love and lose need to stay with you forever. Or at least as long as your memory will allow.

By around eleven o'clock, it occurred to me that if I only kept my own counsel on all that was going on with me right now, I might lose touch with reality altogether. This had been a fear of mine for several decades now. And the decades flew by with the wings of eagles. Clearly, I was not meant to live forever but who to trust with my current situation?

Miraculously I found my little tattered address book and began to thumb through it. Perhaps I should call Emily in Halifax. We'd stayed in touch ever since her daughter — Eva, named after my own dear departed wife — was born in my home ten years ago. Ever since she was born, though, she was called Evie. Em had gone to Dalhousie for pre-med before she dropped out. All the while she had this on-and-off relationship with Brian — not Evie's father, but a good enough lad I suppose. Brian had once lived in the old hermit's shack in the mountains near Margaree. He'd never lost his tree-hugging idealism and I suppose that was to be admired. But before he had made his final exodus from Evie and Em's life he convinced Em that the whole medical system was controlled by big drug companies. So instead of going to medical school, she went to a college for what they call naturopathic medicine. She knew a whole lot more than I did about health and bodies and such but I worried about it. Little Evie had experienced breathing problems when she was a baby and sometimes she was still short of breath. When her mother told me she'd never trust her daughter to a doctor or a hospital and that she would not let Evie get any more vaccinations I was more than worried. With that in mind, I decided not to call her. I didn't want any of her so-called naturopathic advice.

I read through the many other names — so many had passed on. Old Doc Fedder, Lauchie, my devilish brother, and so many others. Sheila LeBlanc. She would be the one I trust. Sheila, who had once run the library's bookmobile around Inverary County, had herself written a novel called *Old and Crazy* about a lovable, wise and eccentric old woman living in rural Cape Breton who can predict the future. The book had been a huge success and made into a movie with Glenn Close.

Sheila had moved up in the world. But she was always there for me whenever I needed her kindness and wisdom.

Miraculously, she answered on the second ring.

"John Alex," she said with joy in her voice, affirming that I had indeed established my name. The reinforcement and hearing her voice elevated my morning to new heights. "So good of you to call."

"And so very good to hear your voice."

There was a moment of silence then — well, twenty seconds maybe — before she asked, "And to what do I owe the pleasure of this phone call?"

So I updated her about my death and resurrection, about the dubious stranger at my dinner table and about my current morning's memory loss.

Sheila, as always, was the kind of take-charge person that everyone needs, even an old loner like me. She had been there when Em gave birth in the middle of the winter in my house. She had remained a faithful friend and inspiration ever thereafter, even though I often failed to keep in touch with her.

"John Alex, this is all both fascinating and troubling. But we're going to look into this together." Just like the old librarian in her to want to get to the root of a good mystery. "I'm going to call that new doctor at the clinic and make an appointment."

"Please don't —" I began, but she cut me off.

"If you put up a fuss, I'll have you kidnapped and delivered to him in handcuffs."

It was a startling image but leave it to Sheila to be so dramatic. "I don't think —" I began.

"Then don't think," she insisted. "God damn it, John Alex, I have a bet going with Margaret Atwood that you will live to be a hundred. If I win, she will owe me an expensive lunch at the Algonquin in New York. If I lose, I will owe her a week touring her around Nova Scotia in a rental RV. I wouldn't mind the company, but I hate losing out on a bet. So I have an investment in keeping you alive. I'll call you right back."

And she hung up.

I sipped cold tea and soon enough the phone rang. "Today at 2:00 p.m. I'll pick you up and drive you there."

I was about to tell her that, if I must go see this new doctor, I would drive myself. But she'd already hung up. I then discovered that I was smiling. Despite my mistrust of the medical profession, despite having to go to meet some smarmy know-it-all new doctor, despite having to disrupt my peaceful contemplative day alone in my comfortable home. Despite all that, I was smiling.

CHAPTER 6

SHEILA DIDN'T LOOK TO BE a day over forty. She had kept her youthful good looks. The term I often used for her was radiant. Brilliant and radiant. That was her.

"John Alex, that's the same shirt you've been wearing for the last ten years," she greeted me as I sat down in her new-fangled electric car. It was a playful taunt, not an insult.

"Wrong. I've been wearing this shirt for at least twenty years. Off and on of course. Time slips by so fast, I hardly noticed."

As she began to back around in my yard, I realized the car made almost no sound. The lack of engine noise seemed very strange to me.

As usual, she was reading my mind. "You get used to the quiet after a while. You can buy a program to run engine noise through the stereo system if you feel you really need it."

"I see," I said.

"Brave new world."

"Is it?"

"Indeed. Listen, thanks for taking me up on my suggestion. Everyone likes this new doctor. They say great things about him. Holbrook is his name. Dr. Holbrook."

"Hrmmph," I responded. I had a million things I wanted to say to Sheila. After all, we had a lot of water under the bridge. But I chose to sit and listen to the quiet of this futuristic car as we drove to town.

The clinic was in a building that was new to me. I swear I hadn't even seen it being built. It was on the same location where the old company store had once existed — the bloody coal company that took your pay at exorbitant prices for the necessities of life. But that was long gone. And good riddance. But who had built this modern box of glass and brick anyhow? And when had that happened? Overnight. Or so it seemed to me.

Sheila parked in front and walked in with me. I was having second thoughts about the visit. It had been such a long while since I'd been to any doctor, and I'd avoided hospitals like the plague. Once inside, everything felt new and sterile and alien to an old fart like me. The receptionist was someone I didn't recognize at all. Another newcomer, I assumed.

Finally, after listening to twenty minutes of the most soulless music piped into the room, the receptionist said, "Mr. MacNeil, you can go in now."

The door closed and I was alone in the office with nothing but the hum of the ventilation system. No doctor. But, as I sat there scratching my unshaved jaw, staring at a poster of the human body — a human body without skin with all its muscles exposed, a real horror of an image — the door opened behind me and someone walked in.

He briskly strode past me and sat down at the desk in front of me.

That's when I realized it was him.

Shit.

"I'm Dr. Holbrook," he said.

"Like hell you are," I snarled. It was the very man who had sat at my kitchen table a few days before.

"Excuse me?" he said, only seeming a trifle rattled.

"We've met before, remember?" There was no doubt in my mind. Different clothes, yes. Now he had on a silly white smock instead of his baggy suit. But the face was the same — borrowed from those Hollywood guys and mushed together. The eyes were the same. Once you've been stared at with those eyes you never forget.

"No, I'm sorry, Mr. MacNeil, I don't recall."

Well, I figured, the game was on. "You sat at my kitchen table and told me my time had come."

"Your time?"

"You as much as told me I was ready to croak. And that I should give myself over to it."

"You must be confusing me with someone else. I'd never use that term and I'm sure I never sat at your kitchen table."

I looked around at the office now, waiting for him to give up the game. There were diplomas behind glass. Degrees from where? McGill. Western. University of London. "Nice office," I said, waiting for him to maybe drop the ball and let slip his true intention.

He cleared his throat and held his cool. Evidently, he was working on an Academy Award. "Well, I am sorry about this confusion but why don't we just get on with it."

"With what?"

"With why you are here."

"You know why I'm here."

"I'm sorry, I truly don't." Okay, I figured, I'd play along. But my mind was racing. Had Sheila known she was delivering me into the arms of Death himself? Was this new doctor the latest manifestation? Would this be it, right here and now? Was I about to be tricked into some kind of quick and easy medical death or was torture in my near future?

I took a deep breath and decided to play it through. "All right, Doc. Here's the thing. I'm certain that I died in my bed the other night. Died and then willed myself back to life. And don't give me that shit that it was just a dream."

"And this seemed very real to you?"

"Very real. And you know it. You were there."

"Well, if it seemed so real, then it clearly had an effect on you. So, in some respects it cannot be ignored."

Psychobabble. But I didn't say that.

"And then what happened?" he asked, as if he had not been there at all.

"I went back to sleep, asshole, and then woke up and there was this man sitting in my kitchen."

"Some man in your kitchen?"

"Yes, some man. He claimed to be Death."

Dr. Holbrook made a small cathedral of his fingers in front of his face and scrunched up his brow. "You had a visitation from someone who claimed to be some — representation of death."

"It was you."

"Someone who looked like me?"

We weren't really getting anywhere. I was looking for my exit. He detected I was ready to scram — or at least scram as well as a ninety-year-old man with creaky joints could scram.

"Okay, okay," he said, waving a hand in the air. "Just relax, Mr. MacNeil. This is interesting."

"So, is this your next crack at me? You somehow lured me into your den here and have some syringe ready to inject in me?"

He flipped his hands out and away. "No syringe. No needle. No injection. Remember, you called here to make an appointment."

"Well, it wasn't really me, but yes, I am here of my own free will. And there will be hell to pay if I don't walk out that door." I admit, *hell to pay* was probably an odd way of putting it.

"I can assure you, you will be able to walk out that door. I'm only here to help. As I have for many other patients in this town since I moved here."

I had to admit his Russell Crowe-slash-Mel Gibson acting job was convincing. "How many have you taken so far?"

"What do you mean, taken?"

"How many have died in your care?"

"I can't say. Not many. A few who were already old and ill passed while in my care as happens for any physician. But, Mr. MacNeil, this meeting is not about me or my skill as a doctor. You are free to walk out that door if you don't want my service. But *you* came to me."

"I did," I admitted.

"And now we have some sort of misunderstanding."

"We do."

"But I have to admit, I'm more than fascinated — well, a little baffled — but fascinated by what you are telling me. I'd like to hear more."

"More about what, goddamn it?"

He took a deep breath. "Okay, let me assume that you did have this nighttime experience — that you believe you died. That it was very real to you. And in the morning, this person — the one who looked like me — was there to tell you it was indeed your time to die. Why do you think this has happened? Have you experienced things like this before? Have you *seen* things?"

"Of course I've seen things."

"Things that may or may not have been there?"

I studied the roof of my mouth with my tongue. "Oh, I see where this is going."

"Look, I'm still getting my feet on the ground here. I don't know your background. You made an appointment and my staff said they didn't have a file for you."

"I haven't been to a doctor since old Doc Fedder died."

"The one they called Shaky?"

"That would be him."

Holbrook just smiled. I could have smacked him just then if I was quicker at getting my ass out of a chair.

"He was the real McCoy," I said in Shaky's defence.

"But Dr. Fedder passed on, what, nine years ago?"

I knew that was true, but it still hit me hard. It seemed like it was just yesterday that Shaky had kicked the bucket.

"Well, my point is, you haven't been to a physician for a long time, I don't have any of your medical records and I'm trying to get some kind of a portrait of your health."

"My health? I'm as fit as a butcher's dog. Ask anyone."

Holbrook unleashed a condescending smile and then took a quick peek at his watch, hoping no doubt that I wouldn't notice. "Do you live alone, Mr. MacNeil? Are you married?"

"My wife died."

"I'm so sorry. When was this?"

When is often a question that is impossible for me to answer. A year? Ten years? No, it had been much more than that. A very long time. But how was that possible? "A while back," I answered.

"You are now, what, ninety?"

I nodded. It was just a number after all. A goddamn number.

"Have you ever thought of moving into extended care?"

"What would you think if I put the tip of my boot up your arse?"

Raised eyebrows but nothing more.

We stared at each other for several long seconds. A tense game of poker. Gunfight at the OK Corral. The Cold War. *Détente.* Something like that. What *was* I doing here anyway? He broke the stand-off by picking up the stethoscope on his desk. "Do you mind?"

I felt like a little kid.

"I'd just like to listen to your heart. It will only take a minute."

I wondered if this was how he would do it. Pretend to be listening to my heart and then drive some kind of lightning bolt from the instrument straight into it. But the pugilist in me said this was *mano a mano.* I refused to appear frightened or weak. "Sure, Doc. Fill your boots."

He smiled. Approached. Like a good little boy I undid the top two buttons on my old flannel shirt. I felt the icy stab of the stethoscope as his even icier hand slid it down past my neck and under my T-shirt. I waited for the jolt. The killer shock.

I could smell his breath — minty, antiseptic. I closed my eyes.

Eva was there in the darkness. My Eva. Waiting for me.

Then nothing.

He slid the silver disc up out of my T-shirt and walked backwards toward his desk.

"So tell me, Doc. Am I dead or alive?" I was willing to go along with this charade that he was truly the doctor and I was the patient. It was becoming clear that if he was going to kill me, it would be bad form to do it here in his office, this doctor from away with his Hollywood looks.

"Most certainly alive. But I hear a murmur."

"My heart has always been strong."

"I can see that. A murmur is just a variation in the normal heartbeat. Aside from that, your heart is strong, I assure you."

"Thanks for the vote of confidence."

"But I really would not advise that you continue to live alone."

"Why not?"

Hands flapped outward, like wings. "No one should live alone," he said coyly. "And I am troubled by what you claim. That you believe you have died and willed yourself back to life."

Was that some sort of admission? Of course, Death would be most displeased with the idea that anyone could do such a feat when the dark doctor comes calling. "I'll consider your advice, Doc. I'll give it some real serious thought."

He knew I was bullshitting. But it looked to me like our little session was over. I put my two hands on the chair and tried to push myself up but I felt powerless. He was up to something, I could feel it. It was like the muscles in my arms failed to respond to my mind.

"Before you go," he said. "Let me get this straight. After your nighttime dream — the event where you believe you died and came back — you found a man at your kitchen table. A stranger. A stranger who looked like me."

"He was you."

Blink. Blink again. A turn of the head. A look at the portrait of the Queen on the wall. As if she was complicit in the conspiracy. "Can you spare a few more minutes? I'd like to change tack."

"Into the wind or downwind?"

"Diagonal."

"Pull in the sheet then."

"Okay. Now that you've got me ever so curious about you and your experience and the unlikely possibility that I was somehow there in your house — and keep in mind, I don't even know where your house is."

He was such a good liar.

"Just for the sake of argument, let's say I was there in your house."

I nodded.

"Why was I there? And if I was this manifestation of death you assert, why didn't I just do what death always does when the time comes?"

Well, that was exactly the question I was hoping to get an answer for. "Well, maybe because you came for me in the middle of the night — a coward's common tactic — and you succeeded at your task but I really did will myself back to life."

"Lazarus back from the grave."

"Don't get Biblical on me, Doc. But yes, something like that."

"Fascinating," he said. "Truly fascinating."

"Where did you say you were from, Dr. Holbrook?"

"I didn't say. But I'm originally from West Virginia. At least that's where I grew up. Coal mining country. Hard people. A hard life. I wanted out of there and far away so I went to university in Montreal. Then I moved around a bit but settled back there before coming here."

"So if you say you settled there, why did you leave? Why did you end up here?"

He was silent at first and then looked out the window. "I felt I was not appreciated there, if you must know. And I believed I was needed here. I heard there was a grave shortage of physicians. Now I hope I've answered all your questions." He sounded annoyed now.

It was then I noticed that the muscles in my arms had found strength and were listening to my brain. As were my knees and legs. Time to leave.

CHAPTER 7

SHEILA WAS LEAFING THROUGH A copy of *Chatelaine* when I walked back through the waiting room. I didn't say a word until we were back in her car. "Well?" she asked.

"Well, I need a drink."

"Okay. The Wooden Anchor?"

"That'll do."

It was only a few minutes past noon when we walked into the pub. All eyes were on us. John Alex and a woman many years younger. Idiots were still playing video gambling machines in the back. Losers were sitting at the bar nursing tall beers. It was quiet as a tomb. Where the hell was some Stompin' Tom music when you needed it?

We sat at a corner table that had the comforting smell of stale beer. The top of the table was notably sticky. I took a deep breath. Sheila was being as patient as a person could be. A young woman — too young to be in a bar, if you ask me — with partially pink hair walked over chewing gum ambitiously. "Whadda I get yas?"

"Could I have a Caesar?" Sheila asked.

The girl nodded. I noted the tattoos on her arms — two dragons woven around each other on one arm. A skull and crossbones on the other. Not a good omen.

"A beer, please," I said.

"Pilsner, IPA, stout, sour?"

Sour? Who would want a sour beer? "Just beer."

"Domestic, Foreign or Local?"

"Just get me a Moosehead."

She clucked her gum thoughtfully. "I'll see if we have some in bottles."

"Please," I said as she walked away, allowing me to notice the tattoos on the back of her calves. An eye on each calf, one winking.

"So, John Alex, speak to me. You walked out of that office like you had seen a ghost."

"Worse than that. But I'd rather not talk about it now."

"Okay. That's fine."

Good old Sheila. Always willing to keep her cool in the craziest situation.

The drinks arrived. Hers was some red thing with a string bean in it. I waved away the glass that the tattoo girl offered with the bottle. I took a slug. It was warm. What the hell?

"I don't know what I'm supposed to say about what you're telling me, John Alex. It all sounds a bit beyond crazy."

"It does," I said, feeling defeated by the truth of what she said.

"But it all has to add up to something," she added, slipping the long string bean out of the drink and eating it.

"But what does it add up to?"

"Well, I've always thought you were the sanest person in town, maybe in all of Cape Breton."

"But?"

"There is no but. I still think you are wise and compassionate."

"Thank you."

"But now this."

"Yes. This," I repeated, starting to lose my ability to formulate a complete sentence.

That's when I spotted Henry, the owner of the place. He must have spotted me as well, because he walked over.

"Out on a date, I see," he said, smiling that smile that had offset any doubts people had about him when he moved to town and took over the old Barnacle, inexplicably changing the name to something laughable.

"Not exactly," I said, but Sheila gave me a funny look.

"It is a date, you old scarecrow," she told me, and turning to

Henry, "I've had my fill of younger men."

Henry laughed. "Well, you can't go wrong with a gentleman like John Alex."

I cringed at the word. Never liked it. Never pretended to be one. "Henry, you were always a poor judge of character."

"Oh, I know a character when I see one," he said. Henry had been part of the ongoing wave of outsiders moving into Inverary. But he'd been in town for a few years, got involved in the Food Bank and curling. Likeable. Very likeable. He'd moved here from Hamilton, Ontario, where he said the crime bosses were giving him a hard time with his little bar downtown. "It's like I died and went to heaven," he'd said about his move here. And he learned early how to deal with the local rowdies and the old drunks. He'd grown up with violence in Beirut before his father moved the family to Canada. He'd seen his best friend blown up by a bomb he had picked up right on the street. I felt a special connection with him even though I rarely darkened the door of his establishment.

"I guess you heard about our robbery," he said.

"No," I answered. "A robbery? Here?"

"Yes, yes. Who could imagine such a thing?"

"Anyone hurt?" Sheila asked.

"Not badly. But young Jenko had a serious scare."

"Jenko? Byron's kid?"

"Yes. He's in the back eating his lunch. Perhaps I should let him tell his story."

Jenko had been one of several generations of punk kids growing up in Inverary who thought that giving grief to old geezers like me was a form of riotous entertainment. But like all of them, he'd grown up, found some semblance of a path in the world and I'd lost track of his progress. I couldn't remember if he'd actually been one of them who had given me grief. It all kind of blurred together — the memories of the many generations of young little scoundrels. But I'd survived it all and even outlived some of them who ended up in car wrecks or fishing accidents.

"Sure, send him out. I could use a good story."

Sheila was checking her cell phone. Didn't everyone do that now? I didn't care. I was glad she was here. The warm beer wasn't doing it, so I motioned to tattoo girl and surprisingly she sprinted over. "Maybe something a tad more tasty," I said. "A smidgeon of whisky maybe."

"A smidgeon coming right up," she said. I could tell she thought "smidgeon" was a funny word. And I'd been noticing that more and more. Language. It kept changing. I was from another time where we spoke a different language. I don't know which of the young punks said it but a while back, a teenage bastard of some sort had openly referred to me as a person "beyond his expiration date." Strangely, that thought had occurred to me more than once. Outlived my brother. My wife. A steady stream of loss documented in the *Pibroch*'s obituaries.

The whisky arrived. "Henry said it's on the house."

I nodded. I sipped. It burned. I sipped some more. Sheila was studying me now. "You're more beautiful than ever," I blurted at her.

She laughed. "Two sips and already you can't focus properly."

"Oh, I can focus just fine," I said. In fact, out of the corner of my eye, I saw the young man, Jenko, walking toward us. I could sense his off-putting attitude, an air about him, even before he made it to our table. Half of his head was shaved clean, the other half had a mane of long dark hair hanging down past his chin. He was nineteen maybe. Could be older. Hard to tell. He wore a black T-shirt that said "Damaged Goods" with and image of a plane crash and an electric guitar.

"Henry told me to come talk to you."

"Have a seat," I said, my thimble of whisky still raised in the air.

"What did you want to ask me?" he asked warily.

"I want to hear about the robbery," I said. "If you don't mind."

Jenko relaxed a little. "Not at all. Told the story a hundred times. It scared the shit out of me. You ever have a gun pointed at your head?"

I actually had on several occasions. "Rifles, mostly," I said. "A shotgun or two."

"Then you know what it's like."

"I have an inkling." Probably another word that wasn't in his vocabulary. "Go on."

"Well, buddy comes in here the other night. Not much older than me. But, like, wired, eh? Like tweaking out on something. Meth maybe. He walks in and he's got this handgun held like sideways in front of him like they do in the cop shows. I figure he's looped out of his mind. Doesn't have a clue what the hell he's doing."

I glanced at Sheila. It was like she wasn't believing his story at all. "Do you know who it was?" I asked.

"It was the devil. That's who it was. You should have seen the look in his eyes. Crazed. Insane. Strung out. I'll never forget the look. I could tell he was ready to blow someone's friggin' head off.

"So who's the lucky one that he picks on? Yeah, that's right. Me. It's like he just zeroed in on how scared I was. Pissed my pants right there. First time since preschool. Hot piss just gushing down my legs into my Nikes. Not good, I said to myself. Not good at all."

"We all get scared sometimes," Sheila said. "You had good reason to be panicked."

"Yeah, I was pretty sure I was going to die. And that look. I really thought he *was* the devil. Like in that Megadeath song. Anyway, I figured I was toast. So he looks around at the sorry buggers sitting at the bar and says, 'I'll blow his fucking head off if you don't all give me your money.' And he looks at Henry behind the bar and says, 'You too, Ali Baba.' Henry nods yes but the other assholes are sitting there with their beer glasses halfway to their yaps and don't do nothing.

"So once I stop pissing myself I start to shake. I'm thinking, I'm too young to die. I don't want to get offed like this. Buddy didn't like that and he starts hitting me with the handle of the gun. Says, 'I'm serious, motherfuckers. Put your money on that table there. You behind the bar, empty the cash.' Henry moves toward the cash register and the guys at the bar start to take out their wallets. It's all like slow motion. But I'm already convinced I'm going to get wasted. I have images of my mother reading me *The Cat in the Hat* when I was little. And I can smell this guy."

"Smell?"

"The drug probably. The shit comes out your pores. It's like sweat and shit and sulphur. And I keep thinking this maniac really is the devil. But he's not. I know that. Still, I know he's high so he could go Vesuvius anytime. He's got me in an armlock now and the gun is still against my head. I'm ready for it now. Nothing left to do.

"He starts to pick up a couple of the guys' wallets and then I see Henry duck down behind the bar. Next thing he's rolling an empty Bud Lite keg at us. The creep shoots at the barrel and misses and I stagger backwards. Then I hear the shot. And I know right then that bullet has my number. I swear I can see it like in the movies. More slow mo. Bullet straight at my skull. Right between the eyes, I figure. Then it all goes black."

Jenko was shaking. Probably just like he was then. I didn't blame him. I felt sorry for putting the poor bugger through the ordeal again. Sheila reached across the round table and put a hand on his shoulder. Henry arrived back at the table, still drying a large beer glass with a bar towel.

Henry pointed to the wall with the towel. A wooden anchor was hanging there and, beside it, the front end of a dory sticking out — some kind of decorative bar thing. He walked to it and put his finger in a bullet hole in the bow then tapped the very front tip of the boat. "The devil couldn't shoot straight. He missed Jenko, thank God. But Jenko smacked his head right into the dory. Out like a light."

Jenko took a deep breath. Henry continued. "The guy just bolted then. I told everyone to stay put. I called 911. Then out of the blue, the new doctor walks in the door."

It was either a cold shiver or a lightning bolt that ran down my spine. "Holbrook?"

"Yeah," Henry said. "It was like he knew something was going on here. He'd never come into my establishment before. I'd seen him around town but there he was. He walked in, picked up on the panic in the room right away. I was about to say, 'Check the kid, Doc,' but I didn't need to. He walked right over to Jenko there on the floor. Like he had some kind of ability to size up what was needed. One hell of a doctor, I'll tell you."

I looked at Sheila, but she just looked away at that foolish cut-off dory stuck onto the wall like the silliest thing I'd ever seen this side of Halifax.

"Why do you think he showed up right then?"

"It doesn't make sense. No reason, I guess. He was just there. He knelt down by Jenko and cupped his hand behind the kid's neck. Or no. Maybe he put his hand around the kid's neck. Thumb on one side, the rest of his hand gripping — tightly. Too tightly I thought. So I said, 'What are you doing?' 'Checking for a pulse,' he said, calm as a cucumber. Then he gave me a look that I thought meant the kid was gone. The guys at the bar were like groaning. Gabe Jarret was crying."

"But he obviously wasn't dead," I said.

"Holbrook tapped the kid on the cheek a couple of times. Nothing. Then he gave him a good smack but then put his hand — it was like a claw — on the kid's windpipe. I swear, he was about to squeeze. Maybe I was overreacting, but I didn't like the look of it. It was all so crazy, so unreal. I was reaching for my hand-gun behind the bar and he said, 'Don't even think about it.' And then he let go and gave me a funny look, like I had misunderstood. And he cupped his hand over Jenko's forehead, opened the kid's eyes and Jenko was back. He got conked out when he backed into the dory. That's all. I'm going to get rid of the damn thing. Put a big-screen TV up there like they have in the Halifax bars.

"Jenko was dazed and confused but that was all. He'd pissed his pants, of course, like he said but it all could have gone down much worse. And the doc, he just got up, walked over to the bar where I still had my hand on the gun, asked for a glass of water, drank it, said something like, 'It will all be okay now,' and left. All's well that ends well, I guess. I'd seen much worse as a kid back in Beirut. I just don't know what to make of it. Something a bit unusual about our new doctor maybe. I could be wrong. Well, the Mounties showed up and we gave them the story, but they didn't have much to offer."

Jenko got up and retreated to the kitchen without a word.

Sheila had finished her drink. "We should go," she said.

"Thanks for the whisky," I told Henry. "Tell the kid if he needs to talk, to come see me."

"Sure. He's been pretty jumpy since that night. Don't know if he'll take you up on it but he knows where you're at. Even the young punks like him could probably still take some ideas from you, John Alex."

CHAPTER 8

"THERE'S A METH LAB IN Southwest Mabou, if you can believe it," Sheila told me in the car. Then she had to explain what methamphetamine was and why anyone would put that crap in their bodies. The stuff makes people crazy once you get hooked apparently.

"Why don't the Mounties close it?"

"Not sure. Used to be the bootleggers they'd turn the other cheek to and look the other way. Now this. Maybe they're waiting for the guys who make the stuff to just blow themselves up. They say that the chemicals that go into it are pretty dangerous."

"So much I don't understand," I said.

"Maybe you shouldn't try to."

"The kid said that this guy with the gun was high but also that he was the devil."

"Don't even go there," Sheila admonished. "Did you see his T-shirt? Heavy metal kid. Death Metal they call it. Obsessed with death, evil, the devil. You wouldn't believe the half of it."

"But this whole death thing. Something is not right."

"I agree."

"What do I do if my visitor comes calling back to me?"

"I don't know. But if it's okay with you, I'd like to stay over for a couple of nights."

"People will talk," I said.

"Let 'em."

I hadn't had a woman in the house for a long time. But there it was.

For the rest of the drive, we talked about the baby she helped bring into the world on that icy day so many years ago. Em's kid, the one we named after my dead wife. Evie was now ten and going to a Buddhist international school in Halifax. Em was deep into her studies of God knows what that would allow her to be a naturopath — a natural healer as she explained it to me. They came to visit whenever Em could swing it which wasn't very often. I missed them both. Evie was a bright shining light in my sometimes dark life. The connection between the three of us would always be there. I'd taken Em in when her parents kicked her out. That was so far back but it seemed like yesterday. All of us old farts say it like that. Like yesterday.

Once at home, Sheila and I broke into a bottle of wine — her idea. Sat at the kitchen table playing cards, listening to the CBC. A bombing in London. Somebody mowing down pedestrians with a truck in Vancouver. Crazy politics in England. Melting ice cap. Right-wing nut jobs in the States. Some new kind of strain of flu or virus in China. The world really *was* going to hell. And the news always made it sound like it was about to get much worse.

"Sheila, do you think we're going to get through it? Or is it the end?"

"I think it's the same old, same old."

"Right." I touched her hand. "Thanks for staying. But I'm not sure why you're doing this."

"Guardian angel," she said.

"I knew it." But I also knew it was just a saying. Not many like Sheila left out there, I was thinking.

"Can you take me to the old settlement?" she asked.

I hadn't been there in at least five years. It was an hour hike up the mountain and back into the forest on a trail that was long overgrown. "Sure. Now?"

"Now."

"I'll get my boots."

The first part was easy. Up the overgrown rutted forest road.

But it was sad to see how it had been defiled by ATVs gouging away at the stones. I didn't say anything about it though, tired for once of being a cranky old man. When we hit the clearing where the old Gillis house had been I pointed up into the sky where two eagles were cavorting. Dancing, Eva and I used to say. The two of them soared and circled and then locked claws and spiralled slowly downward only to break free and glide with their long wings. "Eagles mate for life," I said out loud even though I knew that Sheila was well aware of this.

"Not always," she said, breaking the spell.

I wanted to disagree but I was pretty sure she was right. Nothing was "always."

"First time I saw them do that I was a kid," I said. "Somewhere up near Chimney Corner with my cousin Alistair. We'd go walking in the woods for a whole day and our parents wouldn't think a thing of it, except for the fact we were goofing off. Not doing our chores and all that. The forest was our backyard even if we were miles away." I was thinking again about me being "past my expiration date" or whatever it was.

My legs felt pretty good. My head was clearing. I had this kind person beside me and silence all around except for the sound of birds on the branches in the light north breeze. Too good to be true, the old cynic in me hinted. Or maybe I was truly gone from the old world and this was what you get to do in the afterlife. If there is an afterlife. Best not to ruin the moment.

We walked on beyond where the ATVers had turned their sights on Margaree. The trail was well overgrown as expected. Strangely, my memory in finding our way to our destination was sharp as a knife. Overgrown it was, yes. But I remembered boulders along the way. Once I had given each a name: Superman, Bunyan, Big Tooth, Hairy, Cramps, Jesus, St. Peter. All men for some reason. Each with its own special personality, lichen colony and moss.

And I recognized each small brook, smaller now as if diminished with age. And the trees — the ones that had been big many years ago, now looked older and frailer. But, despite my many doubts, my mind and my feet found their way. I looked at Sheila but she was lost in reverie. For me, time had come to a blessed stop.

When we arrived to where the old settlement once existed, I should not have been at all surprised. The forest had continued to do its work.

"Highlanders," I reminded her. "Refugees. Wanted to be up here high on the mountain, not down by the shore where life would have been a hell of a lot easier. They wanted to be away from that world, not with it. Those are my ancestors."

We stood on a small embankment, a swelling of the ground on four sides that had once been a foundation.

"They had their families and they had God. I reckon that's all they needed." Sheila probably knew more about the history of this place than anyone around here.

"Wouldn't it be nice," I heard myself saying.

"It's the name of an old Beach Boys song," she said, smiling.

"Beach Boys?"

"Sorry."

"Let's poke around. I used to come up here with Alistair or Lauchie and we'd find things. Fragments of old tools, plates sometimes. I found an old buried shoe once but couldn't believe it went back that far. Each time we found something we made up a story about the person it belonged to."

"Stories are good."

Because of my recent frame of mind, and my current obsession with my nighttime trauma and morning encounter, I started to think about what it was like when someone died here.

"They were hard people, I would guess," Sheila said. "They'd lost their homes, their way of life, probably loved ones. They'd been put on unreliable ships and sent off across the ocean. They trusted no one. They were deeply religious but intolerant of other beliefs. And I think they were hard on each other."

I nodded. The visions Alistair and I had created were much different. Carefree, brave, fun-loving, happy in a way no one could ever be in the twentieth century. Pure fantasy maybe, but it was our fantasy. "When it was your time to go, you just died. That was all there was to it," I accidentally added out loud, my mouth betraying my brain.

"No, idiot. You got sick and you suffered and you waited for God to take you. And then your clan mourned you."

"That doesn't sound like any fun." We were poking around with sticks now in what was once a basement. I tapped something solid and it didn't feel like a rock, so I reached down into the soft dark soil. It was the top half of a clay jug of some sort. It had been glazed somehow, which meant it had probably come over with them from Scotland. I spit on it like we used to do in the old days and wiped it with my hand. Some markings that I could not make out but it was clear to me what it was. "So they did have some fun ... while living that is."

"Whisky?"

"I assume so. Would have been double the alcohol what we have today. And I'm sure they would have made their own right here. Supply from the old country wouldn't have lasted very long. They drank it because the Bible said nothing against whisky. Not a word. Jesus had never tasted a drop. Pity."

"But at double the alcohol of what we know, it would have been potent."

"Probably. And God would not have stopped any man from indulging."

I held the artifact up to the sunlight. Sheila must have seen a funny look in my eyes.

"What?"

"Being here, holding this, I feel connected to them."

"You probably are. Do you know your genealogy? The MacNeils. Could be that jug belonged to your great-great whatever."

"No, girl, I don't go for that bullshit. I can feel the connection, but it's not because of the blood in my veins."

"Ancestral memory maybe. Who knows?"

"More bullshit. But this," I said, holding the artifact even higher, "this tells me more about the ones who lived here than any genealogy chart. Makes me feel even more connected to the past." I'm not even sure why I said it but there were many words and sentences that just leaped from my mouth.

"Explain."

Damn her for asking. But it was my own stupid fault. I handed her the piece of the past to hold. "Feel it," I said. She took hold of it and brushed some more dirt from the outside. "Objects remain when we are gone. A favourite cup, a spoon, a letter from the one you loved. They don't change, do they? But they meant something to you. And then you are gone. Like my parents. Saved that spoon, that cup. And the letters from my mother written when she was young in the most beautiful script I'd ever seen. But the words were sentimental and not at all like the mother I knew."

"People change."

"People change but objects live on. If preserved, they are that window into the past and it's a window into a very different world. Don't ask me where that spoon is or those letters. Tossed out, I expect. And all of us are just these tiny candles in the vast dark, alight for such a short time and then extinguished."

Sheila gave me a look — holding back some kind of comment. I knew how that sounded — poetic, sort of, smarmy, geezer philosophical. I took that clay jug, what had remained of it, and studied the jagged edge where it had been broken off. It was strangely sharp. The glazing had held its own all these years. Some potter in Oban perhaps a couple of centuries ago had done good work. If I were to root around in the ground here, maybe I'd find the rest of it. Take it home and glue it back together. But that didn't feel right.

I settled the thing on top of a flat rock and picked up another heavy stone the size of a loaf of homemade brown bread. I raised it over my head and like some primitive ancient brute brought it down as hard as I could on the stubborn reminder of the past. The sound of it breaking was somehow odd and unexpected. The shards were still quite large. It didn't completely shatter. It had been reluctant to give up its form. So I bashed it again while Sheila looked on in disbelief.

When I was done, after a silence, she asked, "Why did you do that, John Alex?"

"I don't know," I answered. "I honestly don't know."

CHAPTER 9

I TRIED TO DISSUADE SHEILA from staying over, I really did. I never fully understood what it was with that wonderful person who always seemed to be there to look out for me. I never truly understood *her,* to be honest. I met her first when she was working the bookmobile for the County. I swear it was her sweetness that turned me from a hick into an intellectual. I read every damn book she told me to after Eva died. She'd pull that big old rig into town and arrive at just the exact time listed in the *Pibroch.* And I'd be there when the door to the library monster opened. Yes, it had been painted up as a sea monster by her own hand so that kids would find it fascinating. Hell, I found it fascinating. And her too.

Why she was interested in me, an old man even then, still perplexes me. She'd have a small stack of books for me each time and I was expected to read them before she returned. Mostly writers I'd never considered reading. Albert Camus. Fyodor Dostoevsky, Dylan Thomas, Robert Burton, Theodore Dreiser and Marcel Proust. Tough sledding, some of that. But I'd read it if she said I should read it.

Some of the old boys would see me carrying my reading for the week into my old truck and let out a hoot. "Pussy-whipped," or something worse somebody would yell. I'd give him the finger as soon as I could pile the books onto the front seat of the truck and go looking for the fucker but whoever it was had always vanished into thin air. People around town were still a bit wary of me back then. Afraid, some of them. Crazy old coot. Now look at me. Still crazy but still living my life as I see fit.

Well, Sheila and I stayed friends — or whatever this bond was

— ever thereafter. When the County cutbacks came, they canned the bookmobile. Tearfully, Sheila told me she was going away to Toronto to see what life there was all about. I felt abandoned, but she wrote me letters that would arrive in my old mailbox down at the end of the driveway. Long letters with words I'd have to look up in the dictionary that sat on the shelf with Eva's old cookbooks. I'd read those letters at night sometimes over and over, marvelling at the handwriting and the language. The woman should have been a poet. Instead, she ended up shacked up with some computer wizard guy ten years younger than her. Said she didn't know quite why, but the two of them started some kind of internet company that offered dating services to lonely folks all over North America. She claimed that he had the technical know-how, and she had the people-savvy and research skills. But then they took the company public (and she had to explain that to me) and it was big. So big that buddy got some wild ideas about expanding into some of the darker corners of the internet. That was when Sheila knew it was time to get out. So she sold her shares of the company and suddenly found herself wealthy. Wealthy and wanting to drop lover boy in the toilet and head on home.

I must say I was glad to see her back in the neighbourhood. Bought the old manse in town from the Catholic church and started living the life of Riley.

And that at least had something to do with why she was always hovering in the wings, trying to watch out for my boney old ass. And so, here she was, asleep in what was once Eva's old sewing room, doing what? Staying on in case Mr. D showed up again. We'd had a long hike, however, and after dinner and a bottle of wine that she said cost over a hundred dollars, I saw she took a pill. Said she had a hard time sleeping ever since Toronto. Nothing too potent. But some kind of sleeping pill nonetheless. She said I could wake her if anything odd happened in the night. But I wasn't so sure.

Well, sleep is a funny thing. A guy like me can nod off at the drop of a hat. But I stayed up after Sheila and her beautiful droopy eyes slipped off to the sewing room. I listened to CBC radio real low and registered the news about the American president proving he was more of an asshole than even I had expected. And then something about China again and the new bird flu or some such malarkey. Terrorists lurking in the most unlikely places. Global warming conjuring up hurricanes and tornados like no one has ever seen. Black people being shot dead by cops. All the same stories, but always with some new twist, some new flavour. Never was a news junkie but now it seemed like we were all headed … somewhere. Best not to think about it.

I brushed my teeth and thought about shaving since I had a guest, ya know. But realized it would be too much trouble. And I didn't have any decent blades. Only old ones that were dull and would probably wreck my pretty complexion. Instead, I lay in bed and conjured up Eva — the first time we met. The first time we kissed. The first time we made love. And, of course, she was the first woman — hell, the first person — who really loved me. You never get over that. Ever.

I could have dozed or maybe I was still awake. I thought I had locked the door — not that it was much of a lock — but maybe not. When I opened my eyes and the image of Eva as a teenage girl faded, I heard the door creak and footsteps on those old pine floorboards. I lay there, not breathing for as long as I could hold my breath. More footsteps — someone, Sheila, I guessed, turning on the tap, shushing water into the kettle, setting it on the stove. I assumed she wasn't as conked out as I had thought. Left it at that. Tried to drift off to snoozeville.

But then the sound of someone humming something. Not a woman. But a man.

I shoved the covers off, jammed my boney feet into my slippers, threw on my old flannel shirt and wobbled as I stood, the blood draining too quickly out of my head. I reached for my glasses right where I had left them for once. A dim light from the kitchen allowed me to see my way. I would have grabbed something if I had the forethought to keep a weapon handy in my bedroom — an axe maybe or even my old baseball bat. But I decided it was just my wits I had for whatever was about to unfold as I shuffled forward.

And yes, there he was. Turning off the stove, pouring the hot water into the teapot, the one Eva had brought into our lives when we married in those most ancient of times. He turned slightly, acknowledged my presence but didn't say anything at first. Nothing in the slightest threatening about him, but there could not have been a more unwanted guest.

"There's an art to steeping tea," he said as casually as he could. He was dressed in what I'd call a business suit. Something new. Something pressed. No wrinkles. He was wearing a red tie like you see on the American politicians. He was wearing white socks and I spied his pointy-toed, polished black shoes by the entrance way.

"Yeah, I realize that," I said, as matter-of-factly as I could. "You boil the water and throw in the goddamn tea bags and then go have a pee and by the time you come back, *voila*."

"*Voila*," he repeated.

"Dr. Holbrook, right?"

He held the pot and swished it around until some of the tea splashed out the spout onto the dull pine boards of the floor. "Oops," he said. "Sorry about that." Then he wiped it up with his sock. "But no, maybe you better check the prescription for your glasses."

"But we spoke today. In your office. Your doctor's office. So don't give me that bullshit."

He set the teapot on the oilcloth table covering and started rooting around in my cabinets for cups. "Look, I thought I'd give this another try. That's why I'm here. I don't usually offer such courtesies but you, I just don't know, something about you, John

Alex, intrigues me. And I liked our little chat before so, I said, what the hell. Have another heart to heart. See if I could make you see things my way."

"But you are telling me that you aren't Dr. Holbrook?"

"Be realistic, my friend. I understand that there is a doctor in town and that you have been to see him and thought he was me and now you think I am him. That's nothing but gibberish. I'm sure there is a reasonable explanation. Trying to understand or explain many of these sorts of things, these misunderstandings, is never easy. Which is why I rarely try to explain. But here I am. It is a courtesy because you are an old man. A unique old man."

"Is that supposed to be flattery?"

"Take it any way you want. Tea?"

He poured into the same two cups Eva and I had used as if it was the most common of social situations.

"When I make appearances — personal appearances, and they are rare — I am a manifestation. You more or less chose how I would appear to you and for some reason you have chosen this doctor."

"But I never met *him* until after *you* were here that time."

"I know. But don't let that worry you. Time is not linear and most of what humans think is true is an illusion anyway. So let's not get bogged down with what is real and what isn't."

"That's no explanation. And don't give me some Albert Einstein line that time isn't linear crap."

"Okay. Fair enough. So let's deny everything we know about quantum physics for now." He was smirking, about to break out into a laugh maybe. He was enjoying this.

I suddenly remembered about Sheila sleeping nearby in the sewing room. Maybe I should wake her. Have her come out here to validate my experience — manifestation or whatever the hell it was.

I guess I was looking toward her room because he interjected,

"No, don't do that. This is between you and me."

Of course. No, I wouldn't wake her. There was danger here. I was expendable. She was not. I nodded. "What do you want?"

"Well, I'm taking it slow with you, John Alex. I think you deserve it."

"But in the end, you'll take me, right? Just doing your jeezusly job or whatever?"

"I thought it would be more interesting to give you a choice."

"It's not some freaking game."

"Well, there are certain rules, and in the end some win — if you call living winning … and some lose."

"But *you* always win in the end."

"Generally. Well, eventually. I know your lady friend has you very well read so have you ever read *The Art of War*?"

"Yes."

"Then you know sometimes the general wins the war by retreating from a battle rather than advancing when circumstances are stacked against him."

"Is that why I didn't die on your last visit?"

"Oh, you did die. You, yourself said so. You died and you came back. It was, in my way of thinking, untidy. And I would say it was untimely. That's why we're still having this conversation. And I'm intrigued."

"How did I die and come back?"

"You willed yourself back to life."

"I didn't know you could do that."

"That's the most fascinating part. I didn't either. So here I am. Studying you."

"What am I, a frigging guinea pig?"

"Well, in a word, yes."

I cupped my hands around the warm teacup for something to do. He had my cup. Mine had been Eva's. I would still pour tea in it occasionally on a damp cold morning and set it across the table from me at breakfast. Old habits die hard. "If I drink this tea, will it kill me?" I asked.

"Anything is possible."

I drank the tea. It tasted like tea.

"How old are these tea bags?" he asked.

"Old."

"You should think about getting some new ones. I'd get the Morse's ones if I were you. Red Rose has those new plastic pouches that don't decompose. I like things that decompose."

"Then you should go hang out with my compost bin. Or better yet, my pile of chicken manure out behind the barn."

"Lovely thought," he said.

"We seem to be dancing around something. I'm not sure I have as much patience as I had as a young man. You seem to have all the time in the world."

"I do."

"Well, I don't. Are you here to bust my chops or is there a purpose?"

"Okay, let me say again, the little incident the other night really tweaked my curiosity. I don't want you to get a swelled head or anything but you are an unusual one. A rare and remarkable case, if I do say so."

"You made that point."

"So I want to figure out how it is that you are different."

"The CBC would tell you it probably has something to do with global warming. Or maybe the earth's magnetic field is reversing."

"That's a good one," he said in the softest of voices. "That hadn't occurred to me. Close maybe, but no cigar. No, the rules are pretty much the same. Gravity. Inertia. Human fallibility. Mortality. Etcetera etcetera. But let me get down to what I have to say here tonight."

"Please."

"Well, it's hard to explain, of course, because you and I have two very different views of reality, two very different reference points. But I'll dive right in because you seem a bit more amenable to conversation tonight. I want to thank you for that. You didn't hit me with a baseball bat ... or what was it you were thinking? An axe? Ouch. Do I really deserve that?"

"I don't know. Do you?"

"Probably. But that is neither here nor there. So let's stop chasing each other around Robin Hood's barn." He cleared his throat and loosened his tie, stretching his neck to the left and upward so I could see the tightness of the thick muscles along his throat. "Each of us — excuse me — each of you are part of a grouping. A circle of people. Sometimes we refer to this as an affinity group since you all have something in common. I could once use the term 'family' but that now has the wrong implications. How to explain this? You are tied to certain other individuals through a bond, a thread, a link." He paused and seemed exasperated. "English is so bloody poor at explaining things. It's like trying to describe an elephant to a cockroach."

"And I'm the cockroach."

"Don't take that personally. I just wish one of your prodigies would come up with a universal multidimensional language."

"I'll get them right on that," I said.

"Don't worry about it. Not your fault. Let me fumble along as best I can. Okay. Let me be more specific. Your circle — your affinity group — has a finite number of people. It's not huge, but it's not small. And keep in mind that everyone has a group they belong to even if they don't know it. Believe me, this is the way it works."

"So I'm part of some ... family, some club."

He smiled. "Yes, okay. Some club. Nice touch. Or think of it as a team even if that helps since you don't have a word in English — or Latin for that matter — that works. Right. So that woman asleep nearby. She's in it."

This made some kind of sense to me. There had been a bond between Sheila and me since we first met.

"You want to know more?"

"I do."

"Okay. Sheila's in it. So is Em and her daughter, Eva."

This too made sense. I felt naked now. Like he knew more about my life than I ever expected. And the fact that he even mentioned the others made me shudder. Were they vulnerable as well to this man … this manifestation? "Have you said everything you came here to say?" I desperately wanted this asshole out of my house and out of my life. Our lives.

"Not by a long shot. You were even in the company of some of the others today. That kid Jenko. And Henry. And you met someone in a pharmacy. Bradley, I think his name is. And you are linked to a few folks you don't even know at all. The methadrine kid who took the gun into the Wooden Anchor. You should really try to do something about him."

"I don't even know who he is."

"Fair enough. But I would expect your paths to cross. There's also another young man living alone out on Wolf Island."

"No one lives out there."

"This fellow does. He's the son of your old hermit friend from up Margaree way. By the way, his father was also in your … circle."

"But Samson Langley is dead. Has been for a long time now."

"Oh and I guess I didn't properly explain that yet. Since you have the privilege of old age, you have outlived many of the most important people in your circle. Mr. Langley himself, for example. That old doctor you like so much — Dr. Derek Fedder. Now there was a character. And then there was Vin McCallum. You remember him, right? Too bad about that gambling problem of his. Didn't leave his wife with much. There are a few more who are still of the oxygen breathing category, but I think that's enough for now."

I was beginning to think this was some exceptionally elaborate hoax perpetrated by someone who had gone to the ungodly trouble of doing in-depth research into my most ordinary life.

"Your brother Lauchie was in there, although brothers and parents are not usually in the same circle. And Eva — *your* Eva, the one whose cup you are drinking from. She was there. I may be missing some, but I don't have my notes with me. So there it is. Are you beginning to understand about your untimely return? Or do I have to spell it out?"

I could feel my fists clenching in a rage then. It was the mention of Lauchie, of course, that always brought mixed feelings. A man who would seduce the wife of his own brother. And the mention of Eva. How could he even know all this?

"What good does it do to tell me all this?"

"I'm telling you all this because you need to understand that there is a *way* to things. An order, a priority. When old Doc Fedder died, it was because someone in that group, your cluster, had to go. So it was, as the cliché suggests, *his time*. And Lauchie. The same. And I'm sorry to say it right now. But Eva as well."

"And you did this? God damn you and your insane bloody system and all this circle bullshit."

He raked his fingers through his thinning hair and thrust out his jaw. "Well, I knew it wouldn't settle easily with you but it is *your* time and I think that, deep down, you know it."

"But ... the other night ... it didn't take. I'm not dead."

"And that's the problem. But since you were capable of this most extraordinary thing, I thought I'd give you a choice."

"What kind of choice?"

"Well, if it's not you, then someone else in your circle must go. I'll let you choose."

CHAPTER 10

YOU MIGHT SAY THAT WHAT followed was a staring contest between this old mortal and whomever or whatever was sitting across my kitchen table from me. I'd never been one to hold eye contact with anyone, but I felt compelled to keep my eyes glued upon my guest. In order to do so, I took off my glasses so he was out of focus and mostly a blur. It was then that I noticed the aura around him. A soft grey metallic glow, you might call it. It could have just been my eyes, of course.

Pretty soon I detected the faint presence of morning light as the sun rose over the horizon to the east and turned the Cape Breton sky a shade of pink that made me think of those old French impressionist painters I'd seen in the library books.

"What?" he said, breaking the stony silence. "You think I'll run off at the first sign of daylight? You're mixing me up with some Hollywood stereotypes, I'm afraid. In truth, I'm more like an accountant than a werewolf or a vampire."

"Accountant, that's a good one."

Birds were singing now. Sparrows. Chickadees. Out in the world, life was coming back with light after the darkness. That's when I heard rustling from the sewing room. "John Alex," Sheila said. "Who are you talking to?"

Jesus, I thought. What now? "No one," I said.

But too late. She was out of bed and opening the door, wearing one of my old flannel shirts. She froze when she saw us. "Oh my God," she said, her jaw dropping.

My guest gave me the oddest sidelong smile, took a sip of his cold tea and held my gaze.

I gathered my wits. "Sorry we woke you," I said, pulling some words, some feeble explanation out of my frazzled brain. "This is Dr. Holbrook," I said, realizing it was the only believable thing to say. "Maybe you two have met before."

"No, we haven't," she said, looking dazed and confused. "But it's, what? Six thirty in the morning."

He threw up his hands and said, "I guess it's shocking to think of a doctor making an actual house call these days. But especially one this early in the day."

Sheila tugged down at the flannel shirt and leaned on the door frame staring at him. Then at me. Her expression was a mix of fear, curiosity and expectation.

"You remember I went to see the doctor yesterday," I said.

"And I don't know why," he added, "but I woke up in the middle of the night thinking about John Alex here. Something he told me got me worried. Those nighttime visions he had, those hallucinations, maybe. It occurred to me he might have had what we call a TIA, a transient ischemic attack. What some call a mini-stroke. I didn't suspect that when he visited but it occurred to me when I woke up. These things need attention. I figured he was an early riser —"

"So here he is," I said, cutting him off. "Imagine that."

Sheila was buying it. "And?"

"And," he said, "now that we've spoken and I've had a chance to make my assessment, I am convinced John Alex is perfectly fine."

"For a ninety-year-old," I added.

"You're only as old as you feel," the man added, sipping his cold tea.

"Well, I feel like I'm ninety," I said.

"But you don't look a day over eighty-seven."

"Thanks, Doc."

Sheila turned to go back to her room. "Let me put some clothes on. I'll come back and make some breakfast."

"Doc" was now shaking his head. "No need. I'm on my way. I have a full roster of patients to see today. Some paperwork to do. It just piles up. I try to get it done before the door opens and the hypochondriacs start pouring in. Gotta go." And with that he put on his shoes and made his exit.

Sheila stood there in the kitchen with a puzzled look on her face. She leaned over a bit to look outside. "I don't see a car," she said.

"I guess he walked."

"Odd," she said. "Very odd."

"Why don't *I* make *you* breakfast," I said.

"I'd like that."

Sheila acted funny all through breakfast. She knew something was up, but I wasn't going to tell her the nature of this latest encounter. Once again, I even felt like the whole thing was a farce of some sort. Or a hallucination. But Sheila had seen him in the flesh. Whoever he was. I tried to make sense of the fact that he played along that he was indeed Dr. Holbrook.

"Em texted me," Sheila said, finally breaking the breakfast silence. "She wants me to drive to Halifax. I think it has something to do with Evie." Eva, who had been born right here in this house. Every time the name was mentioned, it still made me teary. My dead wife's name was given to the child when she was born. Now she was ten. That seemed impossible.

"Is everything okay with them?"

"I don't know," Sheila said. "Em wouldn't say what it was about but it seemed important. Maybe you should go with me."

And maybe I should have. But I had a gut feeling I was not supposed to go. I feared that this connection I had to certain people in my life made me a danger to others — that if I made a wrong move, something bad would happen to them.

"No," I said, "I think I'll stay close to the roost. Tell them I'm thinking of them. Tell them that if they need anything … anything at all, that I can help out."

Sheila studied my face, looking for clues. *What the hell was going on in that old man's head?* the look seemed to say. "Okay. Just take it easy. I didn't like the sound of that ministroke thing."

"Look, he said it was nothing. Freaking doctors these days have a technical name for everything. And a pill. I hear they have a cure for farting now. Just what the world needs. And who doesn't like a good fart now and again?"

"Lovely," Sheila said. "Just lovely." She stood up and kissed me on the top of my head like I was a little boy. "You okay if I eat and run? I really should get going to Halifax."

"Sure thing. I'll just do up these dishes."

* * *

After Sheila left, I settled down on the old chesterfield with one of the books Sheila said I should read. An English translation of *The Stranger* by Albert Camus. Just what an old codger needs to put him in a good mood after another frightening night. "Mother died today. Or it could have been yesterday. I don't know —" *Aujourd'hui,* right? Wasn't that French for today? Something I remembered from school, learning French from a beautiful Acadian woman when I was twelve. *La neige est froid aujourd'hui.* The snow is cold today. She made it sound so beautiful. I wanted to marry her. But I was only twelve. Then she stopped showing up to school. She got sick. Caught something from one of the kids. Jamison from Chimney Corner, I think. Came to school with a cough. Lived in a shithole with an alcoholic father who wouldn't chop wood to keep the house warm. Mother, who couldn't care less about what happened to her kid. Jamison came in with whooping cough, I think they called it. Madame Laforge kept him after school to take care of him.

Then she was the one who got sick. Stayed sick. Ended up in a hospital in Sydney and died there. Jamison got better. Grew up to be a decent sort. Drove a truck delivering potato chips to little mom-and-pop stores all over Cape Breton. He made it into his seventies until he skidded off the road up near Wreck Cove trying to avoid a deer. Died instantly, they said. How do people know that? *Died instantly. Didn't feel any pain.* Bullshit. That's just people trying to use words to make us believe life isn't unkind and cruel. When it is.

When the phone rang, I almost didn't recognize the sound. It had been so long since anyone had called me. And sometimes I'd turn the ringer off and forget I'd done so. This time, it probably rang ten times before I could settle Albert Camus and his dead mother onto the floor and hoist my carcass out of the chesterfield.

"Hello."

"John Alex? Is that you?"

"I guess so. Who the hell did you think you were calling? And who the hell is this?"

"It's Kern. Kern Wallace, down at the wharf."

"Oh. Okay, Kern. Sorry. Didn't mean to bite your head off. It's just —" but I didn't finish because I didn't really have anything to say to complete the sentence.

"Look, John Alex," Kern said, "I'm down here on my boat and I got this new doctor guy on my case."

Oh shit, I was thinking. *This crazy drama is never going to end.* "What do you mean on your case?"

"Well, he wants me to take him out to Wolf Island so he can check on that damn kid — Mason whatshisname, son of that damn hermit from up Margaree and his crazy girlfriend from North Sydney."

Samson Langley was long gone but his son Mason had been a loose cannon ever since he was born. Mental case of some sort. Decided he wanted to be a recluse like his somewhat famous old man. "What the Jesus does this have to do with me?" I snarled at Kern over the pesky phone.

"Well, I told this Holbrook fella my boat wasn't up for hire. I'm just waiting for the lobster season to start. And waiting is as good an occupation as any, I figure."

"So?"

"So he offered me two hundred dollars. And I still said no sir-ree. But then he said I should call you and you'd help square things up and I'd see why I should take him."

At first, this didn't make a lick of sense. Like a million other things in this crazy world. But there he was, this so-called doctor, down on Kern's big Cape Islander wanting to go out to Mason. And hadn't my guest last night hinted that this kid was part of that goddamn circle or whatever it was?

"Two hundred dollars, he's offering?"

"That's what he said. But to be honest, I don't like the look of the guy. New doctor or not. Something feels funny about this."

And indeed something must have been funny. But I figured I was in this whole thing up to my thyroid whether I liked it or not. That man would find his way out to Wolf Island one way or another if he was offering two hundred dollars. And then what would happen to that poor kid? I hardly knew him, but I'd been a good friend to his stubborn old man, living all alone up there in the deep woods. I guess you could say I felt some kind of responsibility.

"Just wait there," I told Kern. "Don't set off until I get there. Looks like I'll be joining your little sailing voyage to the island."

"I don't think I understand," Kern said, and he kept talking but I was hanging up on him anyway. Understand? Who the hell understands anything these days? I wondered.

CHAPTER 11

BY JESUS, I HADN'T BEEN out on a boat in the Gulf for nearly five years. Back then I'd gone mackerel fishing — handlining with old Vin McCallum. Vin said it was the only thing that kept him from gambling. Fishing. If he could just fish for all his waking hours, he said, he'd never touch a VLT machine again. But then the video gambling gave way to online gambling, which was twenty-four hours a day, and his wife said she'd leave him if he kept it up, even though they'd been married for nearly forty years. She was fed up. So to make a long story short, we all had to pitch in and go fishing with Vin whenever he had the urge to gamble online. Funny what you do for an old friend, even the ones who were sort of a pain in the ass. And that was Vin.

So we caught some mackerel that day, cooked and bottled most of it. Turned out he wasn't so good at the whole sterilization process and the botulism or some such set in and took ole Vin right out of this world. I guess you could say he lost that bet on the bottling. But it did stop his gambling. It was terribly sad that he left us, even though his old buddies were getting tired of going out in the waves on those choppy nor'easters to catch oily fish to keep Vin from gambling. Too bad, especially, because he'd just had Dill Weaver dig him a fish pond with his big Caterpillar rig. He had stocked the pond with trout so he could stay home and fish anytime he wanted, day or night, what with those big lights set up down behind his barn. Too bad, indeed. And maybe I should be asking Mr. D or Dr. Holbrook or whoever the hell this was, if he was in on the deed. I mean, botulism from your own bottled mackerel is no way for a good man to die.

* * *

I didn't mean to go on so, but the whole epsiode with Vin McCallum went through my mind as I drove down to the wharf. The place smelled of rotten fish and, strange to say, it brought back fond memories of boyhood and time spent at the old wharf before a government grant gave us a new fancy concrete one. And today, the smell was probably amplified because there wasn't a whiff of wind anywhere — rare for this coast.

I pulled the truck up to a bulkhead and turned it off. There was Kern's boat, idling in the water. Kern must have been in the wheelhouse and there was that damn doctor again but with him was the kid, Brad, from the pharmacy. I couldn't figure why.

When I got on board, it was Brad who greeted me like an old friend and reintroduced me to this chap claiming to be Dr. Holbrook.

"Yes, we've met," Holbrook said.

I nodded. The charade was on again — Holbrook was the doctor, not the agent of mortality I knew him to be. When Kern walked out of the wheelhouse, he smiled when he saw me. "Good to see you, John Alex. You are looking spry."

God, how old farts like me hate it when we are called spry or any other foolish word that is other than the truth. And the truth is I looked old. Felt old. Was old.

I remembered Kern, like so many people around town, from when he was a kid. Now he was maybe thirty or so. A bit over-weight, slightly balding, looking like the spitting image of his father, Munroe, who had styled himself as a country singer and gone on to tour with Ian Tyson, before Munroe accidentally shot himself while buying a used handgun from a crook in Calgary. Another good reason why Cape Bretoners should stay home on our blessed island and not try to get too uppity out there in the rest of Canada. Especially the wild, wild west. I mean it's bad enough when good Capers feel they want to live in Halifax, but there should be someone stationed at the New Brunswick border stopping everyone and asking, *Do you really want to leave? Are you of sound mind? Why not just go back home and see what your mother has planned for Sunday dinner?*

Anyways, there I was with young Kern on his fancy-ass boat. I was tagging along, not because I was asked to, but because I didn't want to see Doctor Doom decide that this poor misguided kid, Mason, son of my old hermit friend, was his next victim. But then I saw that Bradley was a bit shaky, still downright wobbly on his Ontario land legs and not at all steady on the planks of the boat even though, as I said, there was not a spit of wind.

"What brings you here on this voyage?" I asked him.

"Not quite sure," he answered, so the Doc jumped in again.

"I couldn't convince any of my assistants to come along. They all said it wasn't in their contract. And, to be honest, I wanted backup. Second opinion maybe. I know Brad from the pharmacy, of course, and he at least has some medical training."

"I'm not really equipped —" Bradley began to say but the Doc cut him off.

"He'll do fine. It's always good to have a second set of eyes."

"Then why am I here?" I asked.

"Because I requested you come along. You're the only one around who has had much of any contact with Mason."

"Not much at all since his father passed."

"Still, he'll know who you are. Like everyone else around these parts, he probably respects you."

Respect, I was thinking. There was a funny word. I'm not sure respect ever got me a hill of beans in my long life. I think I grunted right then instead of saying anything.

"Ready to head over, Dr. Holbrook?" Kern asked.

Holbrook nodded. Kern flipped off the rope still holding us to dry land and went back inside to rev the engine. We began to slide out of the harbour.

The sky was the colour of old slate. The sea was much the same. Aside from the wake of the boat, there was not a ripple. A heavy blanket of sky was above us but at the waterline the visibility was excellent. I guess you could say, it felt otherworldly. If I gave myself a split second to avoid thinking about our mission, I could almost say, it felt good to be at sea.

Holbrook was at the stern of the boat looking back at Inverary as it grew smaller and smaller. Brad was hanging by my elbow, reminding me of a lost puppy I once had.

"What exactly is it that the doctor wants to do out there on the island?" I asked.

Brad was still shifting his landlubber legs from one side to another. "He says he's been asked by the authorities to determine if the young man, Mason, is … well, mentally fit enough to take care of himself."

"Well, Mason, I suppose, has taken after his old man. This hermit thing they had going. In many ways, I admire anyone capable and why the hell *not* live alone and be self-reliant in the times we're living in. I'm sure the boy *is* a bit off his rocker, but I'd rather be stuck with Mason and his old father if he was still alive than half the men in suits down in Sydney. And exactly which authorities have asked the good doctor to do this?"

"He didn't say. The social services people, I would guess."

Well, that drew another grunt from me. As far as I could tell, the only social service those social service people did was to harass unwed mothers, have jolly old drunks arrested and suck money from honest working taxpayers like me. (Well, I used to pay taxes, but I stopped sometime around 2010 on principle. But don't get me going on that.)

I decided to ignore for the nonce the purpose of this mission and allowed the still grey waters to work their magic on my consciousness. The blissful reverie was soon interrupted by the thought that Mason, Mason out there, was somehow in "my circle" or whatever it was the creep had been going on about. What if we were actually out here, on our way to somehow assist the alleged Dr. Holbrook in taking poor Mason right off his island and out of this world?

"Bradley, son, I have a favour to ask."

"Sure thing, John Alex. What would that be?"

"I want you to watch my back."

"I don't understand."

"Which word didn't you understand?"

He gave me a funny look and I realized I'd been a bit harsh with the lad. "Just help me out," I said in a gentler voice, "if you see anything starting to go badly."

He gave me a very strange look, this Ontario pharmacist. "Sure," he said, finally, but I could tell he was spooked.

"Go ask Kern if he has any coffee." I knew Kern would have some, but it wasn't caffeine I wanted. I wanted a word with that damn mysterious man standing at the rear of the boat. Brad slipped inside and I slid my hand along the wooden gunwale as I walked to the back of the boat.

"What's this really about?" I asked him.

He was staring into the distance toward a diminished Inverary. "Well, back in Montreal people like this Mason character end up living on the street. Eventually they get into some kind of trouble with the law and get jailed. Then someone — often a medical person — needs to determine if they need to be 'taken care of'... by society."

"Taken care of? You mean institutionalized?"

"Not the word we use, but yes, they need to be kept safe. Safe *from* society but also from themselves."

He was still playing doctor. "Drop the crap, would ya? Does this have something to do with me and your goddamn quota or whatever it was you lectured me about?"

"I have no idea what you are talking about. And why do you think this has anything to do with *you* except that we asked for your help?" The look on his face was that of the most skilled of actors, pretending he knew nothing about the conversation we'd had at my kitchen table. The circle. The affinity group. The whatever. I decided not to wade in further. I wouldn't play the game. I couldn't really, because I didn't have a clue as to what the rules of this game were. I'd have to be on my toes. Anything could happen with this guy on board.

Soon enough, Wolf Island appeared like a fortress before us. Tall red rock cliffs. Ragged, wind-ravaged spruce trees up top. Stories about the place being haunted. I'd camped out here as a kid. Twelve years old. I was with my brother Lauchie who was a tad older. We rowed out here in my grandfather's old dory to stay overnight even though everyone said the island was dangerous. Our parents thought nothing of it. "Bring me back some haddock," my mother had said. "And a bit of dulse from the rocks," my father added. That night on the island, Lauchie told me ghost stories that kept me awake as the wind howled and raged around the flowerpot rock formations along the shore. In the morning there was a sudden rain shower and fish fell out of the sky. Real fish that had somehow been sucked to the heavens by a waterspout, we reckoned. "Well, at least our mother will get her fish," Lauchie said. So we filled the dory and rowed home, both of us forgetting all about the dulse and the both of us getting a good beating for it.

But that was long ago. Another lifetime. But then it was fairly common now that most everything from the past seemed like another lifetime to me.

I coached Captain Kern to take us around to the north shore and pointed out a small cove where the water was deep almost right up to the shoreline. He pulled it in nice and smooth and then Holbrook, Bradley and I climbed into the dinghy trailing behind us. Kern stayed behind, saying, "A captain should always stay with his ship." I took the oars and the pull felt good on my old muscles. Real good. I drove us up onto the glistening pebbly shoreline where the sound of small stones shushing back and forth echoed on the high cliffs with a song that, surprisingly, made me happy to be alive.

"This way," I said, leading the two men up a narrow gully along-side a ribbon waterfall that had carved a sloping canyon into the island. I was out of breath by the time we got to the top. Not surprising really, as I hadn't been much on climbing mountains this last two decades or so. At the very top, there was Mason, waiting for us after watching our approach.

"Saw your boat," he said. "Not many visitors out here." Mason was tall and thin. Like his father, he had a comically long and somewhat pointed beard. He had on a leather jacket and thick canvas pants. First impressions would have been someone doing a bad impression of a Harley biker but I knew that was not his intention.

Brad and Holbrook hung back while I walked forward. "Remember me?"

"Of course," he said, eyes shifting from side to side. No doubt, after spending so much time alone, he had forgotten exactly how to have a face-to-face conversation with anyone. "John Alex MacNeil. Father's friend."

"Good man, your father."

"He loved trees like some men love women." Which was a mighty odd thing to say but it was kind of the truth.

"And you, Mason, what do you love?"

"Wind. Rain. Sun. Sea. Solitude." His eyes had stopped shifting about. His gaze was steady, not on me, but on the brooding clouds above. "Could rain any minute."

"Could," I said. "Anywhere we can go inside?"

"All of you?"

"Well, if it's okay."

"Okay. Like I say, I don't get much in the way of visitors. House may not be all that tidy."

"That's alright," Holbrook said now. "We're not that fussy."

We followed Mason, who hobbled as he walked and appeared to be in pain. He led us to a ramshackle cabin with a moss-covered roof and walls made from split spruce tree trunks. Inside it was dark and the ceiling was low. Animal pelts lined the walls and on a table was a collection of animal skulls arranged from small to large. Mouse to moose was my reckoning.

I made formal introductions and Mason asked us if we wanted some Labrador tea. Holbrook said we did. Mason had a fire going in an old Enterprise cook stove and tossed in some sticks of dry wood. Holbrook was studying his every move. Bradley was looking at me with questioning eyes. Mason appeared to be doing okay in his solitary existence and maybe his father had tutored him well enough to be his own recluse on a haunted island. And here he was, fulfilling his destiny.

Mason brought the tea to us in old soup cans with handmade metal handles. We sat quietly at a knife-scarred chunk of lumber that served as a table — something that probably had washed ashore, maybe once part of another Cape Islander. When Mason got up to deliver some more tea to our cups, he winced and favoured his left leg.

"Something wrong with your leg?" Bradley asked.

"Cut my foot while chopping wood a while back. Giving me some trouble."

"I should look at that," Holbrook said.

"You a doctor?"

"Yes, I am. Can I look?"

"Okay." Mason gingerly and with great anguish removed his high rubber boot. There was a smell that filled the room. It wasn't good.

"Let me look," Holbrook repeated, raising Mason's foot and peeling off a dirty old woollen sock. The smell was overpowering. Bradly put a fist up to his nose. Holbrook held the injured foot in his hands, studying it. "You okay if I wash this for you?" The doctor was gentle in his touch — an entirely different entity from my midnight visitor.

Mason nodded toward a bucket, a bar of handmade soap and a rag. Bradley retrieved all three and handed the items to Holbrook who, with great care, cleaned the wound as Mason tried to keep from crying. There was something both professional and fatherly about the way Holbrook was treating him that made me think now that my own notions about this man were completely unfounded.

When he was finished, Holbrook opened the backpack he had been carrying and handed over three pairs of clean white socks. It seemed uncanny that the man was carrying extra socks but as he passed them over, Mason accepted them gladly. Holbrook settled the foot back onto the floor and stood. "Sorry, gentlemen, gotta pee. John Alex, would you be a good man and escort me outside to some place that might be appropriate for me to urinate?" The question was absurd but I followed him out of the hovel.

Outside, Holbrook unzipped his fly and took a piss on a shrub that looked like ground juniper without further consultation. "Okay, John Alex. Here's the thing. That cut. It's infected. If it's left untreated it will get worse. Gangrene is not far off, I expect. I don't have any of the right antibiotics with me and, even if I did, I think this needs monitoring. I know what you are thinking. You don't really trust me. I can see it in your eyes. And you've already said as much. If you believe he has a right to his privacy, solitude, whatever, we could just head back to town and let nature take its course. No one would be to blame.

"But if we take him back to our world, he will be most unsettled. It will greatly upset his equilibrium I guess you could say. I've seen this before, even with homeless men in the city. They learn to survive on the street and when you put them somewhere else, they turn. It won't be pretty. But if he is not treated he may get worse."

"And die? Is that what you're saying?"

"That's not what I said. But it's a possibility."

The doctor had put the decision in my hands, it appeared. Or if this was not "the doctor," it was the other one who had just offered a way out for me as part of that seemingly predestined group that I was tied to.

"Then we have to convince him to come back to the mainland with us," I said.

Holbrook now furrowed his brow. Did I see disappointment in his eyes? Or something else. "Then you'll have to convince him," he said. "He trusts you."

CHAPTER 12

HOLBROOK SAID, "I'LL JUST WAIT out here. You go talk to him."

When I walked back in, I found Bradley nervously hovering near the door. I sat down on an old tree stump that Mason had repurposed as a table seat and looked up at the drying rabbit pelts tied to the rafters. It was dark inside and Mason seemed to like it that way but with the door open, a grey light from outside filtered down on the poor young man who I still considered a boy. The product of his idealistic, crazy-ass father and lunatic mother. The father had been a friend whom I had deeply admired for his decision to protect those old growth trees, if need be, with his life. But the mother. She had been something else. Certainly a sorry soul, lost in the world like so many, but she had come up to Margaree to seduce ole Samson Langley and have his baby. Why, I did not know.

And now, here I was, sitting with Langley's son on an island off the coast of Cape Breton. An island we all thought was haunted by the ghost of yet another solitary man — the lightkeeper of a light now long gone. "Mason, let me have a look at that foot," I said.

Mason pulled up an old plastic milk crate and set his bare foot upon it. I smelled that terrible stench again. Not just a dirty foot but an infected one. When I looked at the gash, I nearly liberated my breakfast.

"What did you plan on doing about it, my boy?" I asked.

"Let it heal on its own. I dip in the sea every day. Pop said the forest could cure all ills. I say the sea will cure anything as well."

"Probably true. Probably true. I sometimes think these sort of things meself. But that's one rangy foot you got there. Hard to walk on, I bet."

"Getting harder."

I nodded. I knew you couldn't rush these things with a lad like Mason. "Ever get lonely out here?"

"Never."

"Scared?"

"What of?"

I sloughed it off. Like father like son. "The doctor says you need something more to properly fix you up. What do you think?"

"He a real doctor?"

I shrugged. "He says he is."

"Something about him. I don't know."

"Yep. I know what you mean. But —" I let the word hang in the stale air beneath the rabbit pelts, wondering how there could have even been so many rabbits on the island and wondering even more what it was like to live here on a diet of rabbits, fish and wild plants. Maybe not so bad at that. "Well, how do you feel about going to the mainland to get you looked after?" I used his term, "the mainland," even though we all knew Cape Breton was an island and merely lashed to the real mainland by a thin strip of rock and asphalt they called the Causeway.

"I don't know, John Alex. Going there scares the bejesus out of me. I'm not good around people. They act crazy. They say things and do things. That's why I'm here."

"I understand, believe me, Mason. I do. You chose a good island for yourself. And maybe we can get you fixed right up. Get some antibiotics in ya and you come right back. I'll see to it myself. Bring you back out in Kern's big boat."

"I don't like big boats. All that noise. I hate it."

"Not a fan of diesel, I get it. But still —"

He nodded. "My father always respected you. I guess I gotta listen to ya, John Alex."

I sat there on my stump wondering if I was being a hero or a traitor to this boy. It was like Holbrook had known what was going to go down even before we arrived here. Like he put me in this spot on purpose. "Close your eyes for a minute, Mason, and ask yourself what your father would want you to do. Maybe he can still speak to you. Does he ever do that?"

"Yes, he does. On those still, moonlit nights when there is not a breath of wind."

"Like today. No moonlight. But no wind. Close your eyes and ask him."

Mason closed his eyes, but I could see them moving rapidly back and forth behind his eyelids. And then he winced in pain. I stared out the door. Bradley and Holbrook were speaking in hushed tones about something. When Mason opened his eyes, he spoke. "Pop says don't do it. He says stick to my guns. Stay put."

I'd gambled and lost. Old dead Samson Langley had betrayed me from beyond the grave. My own stupid fault for saying so. "What about the foot?"

"He says I'll be okay. Just hang tough."

Just like the stubborn old bugger to let me down. I put a hand on Mason's shoulder and then walked out to speak to the other two. Holbrook had his backpack open and was laying out something on a flat rock. Something packaged. Something medical.

"He says no. He won't go," I told them

"And you can live with that?" Holbrook asked.

"No, unfortunately I can't."

"Then we have to act. I've just been explaining to Bradley here what our options are."

"Can't we just bring those antibiotics out here?"

"He needs intensive care and he needs it now. No pills. Intravenous. We have to get him to the hospital."

"He won't go."

"Then we do what we have to do." He nodded to Bradley who

looked more nervous than ever. And then pointed down to the plastic wrapped package on the rock. "John Alex, you willing to help hold him while Bradley gives him a shot of this?"

Bradley was shaking his head. "I don't know. I didn't sign on for this. I work in a drugstore. I'm not a medic."

Holbrook gave him a dirty look. "You give people shots. You're trained. Don't give me that."

"What the hell is it?" I asked.

"A sedative. Heavy enough to allow us to get him ashore."

"Jesus, man."

* * *

Mason knew we were up to something the moment we entered his home. I felt like Judas Iscariot as I walked in, closely followed by Holbrook and trailing Bradley with the needle. My brain was firing an argument back and forth. Was it a trick by my midnight visitor? Were we killing the poor guy? Or was it the only thing to do to save him — even if it was against his will?

I waved Holbrook back and slammed my body into Mason, knocking him onto the table as Bradley grabbed onto his left arm and jabbed him with the needle. I whispered in Mason's ear as he did so, told him it was going to be okay. I promised him I would look after him. The scream that slammed into my ear was something unearthly, I'll tell ya that. Something I would hear echoing in my sleep for days to come. No words, just guttural primal fear. Something that sounded so awful that my stomach twisted into a knot and my brain told me I was doing the absolutely wrong thing.

He didn't give up the fight easily but the scream subsided to a whimper and he eventually slumped over, looking more like a drunk young man than a proud island hermit. Holbrook and Bradley took charge of him at that point and, with an arm draped around each of them, Mason was led out of his house toward the trail leading down to the boat. Still feeling like a traitor, I stayed behind to make sure the fire went out in the cook stove and that the door to the shack was closed tight.

Back in the boat, Kern gave me a look that said, *What the fuck?*

"Just get us back to Inverary," I said. "Please."

Bradley sat on some fishing gear, hanging onto a rag doll version of Mason who kept mumbling something that none of us could understand. Kern stayed in the wheelhouse, not wanting to get involved with whatever the hell was going on. Holbrook just stood at the stern of the boat looking back at the island. I was feeling antsy and needed to be reassured. "This isn't your way of destroying him, I hope," I said. "If this is some kind of rotten scheme, I'll not let you get away with it."

Holbrook seemed genuinely shocked at my words. "John Alex. Sometimes force is the only way to save a life. You must know that. I've been down this road more times than you can count. Homeless men on St. Catherine's Street, drug addicts, severely mentally ill patients. The ones I could save thanked me. So I had to get used to it. Had to be tough. Had to be strong, cruel even if need be to save them. What would you know about it?"

"I know something, damn it," I said. Then turned away. This Dr. Holbrook. Was it possible he was some king of multiple personality case? No one could convince me he was *not* the same man or manifestation that came to me in the night. Yet, here in daylight, he never let on that he had ever met me before I came into his office. A great actor or a serious fraud? I had no way of knowing. He'd convinced me the boy needed saving. The agent of death insisting that this was the only way to live. Nothing, nothing was right about this. But if he had not brought me along, insisted Kern bring me on this so-called rescue, Mason would have most certainly died from gangrene or worse. Whatever medicine the sea could deliver, I was convinced, was not going to save him despite what he or his dead father believed.

* * *

A light breeze had come up from the east and I could see clear skies sending sharp, glaring shafts of light down onto the water, but the sky directly overhead remained a brooding mass of dark clouds. Bradley took out his cell phone and flicked his finger over the screen like I saw all of them do nowadays as he tried to keep Mason sitting somewhat upright, leaning into him. But then something changed. Mason went stiff, then jerked his head up, shook it from side to side.

With difficulty, he shakily stood up. Bradley made a move to brace him and keep him steady but Mason knocked him away. Then he stood up and let go with that scream I had heard before. None of us on deck moved and could not have expected what happened next. Mason stared at the water and then back to his island, ripped off his jacket, kicked off his boots, leaped to the gunwale and dove straight into the water. He surfaced and began to swim, back toward his island which was already more than a mile away.

Kern had heard the scream and bounded out of the wheelhouse. He understood what had happened and hurried back to the wheel to get the boat turned around. Holbrook, frozen where he stood and looking mesmerized, watched Mason slapping the water with his hands in an awkward crawl in his attempt to escape and somehow return to his island hermitage. Holbrook was strangely passive as if watching the activity from a great distance and it wasn't anything of his concern.

"God damn, you, man," I lashed out at him, cursing him as I kept my eye on Mason flapping his arms in the water, swimming clumsily away from us with a great desperate effort. He'd wear himself down in no time. That's when I realized Bradley was the only one on board prepared to do what needed to be done. He shed his fancy hiking jacket, slipped out of his shoes and dropped his pants to the deck, tossed his cell phone onto a pile of rope and jumped into the water. He executed a near perfect breaststroke, the work of an accomplished competitive swimmer, bobbing under and coming up with each stroke. I lost sight of him briefly as the boat began to arc around, but Kern's engine was reluctant to do its proper work. He'd slammed the throttle to full speed and maybe that was a mistake. He cursed and hit wood as the engine sputtered and coughed.

I searched the deck for some floater jackets or life preservers but there was nothing to be seen. The damn fishermen in town would still rather drown than flounder in the cold waters of the Gulf until they died. And indeed the water would still be cold. Mason would not make it to his island. No matter how powerful his desire. I could see now that Bradley was making headway. I had clearly underestimated the young man from Hamilton, Ontario. He took powerful strokes and displayed a keen sense of his own ability. But I also knew that Mason would not want his help. He'd push him away or try to drag him down in his panic.

Holbrook just stood on the deck with his arms folded, calmly watching, not moving a muscle.

As the boat stubbornly resisted Kern's attempt to get her fully turned around, I scrambled toward the captain. "Back off on it, Kern," I yelled at him. "Don't let it stall." He ratcheted back on the throttle and the diesel engine settled into a slower but steadier thrum. We were turning around.

Back on deck, I was shocked at how far away both Bradley and Mason were. I agonized over how long it was taking to get the damn boat to swing around but as she was turning, I stumbled toward the bow and grabbed onto a metal rod that looked solid enough to keep me from falling off. Meanwhile, Holbrook hung back and looked straight ahead even though he was now looking the wrong way.

In silent horror, I watched as Bradley, a most adept swimmer, caught up to Mason but when he reached out to him, Mason flailed and slapped at him. Then he landed a punch to Bradley's jaw. Bradley went under — for a terribly long few seconds. He came up sputtering, got his bearings and then let Mason struggle a few strokes away before coming up behind to loop an arm around Mason only to be elbowed away. Bradley hung back at that point. It looked like he was saying something. They were both treading water and whatever Bradley said, it had stopped Mason from continuing with his attempt to swim away. I could hardly breathe as we now approached the two of them, the engine running smoothly now at mid-throttle.

I ran back toward the stern as we came alongside them, both still treading water in place.

"He says he won't go," Bradley shouted.

"Okay, Mason," I said. "We'll take you back. You win."

Mason nodded. I reached an arm out, half wondering if I'd have the strength to lift him into the boat. It was easier than I expected. I was a bit shocked to realize how frail he was. As he lay down on the deck, he sputtered and spit seawater and I turned my attention to getting Bradley back in the boat only to discover he had no trouble hoisting himself up on his own.

When I stepped back, I discovered that Holbrook was leaning over Mason and jabbing him with another needle. He cut me off before I uttered a word. "Don't say a thing. We're not taking him back to that island. This is for his own good." Mason was breathing heavily and, after his ordeal, I don't think he even felt the needle go in.

I sat down on the pile of rope with Bradley who had been watching with a look of disbelief that this was all happening. When he caught his breath he told me, "That would be enough to sedate a horse. I hope this guy knows what he's doing." And maybe that was the problem. Maybe Holbrook, showing no sign of emotion, knew exactly what he was doing.

Kern peeked out from the cabin, and I twirled my fingers suggesting we needed to turn around again and head to town, me all the while worrying about the kid dying of an overdose.

Mason was out. I felt bad that I had lied to him. Was it really for his own good? Or was I now a traitor to both him and his father? Shit. And now I could see that I'd put another living soul in danger. And that didn't feel right.

"Where'd you learn to swim?" I asked Bradley after a while, who had his head down now between his knees and was working on a steady rhythm to his breath.

"Lake Ontario. Swimming saved my life. I was at the U of T in grad school for pharmacy. Hated it. Was depressed. I had hoped to study to be a doctor but didn't have the grades. Pharmacy was hard enough. No friends. No girl. Hated school. Hated my classmates and their party life. It was March. Still some chunks of ice on the beach. Water was cold as cold could be. I walked down by the park at — the Ex — and the lake looked just so inviting.

"I chucked my coat, my shirt, my pants and shoes. Just walked right out into it. It felt so good. The sting of the cold on every inch of me until I was up to my chin."

"You trying to do yourself in?"

He laughed. "Oddly enough, no. That wasn't in my head. All I kept thinking was, this hurts but it feels good — so much better than anything else in my life. I barely knew how to swim. But I knew swimming would save me. And it did. I flopped around until someone called the police and they made me get out. I was shivering like crazy. And laughing.

"Things looked up after that. Took some swimming lessons at the Y. Bought a wetsuit so I didn't suffer rigor mortis when I swam. But I liked the lake a lot better than the pool. Found a coach for long distance. Read some books. Before summer was out that year, I swam from Ward's Island Beach to Marilyn Bell Park in one shot. Happiest day of my life."

"Well, you did good here today, son. I thank you."

"Better than counting out Flomax pills for old farmers." But before he had finished saying it, you could tell he thought this might have been an insult to me.

"Don't worry, Aquaman, my piss flows just fine without any of the wonders of modern science." I got this thing in my head that Bradley was like the proverbial son I never had. I didn't really know him. But I liked his spirit. And then I remembered what the night visitor had said. Bradley was linked to me somehow. Like those others. Like Mason. And was I told the entire list or only part of it? And was all that bullshit he said that night true or just some kind of whacked-out fiction made up to screw with my head?

Kern never showed his face again until we were pulling into the wharf and I didn't blame him. But he'd radioed ahead for an ambulance to meet us. I saw it parked on the wharf as we approached. There was a Mountie car, too. And that worried me.

When we bumped up against the pilings and I tied us up, Kern cut the engines and two uniformed emergency workers scrambled down the metal ladder onto the deck. A guy and a girl who looked to be teenagers. Nothing new there. Young people were running the world now. With their cell phones and smart-ass attitude. I just hung back as Holbrook spoke with them and then directed them to carry Mason off the boat and into the ambulance. I didn't want to think about what kind of scene it would be when Mason woke up. They'd have to restrain him. No doubt about it. At the very least, it would break his spirit. He'd be just like his old man who'd gone crazy living alone up there in the woods.

Holbrook was talking to Kern, offering him money — a fairly good wad of cash it looked like but Kern was waving him away and then, looking more than a little pissed off, asking Holbrook to get off his boat and leave him the hell alone. As Holbrook made his way up the ladder, a lone Mountie walked over from his car. I figured I should be in on the conversation that was about to happen, lest Holbrook give some cock-and-bull story that might get Mason into deep hot water. I didn't trust him one iota.

Bradley followed my lead up the ladder and we approached to hear Holbrook explain what had just transpired. The Mountie was Sealy Hines, who I had known since he was a kid. Always a do-gooder. Most boring boy I ever knew who was raised around here. But honest as the day is long. And since he took the badge, he did everything by the book. Always by the book. Don't think he ever broke a rule he came across and probably never spit a gob of spit on a sidewalk in his entire life, even if no one was looking.

Sealy nodded at me and at Bradley as Holbrook pretty much reported in accurate detail what had gone down at sea, so I didn't interrupt him.

"Well, there's been talk about Mason out there on his own," Sealy said in a calm voice. "No complaints. Just some folks worried about him. Social Services has a file, but you guys were the first to go out in a long while to check on him. Sounds like you done good."

"We did what needed to be done," Holbrook said, sounding eminently professional.

"Well," Sealy said, "the timing's probably not good, but I've been meaning to come around to talk to you, Dr. Holbrook, about something that has come up. I didn't think I should come to your office. It's sort of a legal matter that has been put in our hands."

"I don't understand, Officer, but let's hear it. Now's as good as any time."

Sealy nodded toward Bradley and me. "Probably best if we do this in private."

I wasn't leaving unless asked to but Holbrook piped up, "Hey, I was just through a very difficult situation with these two gentle-men who acted heroically, so just go ahead. Say what you have to say."

Sealy pulled out a cell phone and began scrolling through what must have been some notes he had on it. It had taken me quite a while to get used to the fact that everyone used phones for more than calling home, so it didn't surprise me to see a Mountie on the wharf squinting into that damn little screen.

"You came here after practising in Montreal, right, Doc?"

"Of course."

"And we were plenty glad to have you. What with the shortage of physicians on Cape Breton."

"That's one of the reasons I came. I felt I was needed. Didn't always feel that way in Montreal."

"Right." Sealy paused and cleared his throat. "So we got this request last week from the downtown detachment there — just looking for some information. Well, not really looking for information. Mostly just a kind of heads-up. It's what we do, share info that seems relevant."

"So what does this have to do with me?" Holbrook asked without a trace of concern.

"Well, do you recall having a patient named Robert Seville?"

"Yes, I recall him clearly. Terminal case. I was his doctor for two years. Advanced multiple sclerosis. We did everything under the sun for him. Including experimental treatment. At his request, of course. One of the hardest things about this profession is doing it all and losing the battle in the end."

"And his death was an assisted suicide?"

"A compassionate suicide. At his request. With the consent of his wife and his family. Perfectly legal in Quebec."

Sealy nodded. "I understand. But apparently the family has now filed a complaint."

"These things happen. We have a procedure in place in Quebec through the medical board. It's understandable but not uncommon."

"But in this case, it seems the wife and son went to the RCMP."

"I'm sorry to hear that. I have my colleagues at the hospital, the medical board and the insurance company who can handle all that as it is their job."

"Okay, Dr. Holbrook. I do understand. And I'm not trying to say anything more than to let you know that the Montreal RCMP are looking into it and were asking some questions of us so, at the office, they said we should let you know, just to keep communication lines open and keep everything on the up and up."

"I understand perfectly. And I thank you for that courtesy."

"So have a good day, Dr. Holbrook." And turning to all three of us, Sealy said, "Sounds like you gentlemen had your hands full out there on the island and on the water. We all respect that. We're all Capers, right? Gotta look out for each other."

CHAPTER 13

I DROVE HOME ON MY own in my old truck, my brain cor-rugated with a million thoughts about what was and what wasn't the right thing to do. Sure enough, I expected Mason would be a maniac once the drugs wore off. I'd read a short story by William Carlos Williams where a doctor has to use force on a child in order to treat her and possibly save her life. I'd never in my life been a fan of using force for anything. The world was full of bullies, although once they were successful or in power, they were never called that. Bullies became heroes in many cultures, including ours. And here *I* was, part of this effort to supposedly save young Mason, and acting like a bully to do so. I'd have to check on the kid in the days ahead. I owed it to my old friend Samson, who had himself passed away all on his own in his cabin up in the Margaree woods so many years ago. He'd left that note saying he'd "died of a broken heart." An old expression you don't much hear anymore. But it made sense to me. Even though the woman he pined for was as crazy as a bat. Mason's mother, of course. Not long after that kid was born, she'd dropped off the face of the earth.

And what about the information Sealy had shared about this Holbrook man and a death in Montreal? Wasn't that all part of this manifestation of whoever, whatever he was? I was wishing I had my own personal guru — someone I could go to for answers. Truth, I guess you'd call it. Someone who understood these things. Father Walenga was a help, for sure. But even he was out of his depth here.

The subject of death, naturally, was something that could drive any of us right crazy. Maybe I shouldn't fear my own impending doom. But wouldn't it be best if each of us could make our own choice as to when and where we wanted to be when it came time to leave this world behind? Maybe it was the randomness of timing that made death so difficult.

As I tooled up the driveway to my house, avoiding the customary jutting rocks that had been lusting after my oil pan for many decades now, I thought that I might just sit alone in my kitchen and see if I could conjure up some calming memories of my long-ago life with Eva. Had things really been as wonderful as I remembered? Or was that just the illusion an old man cherishes to keep from going crazy? I didn't know.

But solitude was not on the agenda, it appeared. Sheila's car was parked in front of the house and there was a little girl in the front yard. Evie, Emily's child. It had been many months since I had seen her, this girl who had been born in my own house, daughter of her sixteen-year-old mother ten years ago. Or was it mere seconds ago? These days time had no stable meaning in my life. More of a trickster than an ally.

I brought the truck to a halt and turned the key. The sun was out now even though the morning had been so gloomy. Evie waved. She was bigger than the last time we met. Ten years old now. Hard to believe. I tried to remember what it was like to be that age, but it was impossible. She walked toward me as I opened the truck door and stepped out onto the crunchy stones of my driveway.

"Jalex," she said, using the name she had adopted for me when she was five. "I've missed you."

"I've missed you too, kid."

The last time we'd met, I was almost frightened by how her speech had become so much like an adult. She'd been talkative since she was two and had a mind that grabbed onto anything. She learned everything so quickly that it was almost frightening. My dark day had just blossomed like springtime flowers.

"Evie, I'm so glad you are here."

"Me too. I always feel at peace when I'm here." Again, not the words you'd expect from a child.

"Maybe that is because you were born here."

"I know. You tell me that every time I come to visit." It was true. I couldn't help myself. "During an ice storm, right? I wish I could have seen the trees covered with ice. Like crystals, you always said."

"Like crystals. Where's your mother?"

"Inside with Aunt Sheila."

"What are they doing?"

"Baking biscuits."

What a curious thing, I thought. "No one has baked biscuits here since —" I let my voice trail off. Not since Eva died. And now, here was this child, her namesake, at my house. What could be more perfect than that? "What kind of biscuits?"

"I don't know. Ones with raisins I hope."

"Me too."

"Jalex, what's wrong?"

"Nothing. What do you mean?"

"Your colour. I see dark all around you."

She'd been like that ever since I can remember. She'd see things that people around her couldn't see. By the time she was five, whenever she'd visit, she'd be having conversations with my dead wife.

"I was at sea. The sky was dark most of the morning. Heavy clouds. Maybe I brought them with me."

"It's not just clouds. It's you."

Sheila was at the door now and Emily was brushing past her, walking toward me. "John Alex, Sheila persuaded me to come. We were overdue for a visit and I needed a break from school. So here we are."

"Thank God," I said.

"You've found religion?" Emily asked.

"It's just an expression."

"Mom, can you see the darkness around him?" Evie asked.

"No," she said. "Stop it." And then turning to me and shaking her head added, "She claims to see colours around people. She means their aura. I think she's making it up."

"I'm not and you know it," Evie said. "Scrunch down," she ordered me. My knees cracked as I lowered myself down to my haunches.

"Lower," she said, so I sat right down on the stones of the driveway. Evie approached me, looking straight at me. "Close your eyes."

"Evie," her mother chided.

"Quiet please, Mom." With my eyes closed I could feel Evie's little hands hovering over my head. She was so close I could hear her breathing and whatever she was doing was … well, doing something.

"There," she finally said. "Darkness gone."

"I do feel better."

She walked backwards now. "Open your eyes."

I opened them. Evie was standing four feet away and squinting. "Red. That's more like it. Maybe a touch of pink."

"Is that good?" I asked.

"Red indicates enthusiasm for life. The pink suggests you are a romantic at heart." Again the language was way beyond her years. I would have to get used to it. "You got me. That's exactly who I am," I said, even though I wasn't sure the reading of my so-called aura fit at all.

Sheila walked over and offered her hand to help me get up. "I never thought that pink was your colour," she said. "But I guess I was wrong."

"Pink it is, then," I said. "And red. I'll have to get a whole new wardrobe, I guess." That's when I smelled the glorious aroma of biscuits baking in the kitchen and wafting out through the open door.

"I should never have allowed her to read those books," Emily said. "This stuff has gone to her head."

Evie shot her mother a dirty look. "I'm just getting in touch with my true calling."

"Oh God," Emily said again. "She's already getting into some serious trouble at school with her claims about her psychic abilities. But sometimes I do think she's just really intuitive."

"Maybe it's the same thing," Sheila added. "And don't hold her back from the books. Whatever she wants."

"Okay for you to say," Emily added. "You don't have to live with her. I'm trying to get through my schoolwork — so many important details to stuff into my head. I don't think I really have the time and energy to train my daughter to be a shaman. I mean, I approve of it, if that's what she wants to be. I just think that maybe she should wait until she's older."

"I think a healer and a shaman would be the perfect mother-daughter combination," Sheila said. "You could share an office. You, Emily, try to sort out people's problems through natural medicines and if that doesn't work, Evie can try to work things out on a spiritual plane."

"Don't encourage her," Emily admonished, but she was smiling.

I was standing now, actually feeling better if a bit light-headed.

"Jalex," Evie said, taking my hand, "take me to the stream."

I had first walked Evie to the mountain stream behind the house when she was three, I think. For her it was a magical place then. Dragonflies. Water striders. Caterpillars. Tiny frogs and minnows. I let her lead me there, me following in her footsteps and saying nothing at all. We sat down on the big boulder in the middle of the shallow rivulet.

"I felt her presence as soon as we arrived today," she said.

"Eva?"

"Yes."

"I haven't had the pleasure for a long time now."

"I know. You've been preoccupied."

"Well yes." It didn't take a psychic to figure that out.

"It's not like before, though. You told me that you used to be able to talk to her."

"It could have just been something I made up in my head. I missed her that much."

"If you felt it, then it was real to you. So it was real."

"Is that what you are reading in those books?"

"Well, yes and no. I'm just beginning to understand. And to trust what my mother calls my intuition."

"We used to say that women had it and men didn't."

"But now that's considered sexist, right?"

"I guess." I picked up a small round pale stone and threw it into the stream where it made the most satisfying plop.

"Quartz," she said. "Funny you should choose that."

"It was just a pretty rock that drew my attention."

"Maybe. Maybe not. Quartz is a rock that's good for starting something new. It can enhance your understanding ... maybe your own intuition."

"Okay. I could use a bit of both," I said, easing off the boulder and stepping across three dry stones to retrieve the small stone from the rushing water. My feet got wet sliding off a moss-covered rock and Evie laughed. But as soon as I sat back down, she tucked her knees up to her chin and got quite serious.

"Sheila said we should come out with her. She said something was up. I wasn't supposed to be listening but I'm sneaky. She's worried about you, Jalex. She said we might help get your feet back on the ground. I wasn't sure what that meant. But I'm glad we're here. Mom has been so stressed out with her damn school."

The word *damn* sounded wrong coming from such a young person. "I'm glad you're here," I said. "And I'm sure you'll 'get my feet back on the ground,' as you say, even though it's your fault they are currently wet."

"They'll dry," she countered. But as soon as she said it, I wasn't hearing her. I was hearing the voice of my long gone mother who always insisted that wet feet were a sign of adventure in a young boy. She'd say that any boy who never got his shoes and feet wet would grow up to be a dullard. I was not one of those boys, thanks to her.

But as I breathed the cool forest air into my lungs, my brain locked onto a new dark thought. I was so glad they were here — Sheila, Emily, Evie. But had I inadvertently drawn them into this unpredictable sphere of danger that had begun days ago with that midnight visitation?

"Your darkness is back," Evie said.

CHAPTER 14

"DID YOU KNOW THAT CATERPILLARS have way more muscles than humans do? Seven or eight times more, I think," Evie said.

"I didn't know that."

"It's a proven fact."

"Ah. Well, if it is a fact, then it is proven, so you don't have to say both words."

Silly of me to chastise the kid. "Well, language is very limited in its ability to express the things that are really important."

"I'll agree to that. But sometimes it's all we've got. Tell me something else you've got in your pretty little head."

"I read somewhere that if bees were paid for their work, a jar of honey would cost nearly $200,000."

"I guess we wouldn't be eating much honey, then. Anything else?"

"Well, I was reading about saliva."

"One of my favourite subjects."

"Somebody did a calculation and figures that in most people's lifetimes, they create enough saliva to fill a couple of swimming pools."

"Well, who would want to swim there?"

"Not me."

"You carry all this stuff around in your head?"

"I do. It's called a photographic memory."

"No such thing."

"You're just like my mom. She keeps trying to tell me I'm just normal and should quit playing games."

"Normal. How boring."

"That's what I think."

"We think a lot alike then," I said.

"Perhaps we do."

* * *

To say that things were idyllic over the next few days might be stretching it but it was pretty damn close. Then Sheila took off to check on her "aging aunt." I chastised her for using that term. The woman was not even eighty. But she was in bad health. The big trouble with most of us old cranks hanging on so long is that we don't always hold on to our health. I felt pretty much like the exception. I had to pee all the time but, aside from that and a few creaky bones, I was as healthy as the workhorse I once had who lived a good long life, at least a long one for a horse. And never once had he seen a veterinarian. I always liked what the old ones said about the first things you see when you get to heaven: your dogs, your horses and your grandparents. But I'd sort of lost any belief I might have had as a child about things like heaven. My own view on the afterlife had taken a vacation somewhere and lately, the whole dark Hollywood horror scenario was more scary than celestial.

The idyllic part was having Emily and Evie staying over in Eva's old sewing room. Evie found every little thing of interest and asked questions about everything under the sun. Her curiosity was nearly endless.

Emily barricaded herself in the sewing room during the day to study for upcoming exams. She said she loved the classes, the professors and her classmates but that it was much harder than she had expected. But she always ended her complaints with the phrase that it was "a means to an end."

And I would sometimes be about to say, "Do the ends justify the means?" but Evie said the words like a mantra before my tongue could even begin to shape the D. I wanted to engage that kid in all kinds of conversation about everything under the sun, but found myself reluctant to get her going, given her mother's advice to not encourage her precociousness.

During the night, each time I awoke for a pee, I'd walk into the kitchen, truly fearing a new visitation. But each time there was nothing but quiet in the house and sometimes the sound of an owl somewhere in the distance or racoons rooting around in my trash cans. Nonetheless, at every wakeful interlude, I was fearful I'd find that unwanted visitor at my table while Em and Evie slept in the next room.

Evie woke up on the third night of their visit and saw me standing at the doorway, staring out at a three-quarter moon. "384,400 kilometres away," she said. "More or less. Sometimes closer, sometimes farther away."

"All I see is the man in the moon."

"Well, the right eye is *Mare Imbrium*. The Sea of Rains. I expect I'll go there some day."

"Really, you want to travel to the moon?"

"I do. I think it would be cool."

"Cool?"

"Well. Cool as in fun. But cold as well. Minus 183 degrees Celsius if you are on the dark side. The Chinese landed a probe there so maybe people will be able to go soon."

"Better dress warm."

"John Alex, why are you up? You seem to be expecting something. Or someone." It seemed odd that she called me John Alex instead of Jalex. Made me feel more like I was having a conversation with an adult.

"Not really. Just looking outside."

"Do you still see her? Do you still speak to her? To your wife?"

"No. Not so much nowadays."

"Why?"

"I don't rightly know. Maybe she's tired of putting up with me."

"Mom told me about you setting a place for her at the table. I think we should do that."

"Probably not a good idea."

"Okay. G'night. I'm going back to bed. Keep an eye on the moon and let me know if you see anything strange."

"I will."

I too went back to bed and slept peacefully right on to morning. It was like the little girl had given me a precious gift of rest and peace. Clearly, she was well on her way to becoming that shaman she wanted to be.

* * *

Evie was the one who first spotted the RCMP cruiser pulling into the driveway. Sealy got out just as she opened the door. "Are we under arrest?" she asked him with only the faintest hint of sarcasm. "Not you, but John Alex. He's under arrest for not having a phone."

Truth was, I had a phone — a land line as they liked to call it these days — but I preferred to leave the ringer turned off.

Evie scowled at him, taking him seriously. "That's not funny," she snapped back, not quite getting the joke.

"Well, it's a little amusing," I added. "What's up, Sealy?" I was looking past him as I asked the question, and I could see two other people in the car. I was pretty sure it was Bradley in the front seat but someone else in the back seat.

"We have a problem, John Alex."

"Of course you do. Isn't that your job? Dealing with problems?"

"I was hoping my job would be going into schools and lecturing kids on bicycle safety. But it didn't work out that way."

"Life is full of surprises."

"Life is full of things that are a pain the ass," he added, but then he looked at Evie and apologized.

"You don't need to apologize," she said. "I've heard much worse on the street in Halifax."

Sealy shook his head. "I can see it's probably not a good time," he said. "But I came about Mason. Things have not gone well."

"How is his foot?"

"Well, he's been getting treatment, but he's been raising hell. They're fed up with him at the clinic. They want to send him to the Nova Scotia Hospital in Dartmouth."

"No. Not the NS. It'd kill him quicker than the gangrene."

"Well, that's what Bradley said."

I looked over at the car and Bradley waved to me from behind the tinted glass.

"Thing is," Sealy continued, "Mason keeps demanding we take him back to the island. But Dr. Holbrook is adamant that if we do, he'll die. They've told him that. But he insists."

"You can't take him back there. Not right now." I was already thinking about Holbrook and his sneaky way of racking up another death. Mason was easy picking and I already felt like Holbrook had made it my call. Does he live or does he die to help fill some kind of godawful quota?

Evie looked like she was about to burst with a thousand questions, but I put a hand on her shoulder and shushed her.

Sealy cleared his throat and looked up at the paint peeling off my soffit above the door. "Well, Bradley has been down at the clinic trying to help out. He figures since he went into the drink to save the poor lunatic, then he has some responsibility for him."

"They say that's an old Chinese custom," I said. "You save someone's life and you are forever responsible for them."

"Well, we're not in China. But he's been helpful. He asked Mason for an alternative. Anything so he could still get treatment."

"And?"

"And Mason said, take me to John Alex. So here we are. Let me get Bradley to help explain. Sealy waved Bradley out of the car and into the conversation.

"I'm sorry, John Alex, but he's a nuisance down there to the workers at the clinic. More than a nuisance, really. He's scared some of the staff. But he claims he'd be okay if he could stay with you." Then, looking at Evie, added, "But I can see now that it's probably a bad idea."

All through my life people have shown up at my door looking for some kind of assistance. A meal. Or some advice. Or money sometimes. Or comfort. I'd never turned a soul away, even after they stole from me or turned on me like I was their worst enemy. Now this. "I can't give him the medical help he needs. Could be a bad idea."

"He doesn't need the IV anymore," Bradley said. "Just pills. And washing the wound each day." He gazed out over my field for a moment before he spoke again. "He says he'd be happy to stay in your barn."

"My barn? Not the most sanitary place for someone recovering from a serious wound."

"I could fix it up," Bradley said. "If you're willing. And I'd look after his meds and the foot."

I looked at Sealy. "And you think this is a good idea?"

Sealy threw his hands up in the air. "No. But it's that or the island where he'd probably die. Or shipping him off to some institution where he might never emerge."

"Great then," Evie insisted. "We'll have company."

I thought about what Emily might think and that this could somehow be a bad move with the two of them staying here. But Evie squeezed my hand.

"Okay, we'll give it a try," I said. "Guess I owe it to old Samson Langley. The guy saved my ass once when a tree I was chain sawing snapped and pinned my leg. I was alone, way the hell out in the woods in Dunvegan. I have no idea how it was he showed up after I'd been pinned there for over an hour. Guess this is what he meant when he said I owed him one and he'd make damn sure I paid him back."

CHAPTER 15

BRADLEY MOTIONED FOR MASON TO get out of the car. Mason haltingly stepped out, took a deep breath, and looked around at my overgrown pasture where I once grazed cows and horses and his face cracked wide open into a smile.

"Heavenly," was the word he uttered. He was on crutches and his bad foot was all wrapped up in white.

"You sure you want to stay in my barn?" I asked him.

"No, I want to go back to the island. But that bastard Holbrook says I'll probably die if the infection isn't looked after."

I looked at Bradley and Sealy. "Holbrook said that?"

Both just scrunched up their shoulders. I wanted to ask each of them their opinions about the so-called new doctor but now was not the time. I was wrestling with the idea that all of this might somehow be of Holbrook's design. What if Mason died while in my supposed care … in my barn? What if this turned out to be a really bad idea that would draw us all in?

"Mason, the chickens are in the shed nearby. That rooster is pretty damn noisy. And I used to keep cows and a horse in the barn. They're long gone but I can't rightly say I ever cleaned the place properly. It's not pretty. I'm not sure this is a good idea."

"No," Evie piped up. "It's a great idea."

Mason looked at Evie now. "Squirt," he said. "Who are you?"

"Evie. I was born here."

Mason looked at me with a big question plastered on his face. "No, she's not mine. But she was born here. Her mother's inside."

"Why'd you call me Squirt?" Evie asked.

"That's what my father called me when I was your age. It was either that or Pipsqueak."

"That doesn't make any sense," Evie said.

"It just means you're little."

"Ten. I'm ten. And you can call me Squirt if you like."

"Thank you."

"Okay, let's get this show on the road," Sealy said. "I gotta be back at the cop shop as we like to call it. We gonna move this guy into the Ritz or what?"

Evie was staring at Mason as he gazed off, surveying the overgrown field and the wooded hill behind it. He had a big smile on his face again. Bradley lifted a hockey bag out of the cruiser and led Mason toward the barn. Sealy nodded and exhaled deeply, turned to me and asked, "Jesus, John Alex, is this going to work? I gotta say, it doesn't feel quite right."

"You're wrong," Evie interjected. "It feels perfectly right. My mom says I'm more intuitive about these things than anyone. Trust me. This is going to work out."

Sealy shot me a raised-eyebrows look that Evie didn't see because she was staring at Bradley and Mason. He blew out a little sigh and said, "I hope so or we're all in —" He didn't finish the sentence as he looked at Evie. "Well, you know." Then he abruptly shut his mouth and strode back to his cruiser.

As he pulled away, Evie was tugging me to follow Bradley and Mason to the barn. "Let's go help," she said.

"No, let's hang back for a little minute."

"There's no little minute or large minute. There's only a minute. Sixty seconds."

"Thanks for the information, but Albert Einstein would disagree."

"Oh, right. But what are you worried about? I can see it in your face."

"Jesus, kid, can you read us all like a book?"

"I can read most people, yes."

"Then what do you see in Mason? He hasn't had it easy. And he's been living all alone out there on Wolf Island for I don't know how long."

"He's what my mother would call a lost soul. Like the men on the street in Halifax. She says that if she can finish her naturopath degree, she'll find a way to help them. So this is just like me and you doing the same."

"What do you mean, me and you?"

"I have this feeling that I'm supposed to be here right now."

"Oh God. Not this psychic crap again."

"Yes, this psychic crap, as you call it. But it's intuition, that's all. Mom says that she expects I'll lose it as I get older. I can already feel it fading. Like I'm getting old and losing it. I don't want that to happen."

"You're ten, kid. Ten. Not even close to being an adult."

"Thank God for that."

I figured I was being a little too rough on Evie. She was a live wire as we used to say and between her and everyone else coming into my life, I could see that I was not in charge of anything here. Events were just moving forward. And maybe that was good. It wasn't too long ago that I was pretty sure I was dead. Not one-foot-in-the-grave dead. But *dead* dead. And maybe I was meant to be here right now helping "lost souls," a term that my mother once used when referring to the drunks asleep down by the old mine shafts.

Emily walked out of the house now and squinted in the bright sun. She still had a textbook in her hand. "John Alex, what exactly is going on out here? Wasn't that an RCMP car?"

"Just Sealy," I said, "delivering the latest patron of the barnyard hotel."

"His name's Mason, Mom, and he called me Squirt. He looked sort of happy, but I could tell he was happy and sad at the same time. Happy up on top, but pretty beat-up deep down. John Alex and I can help fix that, though."

Emily scowled. "John Alex, what have you been telling her?"

"Haven't been telling her much. She pretty much explains everything to me. You know what she's like."

So Evie proceeded to explain the situation with Mason as she understood it and it seemed to make more sense than the way I saw things, so I kept my mouth shut.

Turning to me, Emily asked, "You trust this Mason person?"

"He does," Evie answered for me. "It's a lost soul sort of thing." And so I just nodded.

I could tell that Emily was stirring this around in her mind. "Should I be taking my daughter back to Halifax, then?"

"No," Evie insisted. "I have work to do here."

"John Alex?"

"If you feel you should take her back, go."

Evie had folded her arms in front of her chest now.

"That won't work," Emily said, realizing she was outgunned. She turned to go back inside. "Just keep me in the loop, you two. I need to study."

The big barn door was open and the morning light was spilling inside. It suddenly felt odd that I had so rarely even gone in there in recent years. The smell was that of new mown hay, although any hay left in the barn would have been decades old.

"The roof looks like it doesn't leak," Mason said. "How about that?"

Mason and Bradley had already begun to clean up what had once been my old workshop. The wooden floorboards creaked as we walked in. I surveyed the bench that held my old tools and wondered how it was that I had just stopped using any of them. Stopped growing my own food for the winter, sold off my cows and watched my last horse die. All that seemed a long time ago. A lifetime ago, as I often heard myself say.

"I made a few calls," Bradley said. "A couple of carpenters I met at the tavern. They'll be up this afternoon. Said they were happy to help when I told them it was your place. Said they could round up some used furniture too."

"Just like that?" I asked.

"Just like that," Bradley said. "All I had to do was mention your name."

"Age has its privileges, I suppose," I mouthed the cliché, even though it was a damn lie. "But keep in mind, this is only temporary."

"Maybe afterwards, you can rent the place out on Airbnb."

"What the hell is that?"

"Never mind. Anyway, thanks for doing this."

Mason was looking over my old tools on the bench with great curiosity. "John Alex, I could make things with these. Maybe help pay you back."

"Don't worry about paying me back. Just get well and do what Bradley tells you."

"I will. I promise."

"Outhouse is still standing out back," I said. "Door hinges are probably a little rusty but never had the heart to tear it down."

Mason nodded and went back to looking over my old rusty tools on the bench. A wave of nostalgia flooded over me. When had I just stopped doing all the daily chores and repairs and everything that was once my life here with Eva in our days together? Maybe that's why I never came out here anymore. Too strange to think of my life then, my life now. Just too heavy on my heart to think about that other man who was once me.

"I have a good feeling about this place," Evie said.

"So do I," Mason echoed. "So do I."

* * *

The carpenters were a couple of thirty-somethings from town who brought a case of beer and a boom box with some kind of rap music. They worked like madmen through the afternoon, and I had to keep Evie out from underfoot. She watched the whole thing like it was a stage show as she sat on a bale of hay. By late afternoon, Emily came out and announced she had cooked a big pot of chili with what I had in cans in the pantry.

Bradley had gone off to work, but the rest of us had a picnic out on the grass near the barn. The lads put some fiddle music on the boom box and, as soon as we were finished the chili, they loaded up their tools in a hurry and roared off to town as if it was all in a day's work.

A pleasant quiet settled over us as I helped Emily clean up. Mason sat on an old milking stool speaking in a low voice to Evie, answering her endless questions. I could hear her giving him some kind of advice and it was clear he was taking her seriously.

"Evie does this with everyone she meets," Emily whispered to me. "Tells them what she thinks about them and suggests what they should do. Now people in Halifax come over just to ask her opinion when they have to make a big decision."

"Like an oracle."

"That's exactly what it's like. I try to discourage her. But it does little good. I think this intuition thing — she'll grow out of it."

"She said you told her that."

"Well, if she doesn't, she's gonna have a hell of a time in high school."

"And beyond. But maybe it's a calling."

"Maybe. But I don't think I believe in such things."

* * *

As the sun was beginning to set, Mason announced he was going to bed. The old workshop had been transformed by the young carpenters who had also marvelled at my old tools. It was a single room in the barn, sealed off mostly from the rest of the expanse with rough cut lumber they had brought up with them. Reasonably clean and now furnished with a table and a bed that even had clean sheets. They'd set up a bottled water dispenser with one of those big blue bottles filled with gallons of clean water and had even brought along a camp toilet. Their whole operation had been a picture of efficiency, the likes of which I had not seen since my last barn raising decades ago.

So, for now at least, Mason, the lost soul, was a found soul. I'm sure his chili farts echoed in the rafters as mine did in my bedroom that night. I guess it's not the worst thing in the world if the last thing you hear at night after a good day is the sound of your own farts in your own private space. And I'm sure I'm not the only widowed man who fondly remembers his wife beside him farting in her sleep after a satisfying day in a married life.

Evie had persuaded her mother to stay on for a few more days and I felt blessed with every day that they were willing to remain here.

That night, however, the Holbrook manifestation appeared again. This time I knew it was a dream and, when I woke, I was determined not to mention a word of it to anyone. But it was Holbrook as the death visitor this time and not masquerading as a doctor. He was not at all threatening in my dream but had the demeanour of a trickster. "So now you see," he said, "how you are connected to these people. That circle I told you about. You can't remove yourself or get away from it, and now you are more deeply entangled than ever." In my dream he held out his left hand and I thought I could see a flame emanating from the end of his fingers. "Is that some kind of threat?" I asked.

"Not at all," he said. "Look closer. They are candles. Candles to light up the darkness." But then he blew them out and it was pitch dark. And the dream ended. Like most dreams it didn't really make much sense. But it haunted me through the rest of the night until I woke.

CHAPTER 16

I WAS UP AT DAWN and went outside to take stock of the thousands of spider webs filled with dew in the overgrown field where I had once grazed cows and horses. Mason was outside of the barn already, sitting on an old kitchen chair that was missing the back. He was rocking back and forth like he was in a rocking chair but it was him, not the chair.

"How did it go last night?" I asked the boy.

"Couldn't much sleep. Lots to think about in an old barn like that."

"I suppose so," I said. "Anything more we can do?"

"I'll get used to it," Mason said and he stopped rocking. "I miss the island. She speaks to me at night, you know. The island and the sea. They have a kind of conversation going and they let me listen in."

It made sense. "What are they discussing?"

"Everything. Pretty much everything."

"And they let you listen in?"

"Oh, they know I'm listening. They just feel a little sad that everyone else has stopped."

"Stopped?"

"Stopped listening."

"Oh. Well, did the old barn have anything to tell ya?"

"A fair bit. But it's not the same. What about you, John Alex? Do things speak to you?"

Funny he should ask that. They did and they didn't. "Oh, I don't know," I said. This was an old man's line — tossed off when he didn't want to say what was really going on in his head. I found it worked quite well to end most any conversation. Not like when I was young and yammering an opinion about everything and anything.

"All those spiders out there are looking after you, John Alex." He had noticed the endless rows of dew-laden spider webs as I had.

"How do you know that?"

"I just know."

"Tell them I said thanks."

"I will."

It's funny that he had said that because I always had a good feeling about spiders. And didn't Father Walenga say they were considered to be protectors in parts of Africa? Plenty in the basement of my old house but I never bothered them and they never bothered me. And they ate other things — carpenter ants and powder post beetles that might have chewed through the beams in the old place. Now I had a field full of spiders watching out for me. Guess they'd been doing that for a long time.

"Let me know if you need anything, Mason," I said.

Mason nodded and, turning his head, smiled as he squinted into the morning sun.

Em was in the kitchen when I walked in. She was making coffee.

"Up early," I said.

"John Alex, I need to get back to Halifax. Those exams are coming up. I don't have all my books and I need the college library."

She detected the disappointment in my face.

"Evie says she wants to stay," she added. "She says you promised to take her to the old homesteads up the mountain."

I had never promised any such thing. But I reckoned Sheila had told her about our hike up there recently, difficult but rewarding as it was.

"You know what she's like when she sets her mind to something."

"Yes, just like her mother," I said, smiling. I remembered how strong-willed Em had been as the teenage girl who had stayed with me through her pregnancy and birth. It was a good memory.

"You think she'll be okay here?" There was a fair bit of worry in her voice.

"With Mason out there, you mean?"

"Well, yes, that and, well, you. Can you handle her?"

"I figure I'll just let her take charge. She's pretty smart."

"Too smart if you ask me."

"Takes after her mother there, you know that. We'll make do."

"That's good because I already called an Uber. Should be here soon."

"A what?"

"An Uber. Like a taxi. Someone to drive me to the bus in Port Hawkesbury."

"How will this Uber even find you way up here?"

"GPS probably."

The kettle boiled and Emma poured the water into the coffee pot. I now saw Emma's packed bag on the kitchen floor. It was already a done deal before we had our little discussion. Emma would be off to Halifax and little Evie was staying on.

And sure enough, the Uber arrived ten minutes later — an old Honda driven by a kid who looked no older than a seventh grader. He whisked Emma away back to her books and library and healing school.

When Evie woke up, she didn't speak a word. I scrambled some eggs while she sat at the old wooden table and studied the grain of the wood.

"They say silence is golden in a child," I told her as I slipped the eggs around, trying to keep them from burning in the black cast iron frying pan that had once been the possession of my mother.

"I always wondered who *they* were."

"Well, join the club. *They* were probably a bunch of old farts who had nothing better to do than sit around and come up with stupid expressions like that to hand down to their offspring."

"Offspring is a really interesting word, isn't it? It's like they spring off of their parents."

"It is just that I think. Probably from Anglo-Saxon."

"Do you speak Anglo-Saxon?"

"No. My father taught me a little Gaelic, but it's mostly gone."

"So many things are gone. I don't get it."

I was shovelling scrambled eggs onto one of Eva's favourite plates. "Eat your eggs before they get cold."

"Thank you, John Alex."

"For what?"

"For letting me stay while my mom goes back to her studies."

"Did I have a choice?"

Evie just hunched up her shoulders.

"You'll be bored out of your gourd," I said.

"Very poetic. The rhyming. But no, I won't be bored. I have an agenda."

"An agenda?"

"The word comes from Latin — things to be done."

"So you're studying Latin now?"

"In my spare time. On the internet. It's an online course from Princeton. And it's free."

Nothing this kid said could surprise me. "But why Latin?"

"Just trying to help Mom with her schoolwork," she said with a mouthful of eggs, spitting some onto the table as she spoke. "Latin terms are used for a lot of herbs and plants."

"Of course. And they used to say children should be seen and not heard."

"That's a good one. And whoever *they* were, *they* were idiots."

"I'm not sure you're supposed to use that term anymore."

"Hey, I'm just a kid. How would I know that?"

And the conversation rambled on like that for many more minutes until it occurred to me that I was ever so glad that Evie was here as my houseguest and we'd share the day together. And that

I was on her *agenda*, not mine. Such a monumentally good thing. All I needed to do was keep death away from my door — another old cliché, I reckon, but that was my primary motivation these days.

But what if by keeping Evie here, I was putting her in danger? Or was it just that I was a crazy old man, even crazier than I was when Emma had this baby child here in my house ten years ago? It made more sense that I was simply having visions. Dreams. Hallucinations. Lack of oxygen getting to the old brain, maybe. Alzheimer's. Dementia.

"John Alex, did you know that you're thirty-three times more like to be killed by bees than to win a lottery jackpot?"

"No, I didn't know that. What else you got for me?"

"Well, there's a 99.9 percent chance there is a molecule in the coffee you're drinking that once passed through a dinosaur."

"You get this from the internet, right?"

"I do."

"Who comes up with this stuff, anyway?"

Evie carried her dish to the sink as she answered. "*They* do."

And indeed the girl did have an agenda. "I want you to take me to that place Sheila mentioned, way up on the mountain."

"You want to see where my ancestors lived? There's not really much to see."

"But I want to go there. With you. I like old things."

"Like Latin."

"Latin is okay, but I like to see things for myself. Can we go?"

"I'm not sure I have a choice. We'll need to pack a lunch."

"It will be an adventure."

"Indeed."

I was expecting she would be disappointed. Buildings were long gone, the road grown over with alders and yellow birch. And I wasn't sure I was up for the difficult trek again. "We're going to have to stop for me to rest along the way. A lot. I'm old, you know?"

"You're only as old as you think you are," she replied with fake smugness.

"Please. I'll go as long as we give up the clichés."

"You started it," she quipped.

"And I'm stopping it now."

"Agreed."

It was shaping up to be a fine day and why not pay my respects again to my ancestors that I had mostly ignored in recent years. And, besides, there was no denying Evie's agenda. Sandwiches and water were packed into my old rucksack, and I laced up my old work boots as Evie watched with a most serious demeanour.

Evie had on some kind of fashionable overalls which surprised me, but even more surprising was her footwear — some kind of heavy-duty hiking boots for kids. She saw me looking at them.

"A hundred and fifty retail. Mom got them for twenty dollars on Kijiji."

"Oh, Kijiji. I buy all my shoes there."

"Liar."

We were barely out of the house when Mason walked over to speak to us. "What's up, little one?" he asked Evie, positively ignoring me.

I had been hoping we could get out of the yard without having to explain but Evie told him exactly what was on her agenda.

Mason nodded. "The past doesn't really ever go away. It's always there," he said.

"Metaphorically speaking," I added, hoping to end the conversation.

"Not everyone thinks time is linear," Evie chided me.

"Well, I do, Little Miss Einstein," I said, feeling it was my duty to be cantankerous.

"On the island," Mason said, "one of my favourite spots was the remains of the old lightkeeper's house. Not much left but I felt at home there. Can I join you?"

"Of course," Evie said before I could indicate that I didn't think it was a good idea.

Mason broke out into a broad grin. But then he noticed the look of doubt on my face.

"What about your foot?"

Mason slipped back into the barn and came back with a walking stick he must have fashioned out of my old scythe handle that had been hanging in there. "I can do this, really. I promise I won't slow you down. I'd like to see the big trees up there on the mountain, too. Trees are always comforting to me. They remind me of my father. And there's not a lot of trees on my island. Some wind-whipped spruce they used to call tuckamore but nothing big and grand."

I could see that I didn't have much choice here.

Evie set the pace, a brisk one, up the old grown-in cart track behind the farmhouse. She chanted some kind of nonsense song as we walked.

"Maple, white spruce, hemlock, hackmatack, balsam fir, jack pine, poplar," Mason reported.

I had nothing to add to keep up with the biology lesson.

"I think I'm in love with the forest," Evie said.

"So am I," echoed Mason.

After that we walked on in silence for a long time, Evie looking down at the plants on the ground, Mason looking up to the treetops and me just looking straight ahead, trying to keep in step with them as the path grew steeper and steeper.

It was then I noticed that Evie was breathing funny — a bit raspy. "Evie, you okay?"

"I'm perfectly fine. I still have some trouble breathing, but if I focus with my mind I can make it go away."

And indeed, her breathing became steady.

"See?" she said.

That bit of concern started me worrying again about Mason's

foot injury and I began to think this was all a very bad idea. "Mason, you're not limping. How's that foot?"

"Better," he said. "Much better."

"Maybe this isn't such a good idea."

"I'm okay, really. It's healing. I have it bandaged and have fresh bandages with me. Let's keep going. Please."

So I convinced them to slow the pace — for Mason, but also for me. Evie was the first to break the forest silence after that. "John Alex, you know you don't have to be afraid of dying," she lectured.

"Why do you think I'm afraid of dying?"

"I don't know. Girl's intuition. I just sense you have this dark cloud hanging over you again."

"I don't see any dark cloud."

"I do. But you can make it go away."

"How?"

"Stop worrying."

"I'm not worrying," I snapped back. Although this wasn't true. By now I had convinced myself I was part of some circle of people where someone had to die, as the mystery man had said. And wasn't it always true? Somewhere, in any cluster of the population, *someone* would always have to die. Not necessarily me or you. But *someone*. And it was always a sad loss and there were those who grieved but it was never completely real unless it came close to home. And truth was, I never got over the death of Eva and that was a long time ago. I took a deep breath and tried to sweep those thoughts out of my head.

"Poof," I said. "See, dark cloud gone. Up above only blue sky and white cumulus."

Evie looked up. "And cirrus."

Mason stumbled and I took his arm. He steadied himself and then pulled gently away.

When I indicated it was time to stop for a rest, I don't think either Evie or Mason realized we were there. "This is it," I announced.

I could barely detect where the old loose stone foundations were with their basements filled in, the ground and the growth swallowing up everything, trying to put it back to the way it was before anyone arrived.

"They lived here?" Evie asked.

"Yes," I said. "At least forty families. Came over from the Highlands in a ship, were promised land and here it was. My ancestors. Driven from their homes and glad to be here, far from everyone else. They were actually afraid of the trees at first."

"How could that be?" Mason asked.

"No forests left where they lived. But they adapted. Made peace with the trees, I suppose."

Evie looked around, eagle eyed, until she saw something and her eyes locked onto it. I knew immediately what it was.

"That was the cemetery," I explained. "Not much left, but there it is." The grave markers were crude upright stones that looked nothing like modern-day headstones. But there was an order to them that I had determined years ago, indicating that this is where the settlers buried their dead. "A lot of children died young in those days. No hospitals, no nurses. Many women died in childbirth."

"My mom thought she was going to die when I was born," Evie said. "But she didn't. Thanks to you."

"And your Aunt Sheila."

"She's not my real aunt."

"Guardian angel then."

"I don't think I believe in angels."

"It's an expression. I didn't mean she had wings."

"Oh."

"I like it here," Mason said, resting now on a fallen hemlock trunk that lay diagonally across the old graveyard.

"Sometimes the old dead ones are good company," I heard myself say before I really had a moment to think about what I was saying.

"I'm going to be with you when you die, John Alex," Evie said. "That's one reason why you shouldn't be afraid of dying. You won't be alone." I noticed again that she had stopped calling me by the childhood name she once used — Jalex.

But what a weird thing for the kid to say. "I think you should stop thinking about death, little lady."

"But we're in an old graveyard. What else should I think about?"

"Why don't you think about what you want to be when you grow up." It was a stupid adult thing to say. Like asking, "How was school today?"

"I know what I'm going to be. I'll study psychology at Dalhousie University, get a graduate degree and then become a counsellor — a trauma and grief counsellor. Just don't tell my mother. She's completely opposed to the idea."

"Trauma and grief? And you know this for sure?"

"Some things you just know."

I didn't doubt her at all. But I kept wondering how she was ever going to get through her adolescence and teenage years as such a serious, sensitive, intuitive and weird girl who would probably alienate her peers. I didn't speak of any of this but, instead, let the magic of the place sink into our minds.

"I buried my father myself up there in the woods in Margaree where he lived," Mason said. "The trees were just like this. It was where he wanted to be."

"Of course it was," I said. "I visited him there at his home many times. No one was going to move that man from his mountain or far from his cabin."

"Maybe we should all die as we live," he said.

"I don't know if it works that way. Most folks die in hospitals these days."

"That's sad," he said.

Evie walked away from us and began to touch each of the remaining stones that served to mark the graves. Anyone hiking up here would never have realized these were grave markers. But somewhere beneath this soil were the remains of what had once been my great-great-grandfather and great-great-grandmother. And that was something.

When I'd poked around up here before looking for artifacts I'd always found something, even if small and insignificant. Still don't rightly know why I smashed the last one to smithereens, no doubt making Sheila question my mental wherewithal. Evie walked beyond the grave markers and toward a mound that may have once been a foundation. She stopped and sat down on the leafy ground, then swished her hand back and forth, brushing the leaves away. Then poked her fingers down into the rich soft forest soil until she found something. She rooted away with both hands and then tugged something out of the ground, brushed it off and held it up for us to see. It was a spoon. Looked to me like a baby spoon. Tarnished, corroded, crusted with dirt. But a spoon nonetheless. "Never know what you might discover in an old place like this," Evie said, running to me with her find and giving me a big hug.

I looked at Mason, who now had his shoe off and was replacing the bandage on his foot. "Let me look at that," I said. The wound had healed surprisingly well in such a short time.

"It's better, but I think I'll need to take it slow on the way back," he said.

"Slow is good," Evie said. "Gives me more time to study the forest."

And study it she did on the way back down the mountain, leaving my mouldering ancestors behind and returning to our own century along that overgrown trail beneath a canopy of tree branches. "Maple, red spruce, pine, hemlock, oak," Evie named them as we walked on.

CHAPTER 17

IT MUST HAVE BEEN NEAR midnight when I heard the floorboards groan. Often in an old house like this, you hear sounds — creaks and groans through many nights, but this was the familiar sound of human weight on those floorboards. I rarely locked the door so anyone could have just walked in and sometimes did. But I woke remembering Evie was sleeping here in Eva's old sewing room. I stopped breathing and listened.

Nothing at first. Then the sound came again. Thinking that Mason maybe had come into the house for more water or some other reasonable purpose, I half convinced myself it was nothing to worry about. But instead of calling out his name, I slipped out of bed, threw on my old housecoat, slid my hand across the wall until I found the doorframe and then the light switch on the other side. I flicked it on.

The guy stopped dead in his tracks, the bright light shocking him.

"What are you doing here?" I asked, not wanting to raise my voice and wake Evie.

Before me was a young man with long straggly hair wielding some kind of a knife. He had a nearly cross-eyed, crazed look in his eyes.

"Go back to bed, old man," he spit at me.

"Who are you? What do you want?"

"Just go back to bed, Grandpa. You don't want to fuck with me."

"No, I probably don't. But you're here in my house and I didn't exactly invite you."

"Back off and don't do anything. I just want money. Tell me where to find it."

I kept my eyes locked on him but didn't make any moves. He had a knife. I had nothing but a pair of ninety-year-old hands. The look on his face was something I was not at all familiar with. Desperation, nervousness, fear even, but something much more. The tortured face of a young man on some kind of drugs. It was starting to filter into my brain that this was maybe the same guy who had burst into the pub demanding money. What was it they said he was on? Meth? Whatever the hell that was. They said he was not to be messed with.

"I got maybe sixty bucks in my wallet," I said. "Let me get it."

He thrust the knife forward into the air as I inched toward the old desk where my wallet sat. I fished out the three twenties and waved them at him. He grabbed them and stuffed them in his shirt pocket. "Don't be an asshole, old man. You've got more stashed around here somewhere. I hear you have money hidden away."

"You hear wrong, son. Now leave and I won't call the Mounties. I'll just call this a case of charity under duress."

"You call it what?"

"Charity."

"Don't fuck with me. I told you that. What else do you have here?"

The truth was I didn't have much of anything worth stealing. Never did. Some cash in the back maybe but no mattress stuffed with savings. Not a single item in the house worthy of theft for a drug addict. "You probably need help, son. This isn't the way."

"Fuck you. Where is it?"

I can't say I was shaking with fear, but I didn't like the way this was going. Intruder with a knife. Intruder on some kind of high. Kid asleep in the house. Maybe the jig was up. Maybe this was my time that had been hinted at. I found myself looking at the cookie jar up on the kitchen shelf. My intruder noticed me looking in that direction I guess because he broke away from his knife-wielding stance and grabbed it off the shelf.

Now I was really pissed off. Eva had stuffed it with one-dollar bills in the old days. Ones and twos, actually. Back when we had such things. I had added some pennies to it the year that the Canadian mint stopped making them. It seemed like the proper thing to do. And it added some significant weight. But it wouldn't amount to much for a mucked-up shithead looking for drug money.

He grabbed it but didn't bother to look inside. "What else ya got? I could kill you with this knife, ya know?" The poor misguided lad didn't have much of a knack for threatening conversation.

All I kept thinking about was if I could keep the volume down, Evie wouldn't wake up and this dangerous, pathetic thief would go away looking for greener pastures. "I got nothing else you'd want," I said, as calm as I could muster. "Just leave so an old man can go back to bed."

I reckon that was not what he wanted to hear. "Don't brush me off, you ancient asshole," he muttered. I had already turned my back and, if it hadn't been for the reflection in the glass of an old photo of Eva and me in a dory, I might have missed seeing what was happening. Clearly, I'd pissed him off. He lunged at me with the knife, and I was sure my dead wife in the dory was telling me to deke left. Which I did.

He thrust the knife with such force that it went deep into the plaster wall and must have lodged in the lathes because he screamed out loud at his failure and then tugged hard to pull it out but had no luck.

That's when I saw Evie coming out of her room, rubbing her eyes and trying to make sense of the scene before her. Real fear crept up in the back of my skull as I frantically tried to muster a plan to divert disaster.

"Back in your room," I shouted. "Lock the door." But I knew there was no lock on the door. And Evie didn't move.

My assailant had pulled the knife from the wall now, cutting himself in the process. He briefly studied the blood on his hands and then focused his attention on Evie. In such moments, your mind moves ahead in a flash to what is about to occur, and I knew he would grab her, put his knife to her throat and then want to know where my real valuables were. Instinctively, I kicked this punk in the groin as hard as my old legs would allow, only to enrage him enough in his drug-induced furor that he made his second attack at me, now aiming that knife directly at my balls.

I knew I couldn't move swiftly enough right or left this time to save myself. Evie screamed at the top of her lungs as things fell into slow motion. I didn't even see the new arrival at first, my eyes focused on the giant blade that was about to eviscerate me. But then I saw a hand grabbing the knife and watched in disbelief as Mason threw his full body at my assailant and toppled him to the floor. The guy's face slammed down hard on those foot-worn boards as Mason hammered the back of his head once with a fist so that his chin cracked down with a sound that suggested a broken jaw.

I would not have guessed that Mason would have the strength to keep him pinned but, as the guy squirmed and cursed, Mason slipped off his belt, yanked the sucker's hands behind his back and tied them up. I took the cue and took off my own belt, slipped it around the guy's kicking feet and tightened it. When I could catch my breath and look to see that Evie was okay, I saw her talking on the cell phone her mother had left with her.

"That's right," I heard her say. "Someone broke into John Alex MacNeil's and they have him pinned. I see blood. Someone might be injured. You should get here ASAP."

Who says ASAP in an emergency? I wondered.

As the room came back into focus, I realized this intruder was undoubtedly the same lost soul who had burst into the tavern, threatened and robbed them. But as he struggled, continuing to curse at the top of his lungs in language I wished Evie did not have to hear, I strangely began to feel sorry for him.

Mason looked up at me, breathing heavily, and asking, "Did I do good?"

So I answered. "You did very good. Your father would be proud."

"Give me the cord from that lamp, John Alex."

I didn't quite understand, but I dutifully picked up the lamp, the one Eva used to read by, yanked the cord out of the wall and then out of the lamp. I handed it to Mason who took it and wrapped it several times around the guy's arms.

"Ouch," our thief screeched. "Not so tight."

"What were you doing here?" Mason asked. A silly question at a time like this. Evie was watching the scene with wide eyes, still holding the cell phone in her hand. "I should call my mother," she said.

"No, Evie. Not right now."

"Okay. You're right." Her eyes were fixed on the knife lying on the floor. She picked it up slowly and then backed away from the pinned man on the floor and took it into her bedroom.

"What are you doing?" I asked.

"Hiding it. I don't like knives. They scare me."

"See what you did?" Mason chided the thief who was struggling and obviously in pain.

"What the hell?" the guy said. "Jesus. Mason? Is that you?"

Mason looked down at his captive who now had his head turned to the side. He'd split the skin on his chin but he could talk. No broken jaw, I guessed. Just criminal blood staining my floorboards. "Fowler?"

"Damn, man. Let me up. Take this shit off me."

"No," Mason said. "I can't do that."

"You two know each other?" Evie asked as she came back into the room. I was standing beside her now, realizing if anything else went wrong, I'd defend her to the death.

"Fowler, what are you doing here?" Mason asked him. "Why are you doing this?"

"I'm sorry," he said, sobbing. "They said an old man lived here, that he'd just sleep through it. All I had to do was walk in and take whatever I wanted. I didn't mean to hurt anybody."

"For fucks sakes, Fowler. We were the ones getting the crap beat out of us all the time back at school. When did you decide to start hurting other people?"

"I was desperate. I didn't mean to."

Mason, still surprising me with how strong his skinny self was, picked the hog-tied Fowler up off the floor and sat him down on my old rocker. It squeaked as it took his weight and it seemed like the most unlikely of sounds at a moment like this. Usually I associated a squeaking rocker with someone sitting down with a cup of tea.

"Drugs," I said. "He tried to hold up the tavern, I think, a while back. They said he was on drugs."

"You a drug addict?" Mason asked.

"You always were the smart one," Fowler answered sarcastically.

"And you steal to keep yourself in drugs?"

"Again, Boy Wonder. I'm surprised the teachers never recognized your genius."

Blood continued to drip from his chin. Evie picked up a dishtowel from the kitchen table and dabbed it before I could pull her away. Fowler had stopped struggling but was shaking his head side to side. "What's with the kid?" he asked.

"I never met a real drug addict before," she said.

"Well, now you have," he said.

"I'm sorry for you," she said calmly. "What is it? Heroin?"

Fowler laughed. "Don't they teach you about drugs in school? It's meth, kid. Methamphetamine."

"And it makes you steal things?"

"Apparently," he said.

"I don't understand," Evie continued.

"Don't try."

Mason was hovering, ready to move if Fowler tried to get up, but he didn't look like he had anything left in him. He sat there, his head hung over, as I heard the crunch of tires in the driveway, car doors opening and slamming shut.

When Sealy snapped open the door and walked in, he had his gun raised. Two hands on it with the barrel pointed straight ahead. He looked at Evie first, then around the room, taking it in. "We good here, John Alex?" he asked.

"I don't know. No, maybe yes," I said. "This guy showed up. Uninvited you might say."

He stared at Fowler, more blood still dripping from his chin, his hands tied tight.

"Oh Christ. Him."

"You two have met before?"

"On several unpleasant occasions. Everybody here okay?"

"Everybody but him," I said, not paying close enough attention and allowing Evie to dab Fowler's bloody chin again with the dish towel. Sealy looked on in disbelief.

"That Emily's kid?" he asked.

"'Tis," I said. "Visiting. And then this turkey shows up."

It was then that I heard a second car pull up to the house. Sealy put a hand back on the gun that was in his holster. I pulled Evie to me and we edged backwards into the hallway. There were footsteps and then Holbrook came in through the door. I swear I detected a crooked smile on his face as he surveyed the room, but then it was quickly replaced with a demeanour of concern.

"Sealy? John Alex? What's going on here?"

"I got a thief," I said.

"They told me at the clinic something was up here. The kid there listens to the scanner all the time. All the emergency vehicles were out to some accident up at Margaree Forks. So I decided to come. Everybody okay?"

"Everybody but him," Evie said, echoing my earlier words.

"Who did that to him?" Holbrook asked, pointing to the bloody chin.

"Mason here did what needed to be done," I said.

Holbrook nodded to Mason. "How's the foot?"

"Better."

"Good. Keep it that way."

Sealy's shoulder radio crackled and I couldn't make out what was being said. Sealy heard it loud and clear. "Oh shit. Fight broke out at that accident scene. A couple of hunters. Sounds like they got into it — rifles and all. One damn thing after another. And in the middle of the night. I gotta go. He'll have to come with me."

"Right," I said. I wanted this Fowler guy out of the house. Tied up or not. If Evie hadn't been here, maybe I would have seen things differently. Forgive the bastard and try to see if I could help. Turn the other cheek and all that. But not with the girl here.

Sealy was lifting Fowler up from the chair now and studying the electric cord tied around his arms. "Some serious work here," he said.

"My father taught me," Mason said. "When I was little. He knew every knot that was ever invented."

"Comes in handy sometimes," Sealy said. "Gotta go." As Sealy led this Fowler kid out the door, Holbrook reached into his small medical kit and handed Sealy a bandage. "Put that on his chin at least, so he doesn't bleed all over your back seat."

Sealy took the bandage, but then jerked Fowler's arm hard as he shoved him out the door. We heard the cruiser fire up and barrel off down the road.

A strange quiet settled over the house now with the Mountie and the thief gone but Holbrook still hovering as if waiting for something to happen. He seemed downright cheerful as if he'd found the whole drama entertaining. "Well, aren't you at least gonna offer me some tea?" he asked me.

Evie had been studying Fowler's face as they left. I wanted to ask her what kind of colours she saw over his head but didn't want to go there right now. I just wanted him out of my house. But instead, I put the kettle on and picked up the cordless lamp that was on its side on the floor.

"Might as well have a look at that foot," Holbrook told Mason. "Sit."

Mason sat down in the rocking chair and took off his shoe and sock. Holbrook carefully unwrapped the bandage and looked at the cut. "This is healing up nicely. Very nicely."

"She did it," Mason said, pointing to Evie.

Evie seemed startled. "I didn't do anything."

"Yes, you did," Mason said. "While we were walking. Instead of it getting worse it got better. I don't know how but I'm sure it was because of you."

At that, Evie, shrugged. But she was still studying Dr. Holbrook, trying in her own way to figure something out about him. I'm sure she saw something, maybe something much more than just his freaking aura.

"I might be a doctor when I grow up," she said. "A psychiatrist probably."

"Good," Holbrook said. "The world needs good doctors. Sounds like you are already a healer according to Mason here."

"No," she said. "That's all in his head. I try but I'm not there yet."

The kettle sang and I poured the tea, found some Cheerios for Evie and offered them to Holbrook and Mason. Holbrook drank the tea before it had a chance to cool. It must have been scalding hot but he didn't react. Mason crunched on dry Cheerios. I felt tense, still coming down from the adrenaline rush of the intruder but wanting Holbrook out of the house as soon as possible.

"Everything somehow seems to be connected," Evie said.

"Shush," I admonished. Just like her to get that little brain working and start chatting, trying to make sense of everything when, most of the time, nothing did make sense.

"Well, Mason here seems to have known him from school," Evie said.

"We were both picked on from day one," Mason said. "Never could shake it. My mother eventually took me out of school, it got that bad. Tried living with my father in the woods but it didn't work out in the end. So I eventually moved out to the island. And it looks like Fowler ended up … like this."

"But here the two of you were in the same house," Evie continued. Holbrook was bent toward her, hanging on every word. I didn't like it at all. "But why would he have picked this house, John Alex's?"

"An old man's considered an easy target," I offered, wanting to move this conversation away from where I feared it was headed.

Holbrook sipped more steaming hot tea. "She does have a point, though, wouldn't you say, John Alex? He comes here to your house and living in *your* barn is Mason, who we brought here from the island where he might have died of that wound. And Evie here calls 911 which brings Sealy — didn't you say you were friends with Sealy's father as well as Mason's father?"

I had never said such a thing. But it was true. I gave Holbrook a look that should have shut him down but it didn't. He just kept talking. "What if Mason hadn't come in to help? What would you have done?"

"We would have handled it." But maybe it was a lie.

"You do have to admit that everything seems to be … well, connected in some way."

Evie was nodding her head. I'd had enough.

"Well, Dr. Holbrook, I guess you'll be going. You're sure to have some people you'll need to attend to at the clinic, what with that accident at Margaree Forks and a couple of hunters at each other with their weapons."

For a quiet second or two, Holbrook sipped more of his steaming tea. Evie looked like she was about to say something, but I shook my head and, for once, she followed my lead. I kept thinking about that circle thing. The connections. The need for someone to die. The more I thought about it, the more I wondered if I had planted the thought in my own head. Maybe the midnight visitation had never happened. But I felt for sure I'd seen *him* that night and there he was the next morning at the clinic. *Something* wasn't right here. And with Evie in the picture, it all scared the bejesus out of me.

Dr. Holbrook was standing up now, picking up his medical bag. "Thanks for the tea, John Alex." And turning toward Evie he said, "And nice to meet you, little lady. You have a sharp mind and will make a fine physician."

As he left, I registered how tall he was. He had to stoop slightly to walk out the door and I wondered why I had not noticed that before.

"You don't like him, do you?" Evie asked me.

"No, I don't," I said.

Mason appeared to be lost in reverie, his head bowed over his bowl of dry Cheerios. When he was finished, he stood up wordlessly and retreated to his room in the barn.

CHAPTER 18

EVIE WAS TRACING HER FINGERS through some spilled sugar on the table with a worried look on her face. She was probably distraught over the events that had just transpired but I wasn't sure I could do a good job of making sense of it for her. So instead, I asked, "How about I tell you a story?"

"I'd like that," she said. "But not a made-up story. Tell me something that really happened."

I had lots of stories, but I wasn't quite sure what was appropriate under the circumstances. So, after a lengthy session of scratching my unshaven jaw, I decided to tell her about something that happened when I was just a boy.

* * *

The natural world itself was a magical place back then. One summer when I was nine, I saw a waterspout in the morning and in the afternoon, fish fell like rain out of the sky. My mother collected them as if it was the most common occurrence. We had mackerel that night for dinner and she bottled as many as she could before they began to stink up the yard.

Sometimes I saw images of chariots sailing across the moon at night even though my father insisted they were only clouds. It rained during bright sun and there was a report of a tornado in the valley at Skye Glen. There was a girl once, who I met down by the brook in Deepvale, who was more beautiful than any girl I had ever known. She said she was visiting from England and met me there five days in a row before she vanished. She could have gone back to England or maybe she never existed and I made her up. I was never sure. When I asked questions around town, no one knew of any visiting English family and no one else remembered seeing the girl and, even if there had been a girl, why would any right-minded parents let their child go wandering in the woods up in Deepvale without supervision?

It was a happy summer for the most part and our father had a new pair of horses that he was very proud of. We were poor, I suppose, but we'd always been poor and this summer had been better than most. Lauchie was trying to teach me how to smoke hand-rolled cigarettes made from tobacco he had stolen from the pocket of a drunken man on Main Street but I was a poor student. The drunken man was Goff Higgins and, when sober, he was like anyone else, but after a few pints down at the tavern in the afternoon, he'd fall asleep on the Liar's Bench in front of Wheeler's grocery store and wait for his wife to come retrieve him for supper.

Lauchie was never an out-and-out bad apple, but he was prone to temptation more than most, I would say. First the tobacco and then some more ambitious theft. But only in broad daylight at the Liar's Bench. That was his domain. And being, for the most part, a good brother, he was willing to share his ill-gotten gains.

But there is more to this story. There was a fortune teller who came to Inverary. She arrived one year with the carnival crowd that pulled into town each August. Most years we didn't have enough money for the rides, but Lauchie knew how to sneak us into some of the tents where we saw magicians cut women in half, send doves flying out from the wrists of their sleeves and turn water into wine. Mostly crude magician tricks but they amazed us back then.

So, once again, it was August and the carnival was in town. Lauchie had a few illicitly obtained dollars and explained we needed to spend it right away so that our parents didn't have a clue that he'd stolen from poor old Goff or anyone else. Our first fling was on a rickety Ferris wheel that was not anything like the Ferris wheels you see in books. It was maybe two stories high, it rattled and rocked side to side and it was run by a shirtless man from Quebec who constantly had a lit cigarette glued to his top lip raining smouldering ash on the ground beneath.

The Ferris wheel made me feel sick and I told Lauchie he should go spend the rest of his money without me. But he said, "No, John Alex. I want to share this. What do you want to do?"

"I want to see the fortune teller," I said.

"She's probably not a real fortune teller," he replied, although I doubt either of us knew what a real fortune teller was, or if fortune tellers were even real at all.

"I don't care. I want to see her." I had watched men from town line up at her tent on the weekend and patiently wait for long intervals before entering. I was entranced every time she walked out to greet her next customer. She was a young woman with long dark hair, elaborate dangling earrings and a silk dress. Her eyes were dark like black stones in a deep pool and she flowed rather than walked, carrying herself as if she was liquid instead of flesh and bone. I wondered why it was only men in the line but didn't ask Lauchie. If you were just watching from the front, it appeared as though the men went in but never came out. But Lauchie explained that there was a separate exit. It was just the way it worked.

We must have had a lot of time on our hands that day, which was most unusual since there was an endless stream of chores to do on our farm — feeding animals, weeding vegetables, hauling water from the brook, washing dishes and cleaning up. But this August day was somehow different. The line grew and then diminished. "What is it that she does in there?" I asked Lauchie.

"She tells you your fortune."

"I know. But how does she do that?"

"She has special powers."

"And you think this is for real?"

Lauchie shrugged. "This was your idea. Do you want to pay to see her or not?"

I wanted to do this more than anything in the world. I understood that my "fortune" meant my future. And I had no idea what my future would bring. I was just a kid. Nine years old.

There were a few women in line now, which seemed to make the men uncomfortable as they nervously danced from foot to foot. Two women went in together when it was their turn and then left about five minutes later, breaking the rules by leaving the same way they came in.

And then at around four in the afternoon when the fairground crowds had thinned to a few strangers, the line diminished to nothing. The woman walked out of her tent and smoked a cigarette in a long black cigarette holder, something I'd never seen. She was beautiful but struck me as someone who could be dangerous. I was changing my mind.

"Now or never, little brother."

"No. Forget it."

Lauchie was staring at her and smiling. "No way. I'll go on my own then."

That usually did it. If my reluctance to do anything was apparent, Lauchie threatened to do whatever the deed was on his own and it drove me crazy. I would not be left out. I was on his heels as he marched forward hanging onto what was left of the money that he had stolen from Goff.

Her eyes studied us as we approached. She wore no makeup and moved ever so gracefully and dramatically as the light breeze fluttered through her loose clothes.

"We would like our fortunes told," Lauchie said boldly. I was tagging behind him, downright fearful of making eye contact with her.

She looked away now as if we weren't even there. She took a long, impressive drag on her cigarette and looked up into the clouds in the sky. I could now smell her perfume — overpowering. "I don't give readings to little boys," she said, still studying the movement of the clouds on the wind.

Lauchie had been holding out a single dollar bill but now reached into his pocket for a second one. "This is all I have."

"Not enough," she said. "And like I said, this is not for little boys. Go away."

Lauchie remained rooted to the spot despite the fact I was tugging his hand. She threw her cigarette still in its holder down at her feet. She lowered her face directly into Lauchie's.

"I said leave," she growled. Lauchie jumped back and, as he did, dropped the money from his hand. But I was frozen where I stood, unable to move. Lauchie started to bend over to pick up the money, but she was there hovering over him. He reached for my hand and was groping at air, afraid to take his eyes off the threatening woman.

But then something changed.

She was now looking directly at me, a boy paralyzed where he stood. At that instant, Lauchie found my hand and was trying to drag me away from this frightening scene.

"Wait!" she shouted suddenly.

"What?" Lauchie asked.

"Who is this person?"

"My little brother," Lauchie croaked.

"Name?"

"John Alexander," he said.

"Stay."

"I don't understand," Lauchie said.

"I made a mistake," she said, her voice softening as she leaned forward and picked up the money on the ground. This motion was like a flowing gesture in a dance. Her breasts were exposed as she bent over but she stood up quickly and adjusted her dress. Still addressing Lauchie, she said, "I see something in him, in your little brother. I see something I need to speak to him about."

"No," Lauchie said now. "I think we have to go."

"Please don't," she said. "Let him stay."

It was me she wanted to speak to, not Lauchie. "No. Both of us," my brother said.

A jerk of her head skyward. An exhale of much breath. "Okay. Come in."

Lauchie took my hand and pulled me into the tent. It was dark inside and smoke hung in the air. There were three candles burning and, as she closed the flap of the tent, I felt like I had entered another world. Certainly nothing I had ever seen or felt here in Inverary. She seated herself behind a small round table covered with fabric of many colours.

"Me first," Lauchie said, regaining his big brother courage and bossiness.

She gave him a look. "Let me see your hands."

He held out his hands.

"Palms up," she insisted.

Lauchie turned his hands over and she took his right hand roughly into hers. She pressed her thumb into the middle of his palm and her index finger on the back, pinching him hard until I thought he might cry. She brought his hand close to her face. "Just as I thought," she said gruffly. "Better I do not tell you what I see."

"But you took our money," Lauchie said, indignant. "Tell me what you see."

"You are an arrogant little boy, aren't you? You don't need a fortune teller to tell you that."

Lauchie's lip quivered like I had never seen before. No stranger had ever spoken so harshly to him. He tried to pull his hand back, but she had it in a lock between her thumb and first finger. "Okay, if you must know." She loosened her grip and traced her index finger down the palm of his hand, once, twice, three times. "You are a very bright young man but stubborn. You care too much about yourself but not others. You should be more kind. And honest. And you should not steal."

It was the last line that made us both go a little wide-eyed.

How could she have known? Maybe it wouldn't have taken a mind reader to figure out that a couple of waifs like us were unlikely to have our own money. Lauchie had cringed at the sting of her insults then demanded, "But that's not my future. I want you to tell me about my future."

"Sometimes I choose not to."

"That's not fair," Lauchie said.

She leaned back and lit another candle, this one directly behind her which changed the lighting in the room and put her face in a shadow. "Okay, little man, if you insist." She clasped her hands in front of her face and proceeded. "You will be well-liked by men, but especially by women. And it will not always be well-deserved. You will hurt many along the way, possibly betraying your own brother. Many will think you are important and even successful, but you will know that the truth is otherwise. Should I stop there?"

Lauchie looked defiant. He probably assumed she was just trying to be mean to him now. "No, don't stop."

"You will not get to see old age. You and your brother will have a great falling out and it will be your fault. You will die of an illness brought on by your selfishness."

Lauchie's face gave away his feelings of anger as he rejected her cruel words. He stood up, said nothing, spit on the ground, then turned and walked out of the tent, his hands curled into fists. He did not call for me and he did not turn around. In a second he was gone and I was sitting alone with her. She seemed unperturbed by his reaction and exit.

"And now you?" she asked with a hint of a smile.

I think I was in shock or some other state of distraction because I didn't move.

"My name is Theodosia, by the way," she said in a softer voice. "I am sorry that I was so harsh with your brother. He deserved it. But what I have for you, I am sure, is very different. Will you come over here or have I frightened you?"

She had frightened me of course and here I was, my big brother gone, alone with this woman who had said such cruel things to him. Still, I inched forward and sat down on the stool across the small round table from her.

"Reach out your hands, please," Theodosia said in a voice so gentle I felt like it was wrapping itself around me like a velvet blanket. I held out both hands, palms upward. She placed her hands upon them, palms down. "Close your eyes."

As I did as she asked, I grew dizzy. It felt as though my thoughts began to collide with each other. Perhaps it was because she was reading my mind. I didn't know. I listened to her deep breathing. "Now open your eyes."

As I did, she let go of me but began to stroke the palms of my hands with her long fingernails. "Your story is different from your brother's," she began. "There's so much I could tell you, but I need to be careful. I've learned over the years that people always say they want to know their future, but as you can see with your brother, it does not always make them happy."

I was feeling strangely relaxed now. I had not spoken a single word to her. I reached deep inside to find my voice. "Those women I saw walk out of here. They also looked angry. Why?"

She laughed. "The men are easy. I tell them what they want. They leave happy. They feel they've got their money's worth. The women? I feel I have to tell them the truth because they are all my sisters. The truth is not always easy."

"But you didn't tell my brother what he wanted to hear. Why?"

"Because he was arrogant. I punished him."

"Then what you told him was not true?"

"Let's forget about him and concentrate on you."

"Is it going to hurt like that?"

She shook her head. "Not like that. When I first looked into your eyes, I knew I wanted to talk to you. That's why I changed my mind."

"What did you see?"

"I saw you as a very old man." She ran her finger in an arc across the palm of my right hand. "This is your life line. Interrupted but very long. You are meant to live a very long life. A long, rich life."

"I'll be rich?"

"Not like that. Rich in experience." She traced another line across my palm. "A powerful love life, I see, but I don't know what that means to you at your age."

"I understand what it means," I said, although I wasn't sure I did.

"Good. I also have to say you will suffer losses and feel guilt that will haunt you. But my advice is that you will have to learn to live with it."

"Will I do something very wrong?"

"We all do. But most importantly, you have a powerful spirit. It will put you in conflict often and you will wage wars within yourself and with the world around you. But that will shape who you are. And you must be true to yourself."

"What does that mean?" I asked.

"I can't answer that for you. You'll need to discover that on your own. Can you try to remember that after you leave here?"

"I think so."

"Most people will not recognize you for who you really are and you will learn to accept that. You could be destined for great things, but I believe you will choose to live a simple life. There is nothing wrong with that.

"But here is something that I will have a hard time explaining because I don't see it in your lifeline or your heart line or anything in your hand. I just feel it in my heart. You must remain strong through your life. Stubborn, even. Do not give in to petty jealousy or ambition. And you must keep yourself healthy and strong until you are very, very old."

"How old?"

"I don't know."

"But why? Why do I have to do this?"

"I just know that you must do this because there will come a time, maybe more than once, when you will be needed by those around you. And you must be there for them."

"Who are these people?"

She threw up her hands. "I have no way of knowing."

"And what is it I am supposed to do?"

"I don't know that either. But the things I have said are very important, and you must remember them. Promise me."

"I promise."

And then she took my right hand, pulled it toward her and put it on her chest. She pressed her other hand on top of it. "Do you feel that?" she asked.

I closed my eyes again. "Your heart beating."

"I have a strong heart."

Then she put my hand on my own chest and pressed both of her hands on top, almost squeezing the breath out of me. "Do you feel that as well?"

I nodded.

"Our heartbeats are exactly the same. In some ways, we are the same. That is why I have told you these things, and that is why you must remember them."

I nodded again. When I opened my eyes, Theodosia was blowing out the candles. The tent was very dark. I tried to look at her, but she had turned away and I thought maybe she was sniffling and wiping her eyes, but as my eyes began to adjust, I saw she was tucking the two dollar bills into a pocket on her dress. "Now go home and give my apologies to your brother. But remember everything I said."

"Okay," I said, and with some difficulty, stood up and walked back out into the daylight, my head swimming.

At home when I tried to tell Lauchie about the apology and tell him what she had told me, he didn't want to talk about it. "I don't even think she's a real fortune teller. I think she's a fake," he said.

The next day, on my own, I went back to the fairgrounds to see if Theodosia would talk to me again. There was nothing there but a vacant lot. The carnival had moved on. No Theodosia, no tent, no rickety Ferris wheel — just trash blowing around in the damp breeze off the Gulf of St. Lawrence.

CHAPTER 19

"DO YOU THINK SHE WAS a real fortune teller?" Evie asked.

"I don't know. But what she said made a lot of sense. She seemed to know what she was talking about."

"And your brother died, didn't he?"

"Yes, quite a while ago. Cancer."

"And was he mean?"

"Not exactly mean. Selfish maybe sometimes. Or maybe self-centred is more like it. Perhaps that wasn't the best story to tell."

"No, it was good. Thanks for not sugar-coating it for me. I hate when adults do that. But what happened to the girl? The English girl?"

"I came to the conclusion that I had just imagined her, that my mind was capable of conjuring up something so vivid that it would seem real. That frightened me, too. So I willed myself to never do it again."

"And did it work?"

"Yes, I think so. The girl never returned. The gypsy never came back to Inverary. Fish stopped falling from the sky. I think I made the magic go out of the world. My world at least."

"That's very sad."

"It's called growing up."

Evie waited for me to say something else. But I didn't know what to say.

"Maybe the magic is still there. Maybe most people just can't see it."

"Maybe," I said. "Now enough of that. What is next on your agenda?" There was that word again.

"I'm going to read and try to get my mind off things."

"That's brilliant," I said. "Good plan." I looked out the window where the rising sun melted the darkness of our frightening night. "I'm going to go outside and get a breath of fresh air."

Once outside, I immediately felt the sun warming my face and allowed the oxygen to fill my lungs. I started thinking about Lauchie but then started getting angry all over again about him seducing Eva back when we were still young. I walked back and forth across the yard fuming and then quit altogether and sat down on the chopping block. Through the window, I could see Evie sitting in the old sewing room reading. Best to leave her be for a bit, I thought. Kids don't get enough quiet time these days.

And then I began to wonder what became of Theodosia. I wondered if that was even really her name. Of course I never saw her again. And maybe the encounter and her prophetic words were nothing more than parlour tricks. But there was something about that day that changed the way I looked at the world. Someone drops into your life, says something important, teaches you something maybe. Then disappears. You never see them again. In my life, that must have happened a dozen times or more. Connections. Disconnections. And we're always, always left to make sense of things on our own. Suddenly, there in my overgrown garden, I felt more alone than ever. Disconnected. And I didn't like it.

* * *

Weeding made me feel like an old man. What with the bending over and the weeds talking to me in their most arrogant voices saying, yes, you are an old man and you are not even tending your garden and so we are taking over. To hell with you, you little bastards, I'd think and try not to say it out loud. Once upon a time, weeding was easy. Heck, I even cooked and ate some of them back in the day. Now it was just a battle. Another battle I was losing. And that called for a nap.

When I woke up, Sheila was in my kitchen washing dishes and cleaning up. When she saw that I had opened my eyes, she said, "Welcome back to the world of the living," which under normal circumstances would have been a fine thing to say but it gave me a twinge.

"I've never been revived to a sight more beautiful," I said, the old grumpy curmudgeon in me giving way to a gentleman that I never was or could be.

"I bet you say that to all the women cleaning up your messy kitchen."

"Well, I would if there were more than one."

"Slimy bastard," she shot back, smiling. "Where's Evie?"

"In her room reading, the last I saw of her."

"Her mother called. Emily said she's not able to come back here to pick her up and wants to know if I'll drive her to Halifax. I said yes. I want to check in with my financial advisor, anyway."

"Wanna gawk at your money?"

"Something like that," Sheila answered.

"That kid is gonna grow up to be something special," I said.

"I know. Crazy smart for her age."

"But something else too. She understands people in ways I never could."

Sheila placed a pair of cups on a shelf above the sink. "Yeah, that too. Maybe she can save us all from ourselves."

"Whatever that means."

Sheila walked over to me and put a hand on my shoulder. It was like electricity shooting through me. Just that simple touch. There had always been something physical between us but not in the way that most people would think. She was so much younger but that didn't seem to matter. She understood me. She *got* me, as we used to say. I didn't ever have to explain myself. And yes, I think, people did talk. The stupid idiots in town. They talked when Em stayed here and had her baby. They talked when Sheila's car would be in the driveway overnight and in the morning. But it was never like that. And I could never explain it even to people who knew me. Sheila and I were deep down connected.

There was that word again.

"Sheila?"

"John Alex?"

"How long do you think I got left?" It must have been the lousy weeding that made me feel more mortal than usual.

"Don't ask such a dumb question."

"I was just thinking today I got a lot of unfinished business. Things I'm supposed to do but I don't even think I know what they are."

"Your problem is you have too much free time."

"Time? Time rushes by like a freight train."

"Each day gets shorter to you from the time you leave the womb. Day two is half your life. Day one thousand is one thousandth of your life."

"That's reassuring. Thanks for the update."

"You're welcome." She had moved back to the sink and was drying a cup with a not-so-clean dish towel when she looked out the window. "Oh shit," she said. "What now?"

"What?"

"RCMP."

I heard a car come to an abrupt halt and a car door open.

"It's Sealy."

"What the hell?" I growled.

It didn't take Sealy long to make his way into the house. He was drenched and looking more than a little dishevelled. And he was in a bit of a huff. His noisy arrival must have drawn the attention of Mason because he was right behind Sealy, darkening the doorway with his presence and looking anxious as a cat who'd lost her kittens. As if on cue, Evie came into the room holding the thick book she had been reading with a what's-up look on her face.

Sealy plopped down in a kitchen chair, picked up a stale cold cup of coffee that had been there since the other day and took a good pull on it. "Looks like you need something stronger than that, Constable," I said.

"No thanks. Just let me get my wits and I'll tell you why I'm here."

Evie walked over to me and took my hand like she does sometimes, and we all just stood there waiting for the shoe to drop.

Sealy took another sip of the coffee. I think maybe it was two or three days old. Sealy didn't seem to mind. Finally, he took a big long breath. "Fowler's still in the car. I don't know what to do with him."

"I thought he was under arrest," I said. I could tell Sheila was on pins and needles wondering what the hell we were talking about but I waved my hand to quiet her.

"Okay," Sealy began. "So here's what happened.

"I got up there to Margaree Forks with Fowler in the back. It was dark as a dungeon out. The punk was locked in the cage behind me and seemed content enough to be there, bloody chin and all. Hardly a peep out of him. Maybe the drugs had run their course and he was coming down.

"Anyway I responded to the call like they told me, and I get there and in my headlights I see these two guys standing in the road, each holding a hunting rifle. Probably just .22s but they were close enough to each other to do some serious damage. An old Chev was dented in the front end and it looked like the back bumper had fallen off the pickup truck, so they'd obviously had some kind of accident. So there I am with these two lunatics holding a gun to each other and shouting curses like I never heard in my life.

"Cars had stopped but no one else had gotten out of their vehicle. So there I am, fumbling with my radio, looking for backup but the blasted thing doesn't want to work. Loose wire. Fowler's asking me what's going on, but I don't answer him. So I step out of the cruiser like a good Mountie and pretend I'm all cool and collected and ready to take charge. But before I know it, the one guy lets go with a blast at the other guy and then one at me. Both shots are wild and away so that at least was the good news.

"Well, the second guy shoots out the window of his opponent's truck and then takes a potshot at the guy and makes a run for the Chev. I shout at them to stand down but it doesn't do any good. I'm ready to get my service revolver out and try to put the fear of God into these two assholes but the Chev guy has already made it back into his car and is driving off. He's headed east along the river but doesn't get very far before his road rage buddy fires off two more shots. One shatters the back window and another hits a tire. That makes the car veer wildly to the left, only the driver doesn't seem to want to let up on the gas. Before you know it, he's off the road and straight into the river.

"A lot of rain lately I guess, so the water is high, and he's got the front end of that car planted about as deep as he could get it in the river. I point my searchlight over that way to get a good look and hope I don't get a bullet in me. Meanwhile, the guy who shot up the Chev got back into his truck and is driving off. There's not a blessed thing I could do about that. The other people who are watching don't want to get involved. I don't blame them, of course. And I'm thinking, holy mother of God, now I have to go for a swim to save this idiot. And I don't want to do it.

"But I do. I drive my car as close as I can get, keep my light on the water, and leave my gun on the front seat. Fowler doesn't say a word. I'm yammering to myself the whole time saying I'm just gonna let the bastard drown but my body seems to be doing otherwise.

"Only problem is, I get into the freezing water and it's up to the roof line of the Chev. Buddy's unconscious behind the wheel and the water is up over his head. The door's bent up and jammed shut and nothing I'm gonna do will make it budge. I yell to a couple of men standing there watching, but they both just get into their cars and leave. I figure I only got a couple of minutes at most if I want to do any good here so I'm back at the cruiser looking for something to jimmy open the door when Fowler pipes up saying, 'You got to let me out so I can help. I can hold my breath for longer than you can. I've been practising all my life. It's the only thing I was ever good at.'

"I'm at a total loss. Turns out I don't even have a tire wrench in the trunk. And I'm running out of time if I want to save that idiot in the river. So I throw up my hands and I let Fowler out of the cage. First thing I know he's running like a rooster with his head cut off. At first, I think he's just tricked me and he's running away, but instead he runs down to the river, sloshes right in and makes his way against a stiff current to the car wreck. I watch him go in through the blasted out back window and by now the water's up over the roof and the car's drifting downstream in the rushing water.

"Well, I'm back in the water now, not even sure how I got there, and climbing up onto the trunk of that wreck when I see the head of the guy coming up out of the back window, then his body is being pushed out like a cow giving birth. Fowler is still inside, completely underwater. I guess the bastard really could hold his breath after all. I grab hold of the shoulders of the driver, heave and heave until he's out. But I still don't see any sign of Fowler. It takes all my strength to drag the unconscious man ashore and finally, one of the bystanders, this chubby old woman who looks like my Aunt Myra, helps me get him out of the water.

"I go into full CPR mode and ask her to run back to the trunk of my car for the resuscitation kit. She wasn't much of a runner, but she did as she was told. At this point, I still don't see any sign of Fowler and the car's beginning to slide on the rocks, drifting into deeper water. I'm thinking this is a totally screwed up situation. Do I go and try to get Fowler and leave this turkey to get what he deserves or stay put and try to revive him?

"Fortunately, right about then, I see a hand come up out of that back window and then a head. Fowler comes up sputtering, thrashes himself out of that mess, flounders a bit in the current but eventually finds his feet and comes ashore.

"Auntie comes back with my medical gear and I'm completely out of breath from pumping the chest and giving breaths. I look at Fowler and he looks at me. 'Walk away if you want,' I tell him. 'I won't come after you.' But he stays put, asks what he can do to help. So I tell him how to charge the defibrillator machine even though he's sopping soaking wet. He follows the instructions like a real trooper. I put the paddles on the guy and hit the juice. Once. Twice. Three times.

"Coughing and vomiting is the reward I get but that's good enough for me right about then. Auntie sits right down in the muck and props this guy up and smacks him on the back like a newborn baby and then holds him in her arms while I try to stop the world from spinning. I hear a siren and wonder if it's another Mountie or an ambulance. Fowler just finds himself a rock that he likes and takes a seat like he's sitting in a church pew. He closes his eyes and there's this damn smile on his face. I can't say I ever saw anything like it.

"Well, it's an ambulance which is probably all for the best. A couple of real pros — they looked like teenagers to me, but they knew what they were doing — and before I could say Bob's your uncle, they had that guy strapped down, loaded up, hauled off and headed down the road to the hospital.

"I started walking back to the car, water dripping out of all my pockets. I figured I'd let Fowler do whatever he wanted and I'd try to explain all this insanity to someone back at HQ. But he just followed me back to the cruiser like a loyal hound dog, got in the back and closed the door, locking himself back in the cage.

"When I got in, I tried the radio and it still didn't work. Fowler tried to hand me his cell phone but it wouldn't fit through the wire. I thanked him for doing what he did. He said, 'No big deal. But I didn't think I'd make it back. I can't swim.' I asked him, 'Then why'd you jump in the river?' He just repeated that he was good at holding his breath, that he'd been practising in cold water in bathtubs since he was little.

"I had no idea what to make of that. That's when I decided to drive here."

Evie was wide-eyed. Sheila was still holding the cup she had been drying, frozen in place as if in a painting and I was scratching an itch I had on the top of my head. "Why here?" I asked.

Sealy took another sip of the cold coffee. "I was kind of hoping you might decide not to press charges."

I thought about it for a few seconds while everyone in the room waited for my response. "Good deed cancels out a bad one?"

"Something like that. Probably not something I should be asking."

"Well, you asked it, didn't you?" I said.

I was still gobsmacked by the story, so I wasn't thinking all that clearly except to imagine that here was an opportunity for an old man to offer a life lesson about forgiveness to a ten-year-old girl who may or may not be some kind of child prodigy. So I said, "Okay. Roger that."

Sealy nodded silently, then looked at Mason and handed him the keys to let Fowler out of the car. Soon, the two of them returned. I could tell right away the drugs had run out of Fowler because the look in his eyes was completely different from a few hours ago.

"John Alex isn't pressing charges," Sealy said, trying to sound like a professional lawman now.

"Thanks, John Alex," Fowler said, hanging his head. "And I'm really sorry about last night."

"Don't worry about it," I replied.

"I nearly drowned trying to get myself back out of that car," he said. "That scare was exactly what I needed. I'm going to clean up my act."

It was probably something a drug addict said a thousand times. And never followed through on. I knew nothing about these methamphetamines he was using. But part of my brain insisted this was playing out in a most interesting way. So I decided to let things unfold.

"How are you gonna do that?" Mason asked.

"Cold turkey. Only way for a guy like me."

"Let me help," Mason said. "We'll go to the island."

"Probably not the best idea," Sealy said.

"What then?" Mason asked.

I looked at Sheila, that damn cup and towel still in her hand. I remembered that she was taking Evie back to Halifax this afternoon. Things would be pretty quiet around here after that.

"Let him stay here with you, Mason," I said, "if you think you can handle it."

"Good," Mason said. "Fowler and I have some catching up to do."

CHAPTER 20

WELL, WHATEVER WAS GOING TO happen, I needed to get Evie away from the farm and back to her mother. She wanted to stay, of course, but Sheila, always filled with practical wisdom and know-how, said she'd drive her home.

"But I'll be back," Evie insisted. "It's way more interesting here than in Halifax. And you always teach me so much, John Alex."

I gave a grumpy old man groan. I knew when I was being played. But I looked this kid in the eye and experienced that powerful connection felt when her mother gave birth to her, here, in my house, in the depths of winter. That seemed like a week ago in my mind. But over ten years had passed. I gave her a hug and then she went into the sewing room with Sheila to pack their things. Soon they were out the door, but not before Sheila asked me a very familiar question: "You sure you know what you are doing?"

"Of course not," I answered. "Never did. Life just throws stuff at me. That's the way it's always been. And I make a decision — almost always a gut decision, and not always the correct one, I admit."

Sheila smiled endearingly, took my head in her hands, looked me in the eye and said, "John Alex, I should have married you years ago when I had the chance, but I guess I'm too old for that sort of thing now."

It didn't make a lot of sense as she was many years younger than me and my dear departed Eva was the only woman I'd ever be married to. I swore off marriage as any good widower should. I blushed as she held me like that and then felt like a damn fool for doing so. Old men shouldn't blush at anything. "Off with you two, then," I said. "Just be careful out there. It's a

161

dangerous world, if you haven't noticed." And as soon as I said it, it occurred to me that, once upon a time, things had felt quite safe around here. Quiet. Predictable. But not anymore. Danger was all around. Death was out there. Holbrook was still poking around. Meth addicts in my kitchen. Road rage in Margaree Forks. Not quite sure what to think of it or who to trust. Too much for an old codger really.

As the door closed behind Evie and Sheila, I decided to do the only rational thing possible. I settled down on the chesterfield for another nap.

* * *

Some people will tell you that they can control their own destiny. They make decisions, follow through, control their narrative, as I've heard some say. They claim they shape their own lives and reap the rewards from their efforts or get punished for their deeds.

I'm not one of those people. Lord knows I've tried, but in my experience the world just throws things at you and you have to duck and get out of the way or catch. And, naturally, sometimes you get smacked in the face with whatever is hurled your way. With age should come wisdom but ask anyone in my peer group and you'll see that is not always the case. Just when you think you know what is truly going on, the rug gets pulled out from under you.

Nonetheless, it was a quiet afternoon with Fowler probably out puking in the barn and being attended to by Mason who had suddenly become *his* angel of mercy. Sealy had no doubt gone back to being a regular Mountie who followed the book. Sheila was driving little Evie back to Halifax as the charming girl talked a mile a minute about plants, auras, good intentions or clouds. She had lectured me a few nights back: cumulus, nimbus, cirrus, stratus, nimbo something or other. Each one that she described I knew well but I'd never had the proper nomenclature. At least not her names. I had asked her about a mackerel sky and she said the official term was *altocumulus undulatus*. Imagine that. What about those clouds on a Mother-of-Christ morning? I asked.

"Never heard of it," she said.

"Then you should invent a name for them."

"*Mater Christi mane*," she answered. "It's Latin."

"Of course it is," I said.

Well, quiet never did me much good. Sheila had tried to teach me to meditate but all I could think about was corn pudding and fishcakes. With homemade relish. So this afternoon of serenity wasn't really that at all. An old man alone with his thoughts can be a sad thing, and there's the danger of travelling down dark paths of what if, how come, could have done that, should have been kinder, better, smarter. Should have taken each minute and grabbed its bony legs as it flew by.

Perhaps all this cogitation set off something in the goddamn universal scheme as Sheila once put it. Because, before the clock struck two, as I was dozing off yet again, I heard the familiar sound of tires on gravel. I shook myself like a wet dog to get out of my reverie and went to the door. The damnable doctor's car. Holbrook and Father Walenga were getting out. They looked serious as they spoke to each other and I believe they were saying something about me until they saw me scowling from the doorway.

"Regular Grand frigging Central Station around here," I said by way of a codgerly greeting.

Father Walenga was all smiles, warmth emanating from the holy man from Cameroon as always. Holbrook's face I couldn't decipher. Professional fake smile, hint of mischievousness, pretend nonchalance? Hidden malevolence?

"John Alex, is it not a wonderful afternoon?" Father Walenga asked, looking up at puffy clouds that I now knew to be stratocumulus.

"It is and it isn't," I replied out of a reflexive contrariness so ingrained that I'd carry it with me into my coffin and on to whatever other side of darkness was to come.

"Father Walenga and I," Holbrook piped, "had been talking about a dilemma we have down at Green Park and he suggested we get your input. Your help perhaps."

"My help?" I felt it was a trap of some sort but I could see Walenga trusted the strange doctor like he trusted everyone. Holbrook knew that if he came alone I would have told him to get lost, but I could not be unkind to Father Walenga.

"It's your old friend, Florence Henderson."

"Flossie? Is she okay?"

"She is fine for now," Dr. Holbrook said. "But she's presented me with a great dilemma, and I went to Father Walenga for, um, some spiritual advice."

"Last I heard, she doesn't believe in God."

"Nor do I sometimes, John Alex," Father Walenga replied, "but that is neither here nor there."

"Where is it then?" I asked, perhaps a bit too harshly.

"Can we come in and explain?" Holbrook asked. I had expected the bastard wanted to get inside my door again.

"Of course," I said, waving them to follow me inside, even as I had a stabbing flashback of that terrible night when I'd first encountered that man or demon or whatever he was.

They followed me inside and sat themselves at the kitchen table.

"Make yourself at home," I muttered, failing to keep the bile of sarcasm out of my voice.

I looked at the clock, thinking, *Shit and shenanigans, no nap for you this afternoon, John Alex.* Having come to that sad conclusion, I decided that I wanted a drink.

"Rum, gentlemen?" I asked.

"Just enough to wet my whistle," the father said, with a smile as broad as the Northumberland Strait.

"None for me," said the beast. "I have patients to see later this afternoon."

I ignored what he said and poured them both a serious splash of dark Demerara rum into the old jelly jar glasses that Eva and I had used for such occasions. I gave myself a generous fistful too, and then I lifted my glass in a mock toast. "To the future," I said with as little sarcasm as my voice would permit.

"To the future," they echoed.

"And now?" I asked with a husky voice as soon as the pleasant burning sensation subsided.

Holbrook cleared this throat. "It's like this. Ever since I arrived here, it seems that there's something about you, sir, that keeps coming up. Like you are somehow central to other people's lives and the things that go on here in this town."

This was not unlike what he had said to me on that dark frightening night. And I still didn't like it at all. "That's bullshit and you know it," I countered.

"It is and it isn't," Holbrook said, echoing my earlier words. "To get to the point, though. We are here because we want your advice about Florence."

"Flossie."

"Yes," Holbrook responded. "She has said a most dire thing. She says she wants to end her life."

"She's expressed that to me more than once," I admitted. "It's all talk."

"No," Father Walenga added. "I believe she is serious this time. She's made a formal request for assistance."

"Assisted suicide?" I asked. "I guess the good doctor here knows all about that."

"Do not judge, John Alex," Holbrook said. "This is not a matter to be taken lightly. And it's called 'assisted dying.' Just to be clear."

"Of course," I said, now looking away from the strange expression on the doctor's face. What the hell was that look anyway?

"Explain." I found that I was unable to keep my eyes on him. So, instead, I let my gaze attach itself to the half-full rum bottle I had put back on the counter near the tea kettle.

"Well," Holbrook continued, "we believe she has cancer that has spread throughout her body. But she will not allow me to take a blood sample to determine this for sure or let us do any other tests."

"Flossie had the cancer back when she was sixty and she beat it then. Out of sheer will, if I recall correctly."

"But that was many years ago," Holbrook said. "Her body is not as strong now. The ALS has worn her down and I believe the cancer has in fact spread throughout her body. But, as I said, she will not let me confirm a diagnosis with testing."

"And she wants you to administer some kind of drug to end her life?" I wanted to add, *how convenient*, but I did not.

"She does. But I refuse to do it."

"Because of whatever it was you did in Montreal?"

"That has nothing to do with this. And that was a misunderstanding which will be cleared up soon."

"I see."

Father Walenga stared into his empty rum glass and then held it up to capture the sunlight in its mottled sides. "John Alex, please. We are here to ask you to speak to Florence. Tell her she must take some tests, but also tell her that this decision is not wise for her or any of us."

"But if the blood tests prove positive, then it would be legal, right?"

"There are complications but ultimately it would," Holbrook said.

"And you would make this happen?"

"I don't know. It is never a desirable thing to be involved in. But if she was in pain and if —"

"Is she in pain right now?"

"She says she isn't. But we want you to talk to her. She trusts you and your opinion."

"Because she and I are both old as dust, I suppose."

"Aging is a privilege," Father Walenga responded. "We believe that in my country. Everyone there would say so."

"Well, we don't say that here. No one who is old would say that." My words were harsh and I regretted them as I saw the somber look on the good father, so I added, "But, yes, dammit, I will speak to Flossie."

This brightened the mood. "Would you come with us now?" Holbrook asked.

"Why now?"

"When I told her I would not do her bidding, she suggested she may do something herself."

"Oh shit. I see." I finished what was left of the dark dear poison in my glass. "Yes, now."

"John Alex?" Father said.

"What?"

He nodded toward the kitchen counter. "Take the bottle."

CHAPTER 21

THEY LEFT ME AT THE door of the Allan J. MacEachen Home for Aging Humans or whatever it's called. I carried the rum in one of those black cloth grocery bags from the Superstore that had replaced disposable plastic. I was greeted like an old friend at the front desk, and I could tell that Millie, the receptionist, could smell the rum on my breath but said nothing. No one asked me what was in the shopping bag.

"I came to see Flossie."

"She's waiting for you," Millie said, as if the whole thing had been orchestrated and about to unfold as planned.

"How'd she know that I was coming today?"

"Oh, she knows," Millie said. "She seems to always know what's about to happen. I think she believes she *makes* things happen."

"Maybe she does."

"Maybe."

I suppose it was not an unpleasant place, this nursing home for the elderly, but infirmity was everywhere. Old wrinkly men and women hunched in wheelchairs, a posse of lifeless-looking people sitting in front of a game show in the big room. Old faces that I once might have known, now transformed into something else. I would rather let Holbrook take me from this world than end up here. The rum had lit me up for a while but now I wished I was home taking a nap, drooling on my pillow. Lord help me.

Flossie was sitting up in a finely upholstered red chair in her room looking as healthy as a one-hundred-year-old woman could. She beamed as I walked in. "What's in the bag?" she asked. "I hope it's a gun."

"No gun." I closed the door behind me and lifted the half-empty bottle out of the Superstore bag.

"We're not allowed to drink in our rooms," she said with a serious face. "Cups are in the bathroom. Pour us each a big one."

I always did as Flossie requested.

"Here's to your health," I foolishly said.

"Rubbish," she said as as we both took a sip from the white plastic cups. I sat down on the edge of the bed and studied her. I could see the satisfaction in her bright and shining eyes.

There was a moment of silence as we savoured the slow burn of the liquid sliding down our ancient throats. And then she piped up, "Well, Jonathan Alexander, I didn't invite you here so I could guzzle your booze." She sometimes had a way of twisting my name around but I'd always found it sexy. I could still remember when she spoke to me in her youth. I'd be fifteen and she was twenty-five. We were all in love with her, we horny boys of Inverary. She teased us and led us on because she knew the power she had over us and we were helpless in her grasp. But nothing ever came of it, of course.

"No, I guessed that you didn't. But you've got that determined look in your eyes. Like the time you had your sights set on that priest from Quebec."

"That I admit was a mistake. But he was so handsome and so … well, French."

"And you were determined you could have any man you wanted. Even him."

"I was a stupid young woman back then."

"Now, don't be so hard on yourself."

"Well, clarity comes with age."

"That's a goddamn lie and you know it."

"Well, at least I'm willing to admit my mistakes. I still feel bad that he dropped out of the priesthood and married me. He might have done some good in the world. I guess I should feel guilt."

"But you don't."

"Not really. What's the point?" She took another gulp of the booze. "But that's not why I called you here."

"Well, you didn't exactly call me. But Father Walenga dropped a pretty big hint that I should come for a visit. You didn't try to go after him, did ya?"

Her wrinkled face cracked into a smile. "He's a handsome one, I admit. But I'm too old for that." She paused and looked up at the ceiling. "But maybe not. You never know. He's a good talker, but a bit young. You on the other hand would be fair game. No one could accuse me of robbing the cradle."

"No, they couldn't accuse you of that. So is that why you called me here, to get liquored up so you could jump my bones?"

When her eyes twinkled, I could still see the twenty-five-year-old beauty who had captured my young male imagination so many years ago. "Do you realize that between us we have 190 years of lived experience?"

"You always were good with numbers, Jonas Augustus."

"Come on, now, girl. Stop farting around. Why am I here?"

"I'm old, you see."

"And?"

"I want to die."

"Bullshit."

"No. It's true. Something really big this time, I am fairly certain, is wrong somewhere in me — either my head or my body. Maybe my heart. That strange-looking doctor thinks it's cancer. But I never believed in cancer. I'm just bloody old and my body is telling me it is time to let go and sift back into the planet. But I want some control over how and when I die. I was usually pretty good at getting my way. So why not with this?"

"Yes, you have always been good at getting your way," I said, sarcastically, sweeping my arms around the room.

"Well, that's just it. This isn't exactly the life I envisioned for myself and I've had a good run at 'er. So why not close the chapter with a little dignity."

"I always hated the D word, so don't bring it up."

"I just want out."

"It's a bad idea, Floss, and you know it."

"Don't be silly. You, John Alex, wouldn't know a good idea if it came up and bit you in the ass."

"Don't go making this personal."

"Well, you married Eva and that was smart, I suppose. Made me jealous, you know."

"Don't be ridiculous. You were married to that Italian guy from Sydney who owned a fleet of ships."

"Well, a fleet of ships doesn't help a marriage when he's off in some foreign port with one of his other wives."

"How many did he have anyway?"

"Just three including me."

"The bastard. But you're just joking about offing yourself, right?"

"Is that what they call it now? *Offing* yourself? You must be watching too much TV."

"TV's broke. But stick with the subject. What's this really all about?"

"Point is, I've already made my wishes clear to that new medical man. Doctor whatshisname."

"Holbrook? The man's evil."

"Hogwash."

"I believe he's in trouble back in Montreal over the death of one of his patients."

"If he assisted the patient at the patient's request, it's legal, if you haven't been reading the news. So don't try to talk me out of it. I've already signed the papers."

"He made you sign some papers?"

"He didn't make me. I requested it. The law's still a little grey here, so he wants to cover his ass. But he's willing to do it. To be honest, I think he liked the idea."

"Of course he did. You don't know the first thing about this asshole. He showed up in the middle of the night at my house out of nowhere and told me it was my time to die."

"I'm not sure I'm buying your story. You think that man is your Mr. Death? Don't make up such horseshit. He's odd, I'll grant you that, but at least he's a gentleman. He wouldn't do such a thing. Especially not to you. You have people in your life. That little grandchild. You have things to live for."

"Well, she's not exactly my granddaughter, but yes, I have unfinished business and I told him to go to hell."

"Good for you. But I'm sure you imagined it. The doctor wouldn't do that. I can tell that he's a very caring soul. That's why he's willing to help me out."

"That's not what he told me. He and Father Walenga told me to come here to talk you out of it."

She stared at her empty cup for a very long moment then looked up. "What? You trying to hog that whole bottle for yourself?" So I had to splash some more into her cup.

"I didn't know you'd become an alcoholic."

"Jesus Jones, Johnny, I'm a century old. Do you think it would matter at this point?"

I cleared my throat and tried to clear my head. "What exactly did he tell you, this man of medicine who wants you dead?"

"He said it would be painless. He'd give me an injection of some kind of opiate that begins with an F, and I'd just pass out."

"And wake up in the next world, I suppose. A 'much better place than this one.'"

"No, you handsome idiot. I wouldn't fall for that crap. It would just be done. Done done. Whatever is left of my identity would evaporate and some fool down in Port Hood would shove my body into the cooker and they'd shovel me out like the ashes in your wood stove."

"And you want this?"

"I do."

"What if it doesn't work and you end up addicted to this heroin or whatever it is? I already have one drug addict living in my barn. I don't want to have to come here bringing your latest fix."

"You don't know what you're talking about. You never did."

"Now you're making it personal again."

The spunk seemed to leak out of her. She set the cup on the table and looked me in the eye. "All my life, I made one mistake after another. And then I end up here, an old bag of bones with no one in my life who really cares."

"It's because they're all dead. Be realistic."

"But I hurt people. I lived my life just for me and no one else."

"I don't think that's a fair assessment."

"But now, Dr. Holbrook has shown me a way out that makes perfect sense. Clean. Easy. Complete. Finished. Why not have some say as to how we end things?"

"Because it's not right."

"Who are you to say so?"

"Who am I? A friend. An old friend. Don't do it."

"Well, I haven't set a date. And I told him I wouldn't do it until I talked to you first, explained everything and convinced you it was the right thing."

"Don't think for a minute you've fulfilled that requirement."

"Come on, give an old broad a break. You realize that you are all that's left of the old gang."

There never really was an old gang. I had no idea what she meant.

"Once I convince you it's the right thing, I'll take the doc up on the deal. Not before."

"Good then. That will never happen."

"We'll see."

"Promise me you won't let the bastard talk you into anything."

"I promise."

She leaned forward as though she was going to whisper something, but instead she kissed me full on the lips. "You were always such a sexy man, John Alex. I should have married you instead of those other assholes."

CHAPTER 22

I PUT THE BOTTLE IN a drawer and stood up. "You better damn well be breathing the next time I walk through that door," I told her.

"You know I never let men boss me around," she snapped back. "Not even you."

"Not one ounce of common sense in your body."

"Never was, never will be. Come back to see me, John Alex. Before the ALS gets me or the cancer eats me up."

"I thought you didn't believe in cancer."

"Just trying to lure you back. Don't be scarce."

"I won't," I said and felt more than a little dizzy as I stood up and headed for the door.

I walked out of there in a rummy fog and proceeded to hike home by myself. The thought of cancer set me off thinking about my long-gone lovely wife. The fact that I was responsible for her getting the damn illness. Me with the asbestos from the mines in my clothes that she washed. Why had it not killed me instead of her? I'd been puzzling over that for decades. I wondered how many men walked the face of the earth responsible in one way or another for the death of someone they loved — intentionally or not. There were a lot of us guilty bastards out there. And I knew it.

The more thought I gave it, the slower I walked. The more it made me think that maybe *I* truly was the one beyond my expiry date. Sour milk on a refrigerator shelf. Jesus, I was thinking, can't I even have a decent glass of rum without feeling like shit? Most everyone I ever cared about was gone. My brother Lauchie, bastard that he was, I still missed him after all these years. I never did forgive him properly until it was too late. Both of us victims of a cruel father, we should have stuck together until the end, but he had to go and do that unforgivable thing. That's right — some things cannot be forgiven.

At that point, I must have been wandering like an old senile mule through downtown Inverary. Some might have thought I was an escapee from the nursing home. As I shuffled on, I looked up at some of the faces and kept thinking, *Who are these people?* The town was constantly changing. So many new people living here. Most of them younger. And from away. Why, in God's name, did they want to move here anyway? I almost felt like stopping them and asking. But I figured I wasn't in very good shape for that. *March on home, you jackass,* I told myself.

A young husband and wife walked by and they were wearing some kind of face covering like a surgical mask. Never saw anything like it on the street before. It was the oddest thing. They were bantering in a distinctive Newfoundland accent. And it was he who gave me a funny look — directly into my eyeballs, although I couldn't quite make out the expression because of the mask. The street became a bit of a blur — the old familiar place, not at all familiar now. New stores, new sidewalk. Cars I didn't recognize. Maybe old Flossie was right. The time comes when the time comes. I was ready to walk right back there and tell her she was right. Sign myself up for some of that opium shit the doctor of demise was probably already mixing up in his secret laboratory.

Oh, you could say I wasn't thinking straight. But I'd read enough to know that when your body can't produce enough dopamine or serotonin or whatever the happy shit is called, you might never be a happy camper again. So, at that dismal moment, I was thinking, why not just bite the biscuit?

I had to sit down on a bench and regroup. As soon as I did, I began wondering when Inverary had put in benches. There was a little plaque on the back that read, "In memory of Dr. Derek

Fedder, the physician who served this town so well for so many decades. May he rest in peace." It brought back some memories of the man I once considered my friend, the guy who prided himself on being one of the horniest men on the planet and never let his own infirmity with Parkinson's slow him down. I missed the old boy and the things he used to say to me when I'd go in for a check-up. But he too had moved on from the world of the living. And now all that was left of his memory was this bench here on the sidewalk of a town he wouldn't even recognize. *May he rest in peace.* What a silly thing for anyone to say. None of this brightened my mood.

More people walked by, some openly staring at me. I suppose I made a convincing portrait of an old homeless drunk. Not a single one of them would even know who I was. This pissed me off as well, put me in a darker mood. The world had moved on and I was not part of it. It wasn't until a couple of teenagers on skateboards stopped right in front of me that I snapped. A couple of young louts, one chubby and one lean, squirrelling their damn toys along the concrete and kicking them off onto the curb — really annoying little punks. They danced those damn things in circles in front of me and then the fat one came closer and said, "Hey, old man, you okay?"

He might have even been genuinely concerned, but to me it seemed like a hostile remark. "Bugger off," I told him. When he and his goony buddy kept staring I said, "Didn't you hear me? What's wrong, you don't understand English? I said go away."

It was the skinny one who leaned in close enough that I could breathe some boozy breath into his nostrils as he responded, "No, you bugger off." And I suppose I deserved it. Then they both laughed, jumped onto their skateboards and kicked their way off down the street, laughing as they went.

In retrospect, it was clear I should not have been out wandering the streets of Inverary in the state I was in. I'd always hated seeing the town drunks staggering out of the tavern and making a nuisance of themselves. I'd sworn I'd never be one of them no matter how far down into the cesspool I fell. But here I was.

Trying to get my bearings, I straightened up and looked around. Newly paved blacktop on the street. When was that ever the case? Cars parked between painted white lines, all neat and tidy. I twisted my ancient body around to see what was behind me. It was that new drugstore. Nothing like the old pharmacy run by Ronald Gillis. This was a cloned modern contraption, all glass and metal. Shopper's Drug Mart, the sign said. I had come in here before, I recalled, looking for vitamins and met that young man. No doubt this place was owned by more new blood in the old town.

Well, at that moment, it wouldn't have taken much to get me riled up and there was still enough liquid courage in me to want to go in there and express a few opinions. Not that it ever took rum or any other adult beverage to loosen my lips. Nonetheless, there I was, standing up, countering my stagger with a determined forward advance, walking into the brightly illuminated store and traipsing down an aisle that sold nothing but women's perfumes, asking myself what kind of drugstore is this? Mind you, I'd not walked into a drugstore other than this one in over a decade. I guess they all had degenerated into Walmart wannabees, selling everything under the sun to clutter up your mind and your life.

I asked a woman behind a makeup counter — the one who had orange skin like she had just walked off the set of some silly afternoon talk show — where I might find Bradley Rasmussen.

She stared at me wide-eyed as she assessed me and I surveyed her. But I was too far gone to care. She just pointed to a counter at the back of the store and tried to smile but failed miserably to accomplish that small gesture of courtesy.

It was a long and arduous hike to the rear of the store and, despite what you think, my mind was clear in my newfound intention. My vision was as sharp as it ever was (which is not saying much) as I passed shelves filled with toothpaste and stool softener, shaving cream and disposable razor blades, creams and ointments, condoms and God knows what else. When I finally arrived at the back of the store, I saw young Bradley standing behind the pharmacy counter. He wore a white coat and was wearing dark-rimmed glasses. Naturally, he was fiddling with one of those damnable cell phones and it took him some long seconds to realize I was standing there. When he looked up, he seemed somewhat startled.

"Well, Bradley," I said. "How is your day going?" by way of an attempt at civility.

He cleared his throat and said, "My day is going just fine. Thanks for asking. How is yours?"

"It's the shits," I said. "I visited an old friend who wants to die and she convinced me I should do the same."

Bradley appeared shocked. "I'm sorry to hear that. Perhaps you should rethink this."

It now occurred to me that this young Bradley fellow, whom I had come to respect, had no right to be giving a nonagenarian life advice. "This is one crazy ass place you have here, son," I said, realizing that I was spitting some saliva on his pristine white pharmacist smock as I said his name.

"I guess it's fair of you to say that. But then this is one crazy ass world we live in. Perhaps things will be more sane in the future."

"What future?" I retorted. I realize now there was a certain pointlessness to my side of the conversation, but the liquor in my veins compelled me to challenge this pipsqueak on the pretence that he knew more than me about anything.

"Well, I'm getting married a week after my birthday. So I seriously hope we have a future."

"No shit? Getting married? Really?" Why was he telling me this or even giving me the time of day?

"It's true."

"Am I invited?"

"Well, I don't know. It's in the Catholic church down the street. I guess it's open to anyone if you want to come."

"Who's performing the ceremony?"

"Father Walenga."

"No shit?"

"No shit. We both like him very much, Caressa and I."

The oddest thing about this conversation is that he didn't seem at all annoyed with me. Here I was, a cranky, contentious old fart, drunk as a skunk, harassing him for no particular reason and now I was inviting myself to his wedding to a woman named Caressa. "So do I," I said. "He's about the only good thing I can say about religion."

"I know what you mean," the lad said. Then straightening his glasses, he leaned over and asked, "Pardon me for asking, but are you all right, John Alex? You don't seem like yourself."

"No," I admitted, civility now seeping back into my brain, "I'm not exactly all right." I explained about my visit to Flossie and her plan for assisted suicide. "She says she's going to do it with some drug that begins with an F."

"Fentanyl. A very powerful drug. You need to be careful with it. Who is her doctor?"

"Guess who? Holbrook, of course. Dr. Death. Or maybe Death himself."

"Well, he does seem to take on many of the old folks. But he seems to know what he's doing."

"He knows what he's doing, all right. That's why I'd like a little of that, what is it? Fentanyl. I want the pain to go away."

"Are you in pain?"

"Aren't we all?"

"No."

"Can I just have some of it, please. I've got money."

"I can't do that. You need a prescription."

It occurred to me that, if I understood what Fentanyl was — a painkiller so strong that it could kill you — then the only person who would willingly, gladly even, give me a prescription was Holbrook himself.

"I'll be right back," Bradley said, and I thought that maybe he was going to his boss to see if it was okay to give a drunk old man a package of powerful opioids. I was already having second thoughts as the rum tickled my kidneys and made me realize I needed to pee. Okay, I had bullied myself into a dark little cave this afternoon, all of my own doing and, no, I did not really want to die. But I didn't mind the thought of dancing the demons out of my head with something a bit stronger than forty proof Barbados joy juice.

When Bradley came back, he asked me to have a seat on a padded grey chair. I followed his instructions, but not before discovering that this modern drugstore not only had a waiting room but also a bathroom, so I went in to relieve my bladder. After what I reckon to be one of the most satisfying moments at a public urinal that I had experienced in the last two decades, my mood changed and I decided to be on my way home for that nap.

But when I walked out of the men's room, there was an officer of the law before me. Fortunately for me, it was Sealy.

"John Alex," he said, "we seem to keep bumping into each other."

"You here for prostate medicine? I recall your father had some serious issues in that department."

"No, John Alex. Just here to give you a lift home. Bradley and his boss were both worried about you getting home, so Brad gave me a call. Guess it's my job to keep an eye on you."

"But I didn't get my drugs yet," I said, and then turning back to Bradley, said, "What was that one I was looking for?"

"Fentanyl."

"Yeah, that one. Can you just do me up some of that Fentanyl?"

"Sorry," he said, pushing the glasses farther up on his nose.

"We're all out."

I looked at Sealy, who just shrugged.

"But I'm still invited to the wedding, right?" I asked Bradley.

"We'll be expecting you," he said. "And we'll mail you a personal invitation."

CHAPTER 23

"SIT UP FRONT, JOHN ALEX," Sealy said. "I don't want people in town to get the wrong idea."

I sat in the front passenger seat and stared at the little computer screen on the dashboard. "What people in town? Seems I hardly know anyone anymore. All strangers. Not like the old days."

"That's what my old man used to say all the time. Not like the old days. But that goes for you too. This isn't like you, John Alex, wandering around town in the daylight drunk as a skunk."

I might have taken this the wrong way if he hadn't said the words with such gentleness. In fact, now it finally sank in that I used to be able to drink four times as much booze as I had imbibed with the ole girl today and it would never show. "Must be my age," I said.

"You still don't look a day over eighty," he said as he started up the car. "You want me to put on the lights and siren just for fun?"

"Thanks for the compliment. And sure, if you want, let's put on a show."

"I was only kidding," Sealy said. "I realize now that was a mistake."

"Someone once said there's no such thing as a mistake. Everything that happens happens for a reason."

"Who said that?"

"I did. Once. But not anymore. Let me ask you this, Sealy. What do you do if someone sees a thing that can't possibly be real but it seems real?"

"You get your head examined, that's what you do. But who would we be talking about?"

"No one. It was a hypothetical question. Let's change the subject."

"Okay. You been listening to the news?"

"No. I avoid the goings-on in the world if I can."

"Well, that flu thing, or virus or whatever from China, a whole load of people on a cruise ship have it. And it's turning up in all kinds of places now."

"Hope it doesn't come here."

"Well, it's probably a long way off. But it's one more thing to worry about."

"I've given up on worrying. Takes too much energy." But I was lying of course. I worried about a lot of things.

"What about those two guests you have holed up in your barn?"

"I don't much see or hear them. Maybe they have their own drug lab going on out there with the chickens."

"Could be. If so, I'd have to look into it."

We were in my driveway now and I was noticing how rundown my house looked. "Think I'll give the old place a coat of paint this year," I said.

"That doesn't sound like the John Alex we all know and love. Are you sure you're okay?"

"Of course I'm okay. Don't be foolish."

* * *

And then a funny thing happened. I went inside, crawled into bed to take a well-deserved nap and when I woke up it was two days later. I lost a whole day. I either slept through a full forty-eight hours or I was awake through part of it and couldn't remember a damn thing. Maybe I wouldn't have woken up at all if Sheila hadn't been there shaking my shoulder.

"John Alex, come back from wherever you are."

Wherever is exactly where I was, but I didn't have any recollection of it. "I was just taking a little snooze," I said, not knowing at that point that so much time had passed.

"They say people who nap are smarter than the rest of us."

"Well, if that's true, then I should be a genius, but clearly some-one must be mistaken."

"I tried calling but you didn't answer. So I came right over. When I got here, I saw that the ringer was off on your phone again."

"It's always good to see your beautiful face."

"Beauty's only skin deep."

"Not in your case, Sheila."

"Flattery will get you nowhere."

"Too bad. It used to work wonders."

"Listen, I came because Dr. Holbrook asked me to."

"Holbrook again."

"He said he was out here yesterday to check up on Mason and had a visit with you. Said you weren't all there. Saying things that didn't make sense."

"What's so unusual about that?" I asked, but it was a cover-up. I didn't remember anything about this latest visit with Holbrook.

"Well, he says that you should go see him. He's worried about you — some of the things you said, things you've been doing. He'd like to run some tests. You might have to go to the hospital in Sydney for them."

"The nosey bastard. He should stop conjuring up stories about me. Don't you think there's something just a little — off — about this good doctor?" I decided not to bring up anything about the nighttime visits and the whole Mr. Death routine the asshole had been trying to pull on me.

"Nonetheless, I'm crashing here for the next little while. I heard about your little incident at the drugstore too. That's not like you."

"Well, you know we all change as we get older."

"That's bullshit and you know it. You never change."

"Well, it's probably everything else changing while I stay the same that makes people think I'm crazy."

"You're not crazy. You only wish you were."

"Dementia maybe. I've been toying with it for a decade or so now. They say it's the latest thing for someone my age."

"Idiot."

"I love it when you call me endearing names."

"Buffoon."

"Music to my ears."

* * *

A couple of days slipped by and I do mean slipped. Sheila stayed on and the house felt alive again. I wandered out to the barn on an all too sunny afternoon to see what those boys were up to. I discovered their makeshift bunkhouse was all tidy and neat. The floor of the old barn was spotless. But Fowler and Mason were nowhere to be seen.

I went back in the house and asked Sheila where they had gone and she told me not to worry. Holbrook had told her he'd checked in on them. That Mason's foot was remarkably healed and that he thought Fowler had gotten through the worst of his withdrawal. "Also, in case you hadn't noticed, it seems that the two of them may be in a relationship."

"Relationship?"

"C'mon John Alex, you know what I'm talking about."

"In my barn?"

"Yes, in your barn. Get over it."

I immediately saw her point, even though I admit, such a thing never occurred to me. "Well, they must be out on a date or something. The place is all tidy and they don't seem to be around anywhere."

"So leave it. You got any flour here at the Hilton?" she asked.

"I do."

"Bleached or unbleached?"

"On the third shelf in the pantry. Bleached."

"It'll do."

And it did.

The bread was most excellent, hot out of the oven and smothered in butter. A five-star day. And not a thought about death.

Well, not until the six o'clock news. Sheila turned on my old Emerson clock radio to the CBC. Devastating weather out west and wildfires in California. A couple more cruise ships with that new infectious disease. A school shooting in the States again.

"Not one bit of good news," I commented.

"'If it bleeds, it leads,' they used to say in the newsrooms."

However, there was a local reporter who came on after the world news who was speaking about a fire somewhere near Mabou. Suspected arson, the news guy said but there were reports from locals that the old Beaton house had been bought by someone from Vancouver and that they were possibly in the drug business.

"The meth house," Sheila added. "Someone burned down the meth house."

"Good riddance. I hope the bastards fried with it."

"Shh."

We both listened for more details, but the news guy had already moved on. And then the squeaky but heavenly scratch of Ashley MacIsaac's fiddle filled the room with a strathspey that was so familiar, yet I couldn't come up with a name for it.

Sheila cooked a nice spaghetti dinner to go along with the fresh bread and I must say I felt like a new man. Nothing like a good pasta dinner and news about a meth house burning to the ground to make me feel that all is right in the world.

But that didn't last.

Sheila walked out to the barn while I was washing dishes, lost as I sometimes was, reminiscing about my happily married days. Had it really been so idyllic or was that just my mind again, rearranging the past — the days, the feelings, the story?

When Sheila returned, she said, "Mason and Fowler are back. They're asleep out there. Sound asleep."

"An odd pair, the two of them."

"Not so odd. People need people. They found each other."

"If you say so."

"I say so."

* * *

I went to bed that evening and fell asleep instantly even though I had a dull ache in the back of my head. Nonetheless, I felt better about the world and my place in it, with Sheila in the house.

Around eleven that night, she was in my room patting my arm. "John Alex, you better wake up."

I fumbled around in my brain in an effort to bring myself back to consciousness. Then I had to figure out if I was dreaming or if Sheila was really waking me. That line between dream and waking had become more and more blurred in recent times.

"Is everything okay?" I asked.

"How many people know that Fowler and Mason have been staying here?" she asked.

"I don't know. Um. You, Sealy, Em, I suppose, and Evie. Kern maybe. And Holbrook. Why?"

"Sealy called my cell. He thinks they were the ones who torched that house."

"And they seemed like such nice boys," I said, my own sarcasm convincing me that I was fully awake.

"Well, I don't know about that. But —" she trailed off, lost in thought.

"But?"

"But they can't stay here. The guys who owned the place didn't fry in the fire as you would have wished."

"A missed opportunity."

"Let me get Sealy back on the phone." She tapped her bloody

cell phone and then handed it to me. I sat upright in bed and held the damn thing up to my ear.

"Sheila?" Sealy answered.

"No, it's me."

"John Alex?"

"Of course. What the hell?"

"I need you to take Mason and Fowler back to Wolf Island."

"What? Why?" But it was beginning to seep in through my thick skull. "Get Kern to do it, if they must go."

"Kern is in Florida buying a condo. He wouldn't do it even if he was here."

"I don't have a damn boat."

"The key is in his toolbox. The boat is gassed up. They need to be gone by sun up. I can't help. I'm on shift. If I begged off, someone here would figure it out. I'm sorry. Just say no if you're not up for it."

"Do I have a choice?"

"You do. But I don't have any backup plan except to arrest those two — and try to keep them from getting killed."

"So if I don't do this, you think that someone will die?"

"Yes, I do."

CHAPTER 24

IT WAS A DARK NIGHT with only a sliver of a moon looking down on us when Sheila roused my two barn guests from their sleep and ushered them into the back of my truck. We drove down the driveway without headlights like we were spies in one of those thriller movies.

"I've been dreaming about the island," Mason said. "Homesick, I guess. But now I won't be alone."

"Whaddaya gonna do for food out there?" I asked. Sheila had said we didn't have time to pack much except some basics. We were trying to be out on the water before the sun was up.

"Forage, I guess," Mason said. "My old man taught me all there is to know. Lots of fish out there that the sharks don't eat. Mussels, dulse, berries."

"What about winter?"

Sheila elbowed me to shut up. So I did just that.

"We have each other," Fowler said. "I trust Mason. I'm not worried."

"You boys really burned down the drug house?"

"Yep," Fowler said. "It was my idea, but Mason insisted he didn't want to miss out on the fun."

"You better hope the sea is calm. I don't exactly have my sea legs anymore."

"No wind, tonight," Mason said, looking out the window. "Tide should be high around morning and you can tuck into the Southwest Cove. I'm sorry for the trouble."

"No trouble at all," I said, not meaning a word of it.

"You're a saint. My father always said that."

I wanted to say to Mason that his father was a lunatic who lived alone in the woods and believed the trees spoke to him, that he was a misanthrope and a bad judge of character, that his son should have known better than following his hermit example and that he and his boyfriend should have thought twice before destroying a meth lab run by lowlife wannabees who would now want to kill them.

But I kept my mouth shut, looked up toward that sliver of a moon and made my request to the heavens that all the forces of nature hold off on wind and wave until I figured out how to get these two off the mainland and ensconced on that island.

* * *

It turned out that Mason was more knowledgeable about big boats like this than was myself and he went about unleashing Kern's boat from the wharf and using the aluminum gaff to push us out into the channel. I held off for several minutes and enjoyed the silence upon the sea as we began to drift from shore. The engine started and I had to admit to myself that I was confused as to which direction to go. The light of the moon was not quite enough to guide us but Mason tapped me on the side of the head and pointed in a direction that I was confident was his island.

"Are you sure you want to return to your old life?" I asked.

"I'm returning to the island but not my old life."

I had a thousand questions I wanted to ask him about this relationship with Fowler — this alliance of the bullied — the bullied who had fought back with fire and fierceness. But I decided to let the dull roar of the engine speak for us. It occurred to me that I knew little of what danger I might be in if news got out that Mason and Fowler had been living in my barn.

"I could really use some coffee," Sheila said, sidling up alongside me and looping an arm at my elbow.

"Look in the cabin there. Should be a propane stove and if you're lucky some supplies."

"Aye, aye captain."

Sheila disappeared into the little cabin and I saw a light go on. Mason and Fowler were on deck, looking off into the distance as the faintest of morning light appeared. Dark clouds had formed but there was a band of clear sky to the east allowing the morning sun to shine like a band of gold on the unruffled waters.

That bright horizontal band of light only lasted for a minute or two — first light as the photographers say. But it shone like a beacon into the dark morning. I could see Wolf Island now, appearing like a shadowy hillock upon the flat sea. It reminded me of the summer days when I had rowed out there with Eva when we were young. It was nothing then, the physical labour of rowing a heavy dory out to the distant island. The summers were longer then, the weather of those months at least kinder. We would take the old lightkeeper a gift — often just basics — a sack of flour or rice, a wooden box of tea. He spoke very little but would nod his appreciation. Eva and I would hike off to the far side of the island and pretend we were the only two people on earth.

Now, at the wheel of Kern's boat, I felt that time was standing still. And that was just fine.

Sheila appeared again with two mugs of coffee and I sipped the hot black liquid. I think maybe she was someplace else with her thoughts, this kindly woman who had befriended me through so much of my older life.

When I cut the engine, we drifted so gracefully into the Southwest Cove it was almost like the moment had been rehearsed. Mason helped Fowler into the small dinghy, and I lowered down the packs of supplies we had hastily put together for their exodus from the mainland. They had a gentle way with each other that I was noticing for the first time. Maybe it was just sinking in finally that they were lovers, not just good friends. It now struck me as the most natural thing in the world.

Fowler looked straight ahead at the island, his new home, while

Mason turned and gave me something like a salute. Sheila blew him a kiss, but I just nodded and tried to fix an image of this young man in my mind, wondering if I would ever see him or his companion again. I thought of the generations of men — some married, but mostly loners, who had kept the light here. It would be easy to go crazy living on a rock like this in the Gulf of St. Lawrence. But then the world had gone crazy everywhere — more so in recent years. I felt, as I so often did these days, that I was no longer part of it. My time was done, my life past. I was just hanging on, waiting for the end.

The sunlight split the dark clouds for a brief instant, and the two men in the dinghy landed ashore. Mason launched the dinghy back our way and the current from the stream that spilled into the cove sent it directly our way, allowing me to catch it with the gaff and tether it back to Kern's boat. Before the clouds pulled in and the bright morning light faded, I caught a glimpse of Sheila. She now looked much older than I remembered her. She too had aged.

Despite the low roar of the boat's motor, I felt a peacefulness come over me as we headed back to Inverary Harbour. When such moments came to me, I recognized them as rare pockets of time, completely unlike the great quantity of hours that filled my days ever since I was young. Always at odds with something or someone. It's the damnedest thing, but anyone would think that by the time you hit ninety, you would have some things figured out. That you might look back on your life and see the sense to it. That you might have a kind of wisdom garnered by years of experience with all the trial-and-error of solving your own dilemmas.

But that was certainly not my case. Sheila stood off to the side, leaning against the gunwale facing into the fading sun before it was usurped again by dark clouds that would probably rule the day. Her hands were locked around the metal coffee cup that she held like an offering to the gentle but chilly breeze now coming from the northeast around the cape. Steering Kern's boat homeward, I felt the thrum of the engine, the smooth passage of the hull through the deep channel that I could almost feel through the soles of my feet. And I began to wonder if maybe I'd missed my calling after all. Maybe I should have followed some of my ancient classmates into a life on the sea as a fisherman. I had chosen the land over the sea. Mining over fishing. Plundering the earth instead of harvesting from the sea. And, of course, that had been the mistake that cost me my wife. I had forsaken the life underground after that and lived a more dignified one farming and scraping by with very little, but surviving.

As the shore came into focus, the peace would not last. The past and the present collided when Sheila's damn cell phone chimed. I'm certain we had been out of range of cell service up to that minute, but now the serenity had been shattered. As always, the world had caught up with us. I tried to pick up on what the conversation was about, but it was lost in the shushing of water against the skin of the boat. I saw Sheila nodding in agreement to whatever was being said on the other end. When the call ended, she walked wobbly legged across the deck to me.

"I'm going to have to head off when we get ashore," she said.

"What is it this time?" I thought Sheila might return home with me for a quiet day of doing much of nothing. But it was not to be. There was probably an edge to my voice.

"I just have to attend to some things."

"Vague. Very vague."

"My business, not yours."

"Ouch."

"Sorry. Just get me ashore. I'll find my own way."

"Yes, ma'am."

And so the spell was broken.

She detected my disappointment. "You okay?"

"Of course," I said. "When am I not okay? Didn't we just do a good deed? Shouldn't we feel good about it?"

"Of course," she echoed. "You did the right thing."

I saw the anxious look on her face. It wasn't about me. There was something else. But it wasn't my place to keep badgering. Get the woman ashore and let her get on with her busy important life. I gave the engine a punch and we were soon moving at a fast clip to the wharf, the town growing larger in the dim morning light, me noticing the new houses that had been built near the dunes and the many changes along the coastline.

Once I'd tied the boat, Sheila pecked me on my grizzled cheek the way she always did and squeezed my hand. And then she was off, half running toward town, not even waiting for me to shut down the engine and secure Kern's prized possession against whatever coming storms were headed our way.

I went into the small cabin, cleaned up the coffee pot and tried my best to leave the boat exactly as I found it, placing the key back in its hiding place. I took my time leaving the boat and thanking the sea for an easy crossing. I caught myself staring into the rippling water, still a little disappointed perhaps, maybe even in a bit of a trance you might say. I felt the energy of the morning, the completion of the task, draining out through my feet. Feeling, well … what can I say? … old.

* * *

I can't remember the drive through town or anything much at all about the familiar path back up to my farm in Deepvale. I was in a bit of a state, you might say. A mechanistic machine going through motions. Or an old man tired of living, maybe. Or just tired. The excitement of the morning had been enough for one day. Can a person drive while unconscious? It felt that way. Like sleepwalking. Only it was sleep driving. My old truck knew its own way home and did a fine job of taking me there.

As I got out of the truck, I smelled the gasoline right away. Fuel leak, I figured. Rusty gas tank. This would be the third replacement tank I would have to put in the old beast. Ozzers down at the garage would be glad to get the work. Find me a good used one from out west where they don't use salt on the roads.

But, kneeling down and bending over, I saw nothing leaking out of the truck. And yet the smell was powerful and, even before I could unbend my body, I knew there was something else.

I heard footsteps on loose stones, saw the boots, then the gas can. And when I looked up, a young man with broad shoulders was dropping the container on the ground. He was wearing what looked like a football team jacket, a black toque and a nasty look on his face. "Good place to be old man, on your knees. I like that."

Instinct told me to say nothing, wait for pieces to click into place.

"Your houseguests — or should I say, your barn guests — where are they?"

I said what they say in the movies. "I don't know what you're talking about." I made a move to get up off my knees but they weren't being at all cooperative.

"You do. And you're going to pay for it."

He flicked a small disposable lighter. He nodded toward the barn, then at the house. "Two for one. An eye for an eye."

"Quoting Sobeys and the Bible at the same time?"

"Stupid old man."

"I've been called worse."

"Where are those pricks who hit my place?"

"Don't know what you're talking about." There was no bravado in my voice now. Whatever was about to go down, I was pretty sure I was screwed. I couldn't even lift myself off my knees, for Chrissake.

He flicked the lighter again and I thought for sure he was about to do what he was threatening but then he tucked it into his shirt pocket and took a gun out of his team jacket. It looked like a toy gun to me. I was ready to call his bluff but didn't want to move and make a mistake. Didn't want to see my barn or my house go up in flames either. Strange as it may sound, I found myself worried about the chickens in the nearby shed.

"Look, asshole, I saw where they were staying in your barn. Nice and cozy in there. One of them was that Fowler jerk, I know that. Probably holed up in there with his boyfriend. You let them stay there so now you have to pay. I lost everything thanks to that little shit. Tell me where he is."

Well, the writing as they say was on the wall. Whatever I did, I figured the worst. I heard the click of the gun. Was that the sound of the safety taken off? Whatever I would say, I began to assume he'd take me out, then torch the whole place, home, barn, chickens and all. Not at all the way I expected to go out of this world.

"You won't find him around here. Long gone. Left without saying, the both of them."

"You think I believe that?"

"I'm sorry I can't offer more assistance," I said, trying to sound ever so compliant. I would have preferred to play it Clint Eastwood, telling the creep to get off my lawn. But some higher authority in my consciousness had already determined that the gun was most likely real. As far as I could figure his plan was simple: kill the old man and burn the place to ashes with the body inside. Guess you could call it a discount cremation. "Maybe we can make a deal," I finally offered, even though there was no deal to be made. I knew that.

"Too late, Grandpa."

I must have made some kind of sound — a small laugh, a sigh, an exodus of breath in exasperation. I never made it to Grandpa. No son, no daughter, no next generation. The bloodline ended with me. I begged my knees to do their duty. I was already in the nothing-to-lose department. Was it two for one, or all or nothing? I was deciding that I was ready to dive for his ankles, try to take

LESLEY CHOYCE

him down, probably get drilled in the process. But it was better than staying on my knees in front of this lowlife.

That's when the shot rang out. I waited for the bullet. The pain.

Instead, my assailant fell to the ground in front of me, the gun rattling onto the stones as he reached for the shoulder where he'd been hit. I was up off my knees now and crabbing my way toward him as he reached for the gun and found it. That's when a second shot rang out and he lay flat.

He was unable to get a grip on the gun, but the hand that had been clutching his shoulder was reaching for the lighter. I hadn't yet turned to see who had fired the shots but sprinted — yes sprinted forward like a high school quarterback — and kicked his hand away and pinned it with my boot. I kept my eyes locked onto his as the pain in his face morphed into hatred and he spit something at me.

The next thing I knew, an all-too-calm voice spoke the words, "Step away." But I didn't do that until I had picked up the lighter and then kicked the handgun away. When I stepped away, I saw Holbrook about ten feet away and inching forward. He had a hunting rifle lodged on his shoulder and was aiming it my adversary.

"Don't kill me," the young man pleaded.

"If I wanted to do that, it would be done already," Doc said. "Don't move."

CHAPTER 25

FIRE TRUCKS AND MOUNTIES ARRIVED minutes later. Sealy was not among them and I was treated with something less than respect. But then so was Dr. Holbrook. A couple of the firemen were a bit kinder and when I explained about the gasoline and the creep's intentions, they checked out my house and determined the gas can had not made it to my doorstep. They sprayed some chemicals in and around the barn as a young RCMP officer with a Quebec accent asked me a bunch of questions as to what had happened here and why. I was determined not to say anything about Fowler or Mason, lest they get dragged back onto the mainland into more grief.

Officer Leblanc admitted that he knew who the guy was — Gregory Kincaid, supplier of methamphetamine for half of Cape Breton. He offered no explanation as to why his operation hadn't been shut down long ago. All he would say was that they had been "looking into it."

Even after this cataclysmic event, I didn't want anything to do with Dr. Death. I had not untangled my nighttime visitations from my daytime discussions with the man and it seemed inexplicable that he would have shown up wielding a rifle at just the moment he did. But he insisted on going into the house with me to talk.

"Why were you here?" I demanded even though I should have been thanking him for saving my life.

"I was listening to the police scanner. Someone had called in with a tip about a crime about to go down. Your name was mentioned. Something was up. I was just a little quicker than the RCMP."

"You brought a gun."

"It was my father's hunting gun. A .22. Not an assault rifle. I figured it was better than a baseball bat."

"But you knew this Kincaid guy was here to get revenge. That's uncanny."

"There's a word you don't hear much anymore. But, no, I didn't know who Kincaid was or what he was about to do. I understood that you and maybe your two guests were in trouble, that's all. Where are they anyway?"

"Gone," I said. "Gone."

"Where?"

"None of your business."

"This is what you say to the man who just put a bullet into someone who was about to blow your brains out and torch your house?"

"I say this to a man who seemed a little too comfortable putting *two* bullets into someone. I suppose you were hoping to kill him."

"You suppose wrong. Precision is one of the things I'm most proud of. If I wanted to kill him, I would have. I put one shot into his right shoulder and another into his left upper arm. Neither will kill him, but it put him out of commission and saved your life."

"But you like guns, I see."

"I hate guns. But my father taught me to hunt when I was only thirteen with that same rifle. Like I said, it's only a .22, not much of a weapon, but in the right hands it can do some serious damage. My father taught me two important things — breathing and precision. I could have been a world-class surgeon I was that good — at controlled breathing and using my hands."

I had always hated that term, world-class, but I let it slide. "What happened?"

"Things went otherwise."

"Things?"

"Yes. Things. But you'll be happy to know I never even shot

a rabbit when I went hunting with my old man. If we saw any creature in the woods, I'd miss on purpose and he would call me a pussy."

"Nice guy. I know the type. Where was this anyway?"

"Heaven," he said with a cough. "Well, 'almost Heaven' according to John Denver."

It didn't compute.

"'Almost Heaven, West Virginia.' Or so the line goes. I don't think John Denver ever spent much time in that state. I'd say it's more like hell."

Well, you should know, I thought. Despite the fact that this strange man had just saved my bony ass, I was convinced there was some kind of dual-personality thing about him. I still felt in my gut that those nighttime visits were real, that he and I were in some surreal beyond-the-realm-of-the-ordinary battle of wills. "I thought you were from Montreal where you made your claim to fame by offing sick folks who wanted to die."

"I moved to Montreal to get away from West Virginia. Attended McGill Med School. Was near the top of my class." He was starting to look annoyed now. I guess I pushed his buttons. "And no, assisting the elderly at the end of their days isn't exactly my calling. But it comes with the times we live in. The healthcare system is in shambles. Somebody needs to do something. Even if it's helping someone leave this world with — dare I use the word? — dignity."

"But I thought you told me point blank, I was the one who was supposed to die."

"I never said that. This is part of that crazy fantasy you've concocted. I think you need to get professional help."

"Oh, here we go. Now, the doctor is in."

"Go to Sydney. I'll give you the name of a specialist. I've thought a lot about what you said about me and I don't know where it's coming from. But I have a hunch."

"A *professional* opinion?"

"A hunch."

The hell with that. "West Virginia?" I wanted to change the subject, dig deeper now that we were into it. "No accent. But maybe that's a hillbilly swagger I see sometimes in your walk. How'd you end up in Montreal feeding sleeping pills to old women?"

He laughed at that one. Wrinkles formed around his eyes. I realized that he was maybe a fair bit older than I had thought he was.

"I was in the US Marines, if you have to know. They were going to put me through medical school, but I ended up in Central America when the US government was trying to stage another coup. It was like Vietnam all over again but without the TV coverage. So I bolted."

"You were a deserter."

"I got on a boat headed back to the States. Went back home to say goodbye. Then drove north. Kept that gun in the trunk of my old Chevy. Came to Montreal, enrolled at McGill. Never went back. Never even told my parents or brother where I was."

The way he said it, it sounded fake. Something he'd made up to appease me. I wanted to ask more but the adrenalin was draining out of me fast and I needed rest.

He took the hint. "Guess you want me off your property."

"You do have a habit of showing up here."

"Want to hang onto my father's .22? It's registered. I bet you could shoot it if you had to."

"No thanks. I don't like guns in the house."

"Me neither. Just offering. But before I go, I think you owe me one."

"Here it comes."

"This thing with Florence."

"Flossie. What about her?"

"Her condition is getting worse. She's calling my office every day. You know what it's about."

"And?"

"And I'm gonna need your help. Can I count on you?"

I guess I knew what he was asking, but I was suddenly feeling like things were a bit too … what's the word? Orchestrated.

"I should go check on the chickens," I said.

Holbrook left, taking the hint at last.

CHAPTER 26

THE CHICKENS WERE JUST FINE. Jack was prancing around and the hens were noisy in that happy way that chickens are when they're content. I fed them and collected the eggs in the nests. In the ad hoc guest room in the barn, I noticed again that the place had been left spotless. I felt a strange calmness come over me as I carried the warm eggs in my coat pocket back to the house to cook.

Like many, I suppose, I had come to the conclusion that there was no new news. But now there was this thing that some were touting as "fake" news. The American president speaking on the radio used the term even though he was the one most adept at creating it. It was all a bit much. The new infectious virus was showing up now in pockets around the world. Italy had it. More cruise ships docked in US ports were quarantined, their passengers not allowed to come ashore. Frantic reports on conditions in some provinces in China. Someone telling the CBC he'd seen people hauling the dead out of hospitals there using wheelbarrows. An expert with the Canadian Medical Association saying he'd seen this disease coming years ago. It was only a matter of time.

It was all just a matter of time. I agreed with myself that it would be better keeping the damn radio shut off.

The phone rang, which startled me and made me look down at my plate where the two fried eggs sat cold and staring back at me from their bed of toast. Sheila must have turned the ringer back on when I wasn't looking. Damn her.

I answered. Gruffly. A man stumbling in his mind to get a grip after a harrowing experience that already felt as though it had happened a long time ago. It was Millie from the Allan J. MacEachen

204

home. "It's Florence again. She says you need to get down here. Right now."

"Tell her I just got shot at. Some other time, maybe."

A brief hiatus in conversation ensued. "John Alex, this is not a mere request," the woman said. "Curtail your mean-spirited macho stubbornness for once and do us all a favour. Get yourself down here so the woman will stop harassing the staff. C'mon, John Alex, give us a break."

"Wasn't I just there trying to comfort her?"

"Shall I tell her you're coming?"

"Yes, dammit. Tell her I'm on my way."

As soon as I hung up, I had yet another call. This time it was Sealy. He said I needed to go to the RCMP office and answer some questions about what had happened today. "I'll send someone to you if you feel like you're not up to it."

I told him to kiss my ass.

I knew I couldn't say the same thing to Flossie, despite the fact that my body was telling me I had lived through more than enough for one day. What I needed was another good nap. The kind where you fall asleep at three in the afternoon and wake up the next morning at seven fully refreshed. Well, maybe my old truck wouldn't start and I could use that as an excuse.

But no luck. Fired right up this time.

It struck me as oddly amusing that the day could have gone otherwise if Holbrook had not shown up. Devil or guardian angel or one and the same? Wasn't there an old sixties song about that? What the hell?

* * *

I received my usual greeting at the MacEachen home. All politeness and thank yous for coming, but today was garnished with a sense of relief. Apparently, the old girl had been causing more than the usual fuss. Old people can be such a pain in the ass.

"I'm here, okay?" I announced as I walked in. "Like a regular customer, you might say. But I'm not ever going to move in. Don't ever think I want to be one of your inmates."

"Don't be like that," Millie chided me. "You know we'd love to have you as one of our guests."

"Over my dead body," I said, smiling, thinking of course of the irony of my statement.

Millie smiled what I'd call a genuine rather than a professional smile, and led me down the hall, though she knew full well I knew my way. I wished young people would once and for all stop treating old people like old people.

Old Floss was propped up in bed and beamed a smile like the morning sun in June when I walked in through the door. She was happy to see me, but there was something a little odd about her lopsided smile.

"I'm going to start charging you for these visits," I said. I really was cranky.

"Name your price," she said. "I'll empty my bank account. But the truth is I don't have much of anything in it after being swindled by this place."

"I'll just be on my way then," I said, pretending to back out of the room and trying to keep up the gruff.

"Stay, John Alex. This is serious." Flossie leaned forward. She was sitting up now but in an awkward way and having a hard time keeping her head upright if my eyes weren't deceiving me. "Close the door, if you would, young man."

"Your wish is my command."

"I was hoping you'd say something like that. Now sit down."

I sat down. "If you're thinking I'm going to have sex with you, I'm going to have to disappoint you with my answer."

"You're a lovely man, John Alex, but I'm way out of your league."

I dropped the game. "I know that. I always did."

She tried to lean forward but did so with some difficulty.

"Seriously —" she began.

"Seriously?"

"Seriously, squeeze my hand."

I did as she asked. I took her bony paw into mine and gave it a gentle squeeze. It was limp and frail and I suddenly feared I might break some bones. "Feel that?" she said.

"What?"

"That's me trying to squeeze back."

"Not much of a grip."

"That's my point. I'm losing control of the muscles. Can't grip, can't walk, can't really stand on my own. Can't go to the bathroom on my own. Can barely sit up without assistance. Soon they say I'll lose control of my facial muscles. How hideous do you suppose I'll look then? Speech will go next, if not my mind first."

I could tell from the look of her that what she was saying was not far from the truth. "You're probably exaggerating," I said, not wanting to think about it. "You're probably just fishing for compliments. So if that's the case, I need to tell you that you'll always be a strong strapping beauty as far as I'm concerned."

She smiled what I can only describe as a coquettish smile, if such a thing still existed in this modern world. "Open the drawer." She nodded with some difficulty toward the drawer in the table beside her bed. I opened it. Inside was a small plastic vial of prescription pills and, beside it, an unopened plastic package with a hypodermic needle filled with a colourless liquid.

"What am I looking at?" I asked.

"Dr. Holbrook left them for me. I badgered the poor man long and hard but he said he wouldn't do it. Some trouble still in Montreal. He gave me the whole song and dance, but after they did some more tests, the bottom line was he agreed with me that it was my time, but for professional reasons, he wasn't going to do it."

"He had no right to leave this here. Or to give it to you in the first place."

Flossie's eyes were on fire now. "Before you get all huffy on me, hear me out."

I stared at the needle, thinking that what I needed to do was just close the drawer and walk out of there.

"If you walk out on me, I'll never forgive you."

"Then you may have to never forgive me. You're asking me to do what Holbrook wouldn't do?"

She was agitated now, and still having some trouble holding her head up. "Pick up the file folder under the pills. Read it."

I couldn't bring myself to walk out the door. I carefully slid the file out from under the package of pills and the needle. I opened it. Documents. Medical statements signed by Holbrook. Legal documents notarized by Bentley Wright.

"All the Ts are crossed and the Is dotted. Holbrook said so himself."

"And you're asking me to do this thing? I wouldn't even know how."

With great difficulty she held out her right arm by bracing it with her other hand. "You think you'd have any trouble finding a vein in that arm?" she asked. "Forget the pills. Holbrook said if I took them, I'd get drowsy, probably fall asleep and not feel a thing when the drug took effect. But I'm under the impression there's enough of that juice in there to put down a horse."

"I'm not doing this," I said.

"I can't do it myself."

"Ask your daughter to come up from Antigonish and do it then."

"I'm not asking my daughter to do any such thing. She has a life."

"And I don't."

"You know what I mean. *You* can do this. I know you can. I'm not just asking. I'm begging. Look at me. Mostly gone. Can't you be kind enough to spare me the indignity of what's to come?"

"This is a damn big thing you're asking of me."

"John Alex, I wouldn't ask you to do this if I didn't think you were capable. You lost a wife, you've watched people our age — your age — fall all around you. You're tough. And wise. And I have all the paperwork there to make sure you will not be blamed."

I wasn't knowledgeable enough about the law to know if she was telling the truth or making it up.

"I won't be getting better. Only worse. This is the reasonable thing to do. Forget the 'indignity' bullshit. I shouldn't have said that. This is the practical, sensible, compassionate thing to do."

"You always did have a way with words."

"Words have served me well. And reason. Look, maybe there's some cosmic law that says someone in some community or some random clumping of people has to die. Why shouldn't it be me instead of you or another undeserving person?"

"Who told you that?" It sounded way too much like what Dr. Death had said to me.

"No one," she said. There was something different in her voice now. Not just the agitation. A quavering. Was it fear? "Look, someday very soon, I'll be choking, or I'll be unable to make my lungs work properly and these assholes around here will try their best to keep me alive. They mean well, but they're still assholes. I don't want to see that day. I have this thing. This ALS I've been living with. Now it's cancer as well. Now is my time. Please. I don't want to be punished any more than I already have."

Maybe it was the word *punished* that did something to me. I'd felt myself punished for much of my life. For the death of Eva. For other things I'd done. For me, the punishment was that I had to go on living and grieve the loss of my wife and others. The punishment seemed appropriate and reasonable.

"If you were in my position, what would you want?" she finally whispered. "Please, John Alex. Please." There was a single tear now. Just one. She lifted her hand to wipe it from her face but her hand fell back into her lap and she closed her eyes.

I stood up to go. I believed she was unfairly drawing me into her problem. Why me, damn it? This was not *my* problem.

But before I made it to the door, she let out an ungodly sob that stopped me in my tracks. She whispered my name again, not as an old woman, but more like a lover.

When I reached the closed door, I locked it.

I walked back toward Flossie and took the needle from the drawer. I fumbled as I opened the sealed plastic pack, took it out, held it up to the light by the window. I steadied my shaking hands by taking a deep breath and slowly breathing out.

"Right or left arm?" I asked.

"Right please. I'm left-handed, remember?"

I did remember. What a funny thing to stick in my head all these years.

It was not difficult to find a vein in her frail arm. She had been correct about that.

CHAPTER 27

FLOSSIE'S EYELIDS DROOPED WITHIN SECONDS of receiving the dose. "You have a gentle touch," she said, barely audible. "Thank you. Now we'll be forever young. At least in my mind. Now go."

"I'll stay."

"Stubborn man," she said, but in the sweetest voice I had ever heard.

Flossie's breathing became laboured. I kept my eyes on her as she drifted away from me. The slow breathing changed to short, ragged breaths. I reached over to hold her hand and already it was cool and she had no strength to squeeze my hand. There came a shaking and a series of convulsions as I tried not to react in any way. Her eyes stayed locked on mine even as her eyelids fell. I remembered stories from my old Mi'kmaw friends down in Eskasoni telling me that it was extremely important for someone who cares to be present when a person passes from this world into the next. So I stayed — not at all convinced there was another world any of us were going to.

Once it was over, the room took on an eerie silence. Eerie at first but then strangely comforting. Normally there was noise from up and down the hall. But not now. I allowed the silence to envelope me, refusing to think about what comes next or what my reward for this terrible deed might be. Reward or punishment, you might say.

"Now go," her voice echoed in my head. But I stayed. Minutes. Very long, private and overwhelming minutes. "Stubborn man," her voice echoed next. Hadn't that always been the case?

A calm feeling came over me then even as I was aware I was pushing the panic out of my head. What would Flossie want me to do next? She'd want me to get up and make my exit, preferably without leaving any evidence of what had just taken place. But that felt wrong. I did this deed and now should own up to it, explain the compassionate reasons for doing so, go through whatever legal routine one did after such a thing. Shouldn't I?

Deep down I knew that the panic was only because of the monumental thing I had just done, not because I was worried about what might come next for me. No. At that moment, it occurred to me that I really had little concern for my own welfare. My time was not up yet, I knew that, but maybe old Flossie had shown me the way out for whenever I had grown entirely tired and disenfranchised with life on this planet.

There was a tentative knock on the door. "Housecleaning," an unfamiliar voice said.

"Not now, please."

"I'll be back later," she said.

Contact with the living reminded me, I suppose, that I was still one of their tribe. I decided it was time to depart. I took a deep breath and surveyed the scene. Everything looked perfectly normal except for the needle lying on the blanket beside her right arm. I picked it up, having a hard time believing this was the instrument I had used to end her life. I placed the small plastic cap carefully back on the sharp end, slipped it into the wrapper and pocketed it. I then found the vial of unused pills and slipped them into my pocket as well.

Aside from the tiny dark spot on her arm, there was very little evidence as to what had transpired here. There was no bleeding. I tucked her arm back under the blanket. Was I really trying to cover up what had just taken place? "Now go," I imagined her saying to me again, the voice as clear in my ear as if she were still alive.

There was something terribly odd about what it felt like to

212

stand upright. It was like my leg muscles had seized up, as if I had forgotten how to command my body to get up and walk. So I performed it methodically, awkwardly and with considerable mental and physical strain. Before I left, I leaned over and kissed her forehead.

I left the room, closing the door behind me. There was no sign of the housecleaner. The hall itself was unaccountably empty and when I walked by the front desk to leave, everyone was preoccupied and didn't notice me except for Millie, who almost always had something clever, funny or teasing to say to me. This time, she just nodded ever so slightly to acknowledge my leaving.

And then I was in the parking lot, dazed now, surveying the scene. I had no memory of driving here or parking my truck. I looked around until I saw the old Ford parked imperfectly in a spot as far from the front door as I could have managed.

I opened the driver's door and the loud creaking of the unlubricated door hinge almost brought me out of my state of shock. I put two hands on the steering wheel but was unable to start the truck or even think about anything except sitting there gripping the wheel. As I stared out through the windshield, I was looking at nothing at all. My eyes could not focus but I was not deep in thought as one might expect. I was nowhere and felt like no one. Like my own identity as well as my past had been sucked out of me.

It was not guilt or remorse or pain. It was an absence of everything, a seizing up of the senses. I did not know the time of day or the day of the week or the month for that matter. It was a paralysis that I had never felt before, even at the death of Eva or Lauchie. If I had any desire at all, it was for the world to go away and for me to go with it.

When I could conjure together a thought at all it was this: what have I just done? Was it a mistake? How long I lingered there in no-man's-land is hard to say, but I believe the sun was setting behind me because a ray of sunlight slammed into my eyes, reflected from the rear-view mirror and, as if on cue, there was a sound. Someone was tapping on my window. As I turned to look, I could see that it was Sheila. She looked concerned. Troubled. How could she know? I opened the door.

"Are you all right?" she asked.

I couldn't speak.

"John Alex."

Yet another voice, something like a distant echo in the far back canyons of my brain, was telling me I had to come back from wherever I was. "I'm here," I said finally, my voice sounding like a stranger's.

"I see that. Are you sure you are okay?"

"As well as I could be under the circumstances, I suppose. Why are you here? How did you know?" The cleaning person would have found Flossie and alerted the nurses. Pieces of the puzzle would have fit together. Had someone called Sheila?

"You'll have to come with me," she said.

"No," I said. "I think I should just sit here and wait for the consequences."

"What consequences?"

"In there," I said, nodding toward the building.

"I don't know what you're talking about. I suppose you pissed off the hired help again in the home. Don't worry about it. This is more important. You have to come with me."

"How did you find me?"

"I came looking for your truck. You were here."

"Here I am."

"Well, we have to go. I'll get you some coffee or something. You look blitzed."

CHAPTER 28

"WHERE DO WE HAVE TO go?" I asked.

"Halifax," Sheila said.

"I thought you were just there."

"I was. But now I have to go back. And I need to take you."

"Why?"

"I'll explain on the way. I'm sorry to have interrupted your nap or whatever. You're needed, John Alex."

There was no stopping Sheila when she set her mind to a thing. She eased me out of the truck, pocketed my keys which I had not realized were in my right hand and led me to her car, that extravagant looking Subaru she had bought brand new from the dealer in Sydney after the third ice storm of the year last winter. She pulled into the drive-through at Tim Horton's and ordered me a large black coffee and three donuts. "I need you fully awake and well fed," she said, trying to lighten the mood as she pulled back onto the road." I had never thought much about donuts or their value as food, but I bit into one and took a sip of the hot black liquid.

"You were visiting Florence, I suppose," she continued as we left town and the green hills appeared on either side. "How is she?"

It was obvious now that she did not know. How could she? "She's where she wants to be," I said.

"You two go pretty far back, right?"

"Very far indeed. But remember, she's ten years older than me." And I realized I referred to her in present rather than past tense. I decided not to correct myself. "She was almost a teenager when I was still in diapers. But time has a sort of levelling element to it, doesn't it?" Maybe thanks to the caffeine my brain was working well enough to string some words together. I was thinking maybe now was a good time to confess to someone — to Sheila, here, of course — what had just transpired.

"I can picture you in diapers," she said. "I really can."

"Well, maybe I'll be back in them soon enough."

"I doubt it. There's nothing wrong with you. You're healthy as a horse."

I didn't feel healthy. I felt like a man who once knew who he was and now seemed more like someone stumbling around in a wilderness of his own creation. I chewed on my cherry-filled donut. It vaguely reminded me of the cherry pies Eva would make from those sweet canned cherries, so sweet it would make your teeth ache as they did now.

I tried to put Flossie out of my mind. I had helped the old woman die and now was fleeing the scene. I had even left my truck in the parking lot.

"Now tell me, why are you driving me to Halifax?"

"This will be a little hard to explain," Sheila began, looking straight into the windshield as the light was slipping from the world, the sun sinking somewhere into the Gulf of St. Lawrence to our west. "Evie is sick," she continued. "Right after I took her back, Em called to ask if she had been around sick people here. I told her no and she figured it must have been something she picked up at school."

"A bug, as they say."

"A bug, yes. But I'm sure it's worse than that."

"Emily is the one studying health and healing, right? She can handle it."

"Emily is studying to be a naturopath, not a doctor."

"Natural healing, she calls it. I'm all for that."

"I would be too under normal circumstances, but, John Alex, you need to understand this is different. She might have caught this thing — this corona virus thing — from one of her classmates at school. I think Evie might have what they've been talking about on the news."

"I did hear about that on the CBC. Some folks on cruise ships got sick. Something like a flu, this corona virus."

"Like a flu but worse. And it's not just cruise ships and China. It's spreading."

"A new strain I suppose. Every year there seems to be a new one. Never got a flu shot myself. Healthy as a horse like you said, I suppose."

"This is different. And Evie is sick. According to her mother, real sick."

"Her breathing problems?"

"And more. And this new disease is something deadly."

Now it was starting to sink in. "Jesus. That would be terrible if she came down with such a thing. I love that little girl more than life itself. But why are you taking *me* to her? It sounds like she should be in the hospital if it's that serious."

"You're right. She should be. But Emily doesn't get it. And this scares the hell out of me. Remember that she and Brian got into that whole thing about the big pharmaceutical companies making us all drug dependent with their prescriptions and vaccines? How they are all tied in with the medical profession and we're all just being poisoned and sucked dry for the money?"

"I didn't pay that much attention to her. I thought it was just a phase."

"It wasn't. It's why she dropped out of pre-med, didn't finish university and decided to become a naturopath."

"Right, the whole natural healing shtick. Sounded good to me."

"Sounded fine to me too. But this is different. Evie is real sick and her breathing is not good and these so-called natural remedies are not working." Sheila took her eyes briefly off the road and looked at me as she took a deep breath. "Evie is getting worse and Emily refuses to take her to a doctor or a hospital. I tried to talk Emily into setting aside her beliefs for now, for Evie, but she wouldn't listen. Maybe she'll listen to you."

We sat in silence for several miles down the road as the last rays of sunlight disappeared from the sky and I noticed how poor my nighttime vision was, another sign of my body betraying me as I grew older and older.

"And if she doesn't?"

"Then we'll have to do something."

"You think it's really that bad?"

"It is. I saw her. At least I saw her from her phone. On video. And I've been following the news. There's only a few cases of the virus in Nova Scotia right now. And no one really has a handle on it since it is so contagious and so new. Evie should be in a hospital on a ventilator or at least round-the-clock care. And she needs to see a real doctor."

Already, my afternoon seemed a million miles behind me. I pondered if Flossie was the one from that so-called circle that took my place in death. But then, what if Evie was intended to be the next victim?

"I've already talked to Dr. Holbrook," Sheila continued. "If you can't convince Emily to take her daughter to the hospital, we'll bring her back with us."

This caught me off guard. "We can't do that."

"Emily is being irrational. You talk to her. Tell her that kid needs to be in a hospital. You know I would not exaggerate. Holbrook agrees. Evie's breathing was already compromised by her condition. This has made it much much worse. She has a fever that has not gone away. We have no choice. Make Emily see what needs to be done."

* * *

The road to Halifax had never been longer. The burden of responsibility had never been heavier. Was Sheila really considering taking

Evie with us against her mother's wishes? The prospect was almost too bizarre to ponder. And how was it that Holbrook again was somehow attached to this drama, this crisis? I'd just watched the guy shoot a young man twice with a cool, clinical attitude. I'd seen him in a much nastier mood in my kitchen on a dark night. And he was the one who had orchestrated my involvement with Flossie. And with Mason. There was much to consider here, but the pieces didn't fit together all that well.

As we veered off the TransCanada at Truro and merged onto the 101 to Halifax, Sheila turned on the radio and we listened to the national news on CBC. She did this on purpose. She knew what would be on the news. More reports from around the world about this new virus. The word "deadly" was used more than once. Canada, like most other nations, was completely unprepared for what could come next. Overcrowded hospitals, a health system incapable of keeping up with the sick. The elderly would die first, one expert said, but so would those who already had serious respiratory issues. It was like Sheila had somehow conspired to have this report hit me between the eyes right at that moment.

At first, Emily seemed surprised to see us. "Why are you back?" she asked Sheila in a voice that told me there had already been a scene, an argument, lectures back and forth. "And you, John Alex, why are you here? You never come to Halifax."

"Can I see Evie?" I asked. "I hear she's sick."

"Of course you can. Come in," but she glared at Sheila as we walked into the apartment. Evie was asleep but her breathing was laboured. There was an old-fashioned vaporizer puffing out a steamy cloud of something that smelled like mint. I felt the child's forehead and she was burning up. I had no way of knowing if this was just another kid with a common flu or something much much worse. But I trusted Sheila.

"We need to talk," I told Emily.

Sheila sat with Evie while Emily and I retreated to the kitchen and I said my piece. "She needs to be in a hospital. This is serious."

I guess my ability to persuade had not been as powerful as Sheila had led me to believe. Emily launched into a lengthy discourse of the evils of modern medicine and the amazing healing properties of natural medicine, all of it backed up by reports she had read on the internet. She finished by explaining how her schooling had taught her that for every illness that exists, somewhere nature has a cure. And that cures for ills at home are one hundred times better than what can be had in any hospital where the risk of getting a new infection or disease is almost guaranteed. I did not try to counter anything but let her say all she had to say until she wound down and I saw tears form in her eyes. And then she wept. "But I'm scared, John Alex. I'm so scared that Evie will not be okay."

I imagine that Sheila had been listening in because it was then she walked into the room. "Emily, you need to hear this." She held out her phone and on it was a video call of Dr. Holbrook sitting in his office. I knew that young people were doing this thing where they could see and hear each other on their phones but it was the first time I had seen it for myself.

"Emily, I'm Dr. Holbrook, a family physician in Inverary. I've trained as an infectious disease specialist as well so I want you to hear me out." He paused and his image flicked off for a second and then back on. I half expected Emily to push the phone away but instead she sobbed and wiped away her tears. "I see that you are upset," Holbrook continued, "and there is much to be concerned about here. Sheila held her phone up to your daughter. I listened to her breathing. I understand she has a high temperature as well and, if I am told correctly, it has lasted for more than twenty-four hours. Are you listening?"

Emily nodded.

"I urge you take her to the hospital immediately. She may need to go on a ventilator. They'll know what to do."

Emily was shaking her head. "I won't do that. I'm sure you

know that I have my reasons for not wanting to go to the hospital but, more than that, I've heard that the sick ones who are being put on ventilators are the ones who die."

"That's true," he said. "But that's usually because they arrive in hospital too late."

I could see Emily's resolve returning even before she spoke. "I won't take her to any hospital in Halifax."

"Then bring her to me," he said.

"No," she said flatly.

"Then take her with you to John Alex's and I will meet you there. I will not send her to a hospital and you can stay with her every minute. I promise to administer the absolute minimum dosage of whatever she needs and I have a recovery plan that you can live with as a naturopath."

Emily shoved the phone away, knocking it to the floor. As Sheila picked it up, Emily looked at her and asked, "Why should I trust him?" Sheila was about to speak but Emily had already turned to me. "Can I trust this man, this doctor?" she asked.

I looked deep into Emily's eyes and remembered the hurt, alienated young woman who had first come to me when she was pregnant, carrying the beautiful daughter that came into the world in my humble home. I also remembered the Holbrook I had first met in the middle of the night, the night I was convinced I had died and willed myself back to life. But now we had reached an impasse that if not resolved could ultimately be fatal for the child. "Yes," I said. "You can trust him."

CHAPTER 29

IT WAS MIDNIGHT WHEN WE packed Evie into the car, Sheila and Emily on either side of her in the backseat. I was the driver. Part of me realized we were heading in exactly the wrong direction. The care she needed was at the hospital in Halifax and we were taking her a hundred miles away to Cape Breton.

I kept my hands locked onto the steering wheel with my eyes riveted on the road. My nighttime vision was worse than ever but I did not speak of it. I listened as best as I could to every breath ten-year-old Evie took. Each one sounded like work. Occasionally she paused as she breathed and struggled to take the next breath. None of this was good. Sheila and Emily spoke to each other in hushed tones. I couldn't hear what they were saying and, after a while, I thought they must be having a secret conversation I was not meant to hear. Despite understanding the urgency of the situation, I was confounded by this strange and frightening turn of events. I even started to feel sorry for myself, for everything that had transpired on this day. An old man like me should not have to deal with things like this. And, yes, I was bone weary. Tired of everything, wishing I could lie down somewhere and rest. And maybe never have to wake up again to deal with all the pain of living.

The highway miles crept by. Eventually we crossed the Causeway and headed up Highway 19 toward Inverary. The familiar little communities of Craigmore, Judique, Port Hood and Mabou rolled by. But none looked familiar tonight. The houses all seemed dark and sinister.

More than once I wanted to voice my concern or confess that

the day had taken a toll on me and I was too tired to drive. But I realized that would not do. Hands on the wheel. Eyeballs glued to the road ahead. The voice of Eva telling me I could do this. The voice of reason countering her and saying that what we were doing was all wrong.

* * *

As we pulled up my driveway, I could see that the lights were on in my house. Evie was sleeping as the two women carried her into the house. Holbrook greeted us at the door. The house was bright and warm as he had taken it upon himself to come here without asking permission. He had a hospital bed set up in my living room where he had pushed the furniture against the walls. He was wearing the same formal attire that he had worn the night he had first appeared in my house. When he looked at me, I could not read the look on his face. Some may have called it serious concern. But I saw something else.

"You did the right thing, John Alex," he said. "But you should stay away from Evie. This thing is highly contagious."

"Don't tell me what to do," I snapped back. I was dead tired. I did not trust this man and I could not say out loud what I was feeling.

Holbrook motioned to the bed. Sheila and Emily placed Evie on it and tucked her in. He felt her forehead and listened to her breathing, then walked to the sink and washed his hands with dish detergent. "You're all likely to get this, you know?"

I don't think at that point any of us understood how serious this illness was. Maybe Holbrook did, but to most of the world, it was just another flu. "I don't get sick," I countered. "That's how I got to be ninety."

Holbrook didn't like that. "You got to be ninety by sheer luck. If anyone is going to get this, it will be you. You don't know what we're dealing with here."

Right then I hated this man and was certain we had made the wrong decision. I felt like I had betrayed the people I loved. "And you do?"

"I understand that her situation is critical. She should be in a hospital. I don't like this any better than you do. But Sheila explained to me that the girl's mother will not allow it. We're in this together, John Alex, whether you like it or not. All of us in this room. There is a bond between us that has brought us together. So now we each have to do our part."

Here again was that notion about people's destiny linked together, that affinity group thing. Now, as before, I wanted to believe it was all bullshit. "Just make her better. Cure her. Be a doctor. Cut the crap."

"Just what I need, a lecture from an old lunatic like you," he said in a quiet voice but a most unprofessional manner. "This from the man whose ass I saved by putting a couple of bullets into a criminal who was about to kill him. And guess what? When they wheeled that guy into emergency, I was the doctor on call. I had to take those damn bullets out and stitch the bastard up. Do you think he thanked me?"

It was rhetorical question. So here was the rough side of Holbrook his patients didn't see. I was too tired to keep up the conversation, but I needed to know what his plan was. "How is this going to help her? Being here?"

Holbrook took a deep breath, regained his professional demeanour. "I'm going to try to persuade the mother to let me administer something to lower the fever, improve the respiration. And I put a call into to a medical supply agent I know in Sydney. He's going to bring us what we need. I believe it will help immensely. Now get some rest."

I was already asleep on my feet, still roaring mad inside, fearful, angry, uncertain, but I would not leave the room or go to sleep. I would keep a vigil. It was my house, my watch. I made coffee, offered some to everyone. No one spoke for a long time as we listened to the poor child struggling with each breath.

Emily began to cry in the early morning. Sheila consoled her, tried once more to convince her that her daughter needed to be in a hospital where she could get serious medical care.

"I know that if she ends up in a hospital, we will lose her. I know this. I'm certain of it because I feel it in my bones. We can't do that."

Holbrook listened but said nothing. I said nothing. I kept second-guessing myself. When Sheila had first mentioned driving to Halifax, I thought maybe we were going to take Evie against her mother's wishes and do what needed to be done. Kidnap her and take her to the QEII Hospital. But now here we were, in my old farmhouse, waiting for what?

* * *

It was Father Walenga who arrived at dawn with Bradley from the pharmacy in tow. Father Walenga knocked on my door and I went to open it but was stopped by Holbrook with a firm hand to my chest. He then walked across the room and opened the door himself but held his hand up for Father Walenga. "Don't come in," he said.

Father Walenga looked shocked, and I jumped up to shove Holbrook out of the way. "You can't tell someone they can't come into my house," I snapped. "And it is *my* house, not yours."

Father Walenga looked more than baffled.

"We have the machine," he said.

"What machine?" I asked Holbrook.

"Just leave it," Holbrook said.

"No. Come in," I said.

Father Walenga looked at the doctor, at me and then walked in. "I would like to see the girl," he said as he stepped past Holbrook and into the living room. He knelt down beside the sleeping girl and began to pray. Holbrook just shook his head. "This is all wrong," he said.

Bradley was at the door now holding some contraption that looked like an industrial vacuum cleaner. "What the hell?" I said.

"It will help her with her breathing," he said. "Where can I plug it in?"

I didn't like the look of it. Emily's eyes were enormous, and her hands were gripping each other hard enough to make her knuckles white. She saw Father Walenga praying and panicked. "No!" she wailed. "No!" Her shout pulled Walenga to his feet and he waved his hand. "I'm here to help," he said as Emily leaned over her daughter and put her ear to Evie's mouth.

"I thought —" Emily began. I walked over to her and put my hand on her shoulder. I didn't know what to think about all this.

Bradley had found the wall outlet and plugged in the machine. Emily was looking at him with frantic eyes. "What is this?"

Bradley was fiddling with the dials on the machine now, untangling a tube and unwrapping some sort of mask. He was acting very cool and professional in the midst of so much confusion in the room. "It's not a ventilator," he said. "It's really fairly old technology. It concentrates the oxygen that is in the air. It will help her breathe more easily. I've used them before." And then he added, "In India."

Emily was shaking her head and walked to the wall to unplug the contraption. Bradley held up a hand to stop her. "I volunteered in India for a year. There were always too many sick people for the hospitals to handle. We had a community group that bought one of these and we'd go around to houses to help people with respiratory illness. Here." He held the mask up to Emily and then switched on the machine. Emily hesitated as Bradley adjusted the flow of air. "Please," he added.

Emily put the mask over her face and took a deep breath.

"This machine is called an oxygen concentrator. It provides 90 percent oxygen. More than you get from the air itself. Believe me, it helps. It can make a world of difference for your daughter."

Sheila was beside me now, whispering in my ear, "This is good, John Alex. This is good. Let them do this."

I felt that everything happening was somehow wrong. Things were happening over which I had little control and even less understanding. Sheila's words were comforting, but my mind was a swirl of confused thoughts. The room was too crowded, the noise from the machine disorienting. Holbrook stood back as the young pharmacist placed the mask over Evie's face and gently secured it. Then he sidled across the room toward me and asked me to walk with him outside.

I clenched my jaw and shook my head no, but Sheila elbowed me in the ribs and nodded. I followed the man outside into the bright morning sun.

"I gave Evie an injection in the night. Something that will ease her breathing a bit and keep her sedated. But it will wear off. And I may not be here."

"You went against her mother's wishes," I said.

"I did. I did what needed to be done. But now, we are going to have to hope that the machine will do its work."

"But it's just a machine."

"It is. But it will help. It won't cure her, though. This virus is new and extremely virulent. People are dying. There are other cases in Canada now. It will continue to spread. You all are quite possibly going to get it. And if you are one of them, well, it will be worse for you. Maybe you should leave this to the others. They are younger. Stronger. More likely to recover if they get infected."

"I'm not going anywhere," I said defiantly. "I'm staying here."

He almost smiled then. Almost. "I knew you'd react that way. I know you, John Alex. I know you well."

"You don't know me at all."

He sighed. "That's neither here nor there. Stay then. Be the hero."

"I'm no hero."

"None of us are. We're all just doing the best we can with what we have."

"Why did you come to Cape Breton, anyway?"

"Like I told you. I didn't like the way things were going in Montreal. I heard you needed more medical help down here. I wanted to be somewhere that I was needed. But now I don't know."

"What don't you know?"

"I don't know if all the decisions I've made are the right ones."

"None of us do."

"Yes, but I'm a doctor."

"So you say."

"Look, you've told me your story. You died and you came back. And I was somehow there asking you to die, offering some kind of bargain. It sounds like a dream or a legend."

"I did die. I'm certain of it."

"It's possible you had what they call a near death experience."

"I died and I willed myself back and you appeared and said my recovery was, what? Bad timing?"

"I was not there, and I never said any such thing. Look, old man, I could offer up a dozen possibilities of what you experienced. Some form of dementia or maybe even something caused by a small brain tumour. You've done a few crazy things around here. Speaking to your dead wife and all that. I'm not about to diagnose you or try to convince you of what is real and what isn't except to say, what's going on in your house right now is as real as it gets. Everyone seems to think your opinion matters. I don't know why but they do. So, you need to see this through."

I'd been living with the notion that I was old and crazy for at least ten years, but I refused to buy into his bullshit about dementia or brain tumours. Sure, I was feeling crazier than ever right then and, despite his reasonable sounding words, none of this made sense. My vision blurred and I felt a tingling in my fingers and when I looked at this man with the morning sun behind him, I found him frightening. My brain was on fire with trying to understand what was going on.

"Take me, not her," I blurted out. "You explained it, didn't you? We're all tied together and, for whatever godforsaken reason, somebody has to die. So now I'm accepting the deal."

"John Alex, you're not making any sense. This isn't about you. It's about Evie."

I'd lost my ability to speak. I turned and walked back into the house. Inside, Emily walked over to me. "She's breathing a bit better, I think."

Father Walenga was sitting in a chair now with his rosary beads. When he finished, he stood up and signalled to Bradley that it was time to leave. I was still speechless as Bradley spoke to Sheila and Emily about the machine and handed them a card with his phone number. "Keep it running. Call me if there is a problem." They both nodded. Then the two men were out the door and the sound of the oxygen machine filled the air.

I walked over to Evie and put a shaking hand on her forehead. She was still very warm. Her breathing still did not sound normal to me. The mask over her mouth and nose made her look so strange. Then things went foggy for me. I was there but not there. Sheila was speaking to me as she sat me down on the sofa but the words sounded foreign, indecipherable.

CHAPTER 30

THE NEXT TWO DAYS WERE a blur. I found talking somewhat difficult. I felt tired and confused and was well aware that Sheila and Emily were worrying about me now as well as Evie. Sheila tried to convince me that perhaps I'd had some kind of ministroke, a term I'd heard before but never given much credence. She fed me aspirin as Emily scowled, but they both pampered me and I soon realized I was doing little to help the overall situation. Just old and in the way.

The sound of the machine continued night and day. I disliked it at first but counselled myself that it was for Evie and helping her breathe, allowing her to get through some critical phase of this mysterious disease so she could recover and get her childhood back. I could finally convince myself that the thrum of the oxygen concentrator was like an endless mechanical chant, a sad but wonderful drone like the pipes in an old traditional lament. The days passed in a quick succession although I must have been sleeping through much of the daylight hours as well as the nighttime.

On the fourth day of Evie's tenure in the hospital bed in my living room, I was out by the barn feeding the chickens, my mind somewhat clearer, my strength somewhat returning to me. An RCMP cruiser pulled up in the driveway and when I went to the barn door, I could see it was Sealy. He was speaking to someone on his radio and then turned off the ignition and waved a hand to me.

He slowly got out of the car, put on his cap, the way that cops do in the movies, and approached me.

"How's the little girl?" he asked.

"Better, I think."

"That's good. That's good. Back in Halifax, there's quite a few more cases now. Not really any sign of it here yet. But it's coming."

"The plague?" It was the first time I'd said the word out loud.

He looked down at the driveway stones. "I don't think they're calling it that. But I'm supposed to tell you that you all should stay put here and isolate. Not come into town."

"That suits me just fine."

"I knew it would. But pass it on to the others. Bradley said he'd bring you anything you need and leave it outside."

"Makes me think we're like lepers."

"Don't get all Biblical on me now, John Alex."

"Haven't read the Bible in years."

"I didn't just come here to tell you to stay put, though."

"Sealy, ever since you were a little kid, you always showed up with something important to say."

"I never thought about it that way. But you've known me a long time so I guess you must be right."

"At least I'm right about something. That's a bit of a rarity these days."

Sealy looked over at the chickens now pecking about the dirt and eating the cracked corn on the ground in their outside pen. "That still that same old rooster?"

"Jack? Yeah, that's still him."

"He must be the oldest chicken alive."

"Could be. I've lost count. He's survived all these years, I think out of sheer cussedness and a strong stubborn streak."

Sealy smiled slightly. "Kind of like you, I guess."

"Just like me, you young bastard."

He shook his head. "Hey, you can't say that to the law."

"I said it. So shoot me. Or arrest me."

"Jesus."

It felt good to be bantering like this. Sheila and Emily were treating me with kid gloves and I couldn't goof around with them.

They were all wrapped up in caring for Evie, worrying about her and me. But now I was pretty sure I was back on my feet.

"Well, here's the thing. You want to sit down first."

"Don't be an ass, Sealy. I don't want to sit down."

"Okay. Well, I've got a few things I need to say. And I hate delivering bad news."

"A build-up like that only makes it worse."

"It does. I know." He sucked in his breath and finally said his piece.

"Well, I don't know if you knew it, but Florence Henderson passed on a few days ago. I know she was a friend of yours."

"She was and I'm saddened to hear of this." It was beginning to occur to me that Sealy was here because someone at the home had figured out I was the one who had assisted in her death. I can't say I felt scared at that thought but almost curious as to where things would go from here.

"Well, it appears to be some kind of assisted suicide."

"Poor Flossie."

"She was not long for this world. Everyone knew she wanted to end her life. I think she was unable to do it herself. She was a tough old bird so I'm sure she would have done so if she could have."

"She was tough, yes. But a beautiful person, a beautiful soul."

"I don't doubt that for a minute. But because of the nature of her death, it had to be looked into."

"Of course." A peaceful feeling came over me just then, even a kind of clarity I hadn't felt for days. Whatever was to be said next would likely complicate my life and ruin whatever serenity there was to milk out of my days ahead. "Go on."

"Well, Dr. Holbrook had visited her that day. The staff was aware of his visit. The woman at receptions said she remembered it well, that she always looked forward to his kind words and warm spirit."

"That doesn't sound like the doctor I know, but go on."

"Well, no one saw him do it. But when he was questioned by my chief, he admitted to giving her the drug and said that he administered it as well."

I was once again at a loss for words. I wondered why he would say that. "I don't think that's the way it played out."

"Well, he stated that it was him. Florence had requested him to provide her with the means and he did."

"But certainly this sort of thing happens these days. It shouldn't be considered a crime, right?"

"Well, there's a lengthy procedure. Interviews with the patient, a committee that has to make the decision. There was none of that."

"But he didn't do it."

Sealy looked a little baffled now. "How could you know that?"

"I just know. That's all."

"This doesn't have anything to do with your truck being left in the parking lot there, does it?"

I was ready to tell him the truth. But something held me back. Voice of Eva in my head again, maybe. "Just had some engine trouble and decided to leave it there is all."

Sealy shook his head and kicked at some loose gravel under his shoe. "Well, I guess it doesn't matter now. Not really. Dr. Holbrook took his own life not long after he was interviewed. Different drug but same result. It's all a moot point now as to who's to blame."

The news shocked me to my core. "Dr. Holbrook is dead? Why would he do that?"

Sealy hung his head low and stared at his shoe. "I don't know. It's like a thousand other things I've seen in my job. People doing crazy things. I mean, he would have been in a bit of hot water here. And he had that other thing hanging over his head in Montreal. Something pretty much like this. You knew about that, right?"

"I did. But Holbrook was just here a few days ago, helping out with Evie. He got us an oxygen machine. He may have saved the girl's life. That's got to be worth something. He didn't have any reason to kill himself."

Sealy shrugged. "Who knows? Maybe there was a lot more to it. We'll never know. The man seemed okay to me. We all thought he was a bit of a character shooting up that jerk who tried to burn this place down. We even heard that he had to stitch up the guy after putting two bullets in him. Quite the doctor, he was."

I let it all sink in. Tried to make sense of what I knew — and what I imagined I knew — about this strange medical man who had come into our lives. "What about his family? He never said a word about his family."

"No family connections we could find. Found out he came north from West Virginia quite a while back, but it seems everyone from there is already dead. No wife. No kids. Nothing. Sometimes we run into that but it's rare."

I didn't know what to think. "Gonna be some kind of service?"

"Naw. He had a pretty clear will. Cremation. No service. Nothing religious. Nothing at all. Left some money to the local hospital. End of story."

But I knew that for me the story was not over.

The door to the house opened just then. Emily was standing there shielding her eyes from the sun. "John Alex," she yelled. "Get in here. Right now."

CHAPTER 31

I MADE A BEELINE FOR the house, hearing the urgency in her voice. Sealy was right on my heels. When I walked in, it took a few seconds for my eyes to adjust to the light. "What?" I shouted. "What is it?"

"Look," Sheila said, pointing to the hospital bed in the living room.

Evie was sitting straight up. She had the mask off. The room was strangely quiet. "Where were you?" she asked me in a hoarse voice. "I woke up and you weren't here."

"I was just out with the chickens," I answered.

* * *

Holbrook appeared to me once more in the midst of a troubled sleep on a windy night not long after I'd heard the news of his passing. I know that most would say I was having a dream or, topping that, a night terror. I was only vaguely familiar with the term, but I remembered Vin McCallum once telling me about his horrifying experiences when he was trying to kick his gambling habit. First there would be the feeling that you are wide awake. And then the paralysis would set in, followed by something so real and frightening that you'd lose the ability to breathe.

The first thing I realized was that the house was completely quiet. And it was in complete darkness. There was nothing emanating from the nightlight over the kitchen sink that I always kept on at night.

I awoke immediately when he entered my bedroom. The door opened with its usual creak. The floorboards complained of the weight. There was light in the room — an unnatural silvery moonlight but there was no moon in the sky. "The dead don't stay dead," he said — a real voice I am sure. Not just a voice inside my head.

Local stories of ghosts and apparitions never meant much to me. Each of us believes what we want to believe, and it shapes our lives in powerful ways. Eva had stayed with me long after she was gone. She had always been the most welcome of guests in our home. I grieved when she left me for the second time. But here was the most unwanted guest of all.

I tried to prop myself up on my elbow, but I could not move as he approached my bed and did the oddest thing. He knelt down on the floor beside me so that his face was close enough to touch. Even in broad daylight I had found it difficult to look straight at him. His eyes would penetrate deeply into you no matter what the subject of conversation. Now, in the cold silvery light, he glowed with a kind of electric energy that I could feel on my skin.

I tried to roll over and look away but I was paralyzed. Frozen. Unable to move. Unable to take my eyes off him. "Relax," he said. "Just try to relax, John Alex, and go with the flow."

"I can't move," I said. "How did you do this?"

He looked at me with haughty disdain. "I didn't do anything. You did."

I didn't know what he meant but I had a notion or two as to why he was here. "I brought you here tonight, didn't I?"

"You did. More or less."

I gave up trying to raise myself. "Why is it that I can talk?"

"Because we need to have this conversation. We need to tidy up some unfinished details."

"But why is the oxygen machine not working? Why is it so dark?"

"The power is out. Not so bad right here in the valley but strong gusts of Les Suêtes up in Cheticamp, I would guess."

"What about Evie?"

"Evie is okay. I promise you."

That wasn't enough to calm me down, but I could not move let alone get up. I considered shouting out so that Emily and Sheila would wake up but realized that if they did, they would see him as real as he was to me. And I feared that might lead to something worse.

"I promise you," Holbrook continued. "No harm will come to her tonight. This is about you, not her."

I tried to stay calm but my breathing was ragged, laboured.

"John Alex," Holbrook began. I could hear the impatience in his voice. "I'm here because you have unanswered questions. I like to think I'm a man who tidies up loose ends."

It felt like whatever hands were gripping my lungs so tightly had suddenly let go and I could breathe again. "Why did you say that you were the one who administered the shot to Flossie? I don't understand."

Holbrook shrugged and turned his face slightly away toward the window. "I had provided the means to her end. But she had said she didn't want me to do it. She said specifically she wanted you to do the injection."

"Why me?"

"She said you were the only one. The only one who would really understand."

"No, I don't understand."

"Well, don't bother sorting it out. Living is complicated enough without trying to master the lessons of dying. You all sort that out when the time comes, some better than others, but it amounts mostly to the same thing."

"I feel guilty, though, that you took the blame."

"Well, there's a kind of equation to these things. At least that's the way I see it. You were in the circle."

"Right. The circle."

"It's just an expression. The circle, the group, call it a kind of family. Remember, I tried to explain this before. The affinity group. My group was fairly large. I knew others in Montreal who were part of it. Then I came here and there was you and Florence and others. And Evie, of course."

"Evie? How does she fit in?"

"Relax. I brought her the machine, didn't I? I kept an eye on her until I knew she was going to be okay. Ask her sometime what she saw, what she felt, when she was so sick. She understood. Just don't ask her until she is older." He paused and turned his face back toward me. "Well, maybe that was the wrong thing to say. You may not be around."

Him talking about Evie made me nervous, but now the fear was draining out of me. I was still mostly paralyzed but my mind was ablaze. "No, I may not be around. I suppose you can foresee my death?"

"I can foresee many deaths. I think that in part is why I didn't want to hang around for the next few years. They are going to be bad ones, I'm afraid. It would be so hard on a physician. Hard enough as it was. But the coming months … it's just going to be crazy."

"What about Evie?"

"You'll see soon enough. And then, I'll be out of your life. You won't have old Doc Holbrook to pester you anymore."

"Why are you here? Why are you here tonight?"

"Unfinished business, I guess you could say. You probably don't realize this, but I'm a kind of mentor to you."

"Bullshit."

"I know. You're a stubborn old goat, so you need to say things like that. Don't worry, you can't offend me. The dead take little offence."

"That's good to know. If you are my mentor, what is tonight's lesson?"

"You really want to know? Are you sure you're ready for this?"

"Well, I seem to be what they call a captive audience."

"You are indeed. I was thinking we could just chat some more first."

"Please," I said, "spare me the small talk."

Holbrook stood up and, as he did, the light began to fade from the room. I wanted to reach out and hit him but my arms refused to work. I was breathing hard, labouring to put oxygen in my lungs. It was getting harder and harder. When I went to speak now I could not. And then I discovered I was now unable to breathe.

"Goodbye, John Alex. It's been nice to know you."

I didn't hear him leave the room. My eyes were wide open but unable to see. There was no sound. My lungs failed me. The paralysis was complete and that was when I realized I was dying.

The fear swallowed me like an unseen whale. I felt pain but I could not determine where in my body the pain resided. And then the fear and pain translated itself into something else that I have no words for. Something that was not terrible, but so powerful and overwhelming that I could not even begin to relate it to anything I had known in my long life. There was no visual context, only darkness. I was searching for a word to describe it, to understand it. The word that finally came to me then was something very simple: loneliness. A sudden and horrible sense of being totally alone.

But then that changed as well. The loneliness softened, I guess you could say. It melted and I was not alone at all. Close to me were others — people both living and dead whom I had cared for. I could not see them or separate one from the other, but they were definitely there with me. The comfort they provided guided me to something, some place, some feeling that was so overpowering and beautiful that all else completely dissolved and melted away.

At last, and truly for what may have been the first time in my life, and now in my death, I was at peace.

How long this lasted, I have no way of knowing. But then an even stranger thing happened. The warm mass of loved ones started to dissolve and I began to hear a voice. It was the voice of Evie, screaming. Screaming loud and terrible. Screaming my name at the top of her lungs.

And I had no choice but to will myself back to the living.

CHAPTER 32

IT WAS A COOL, CLEAR morning when Evie asked me if we could walk up the mountain to the abandoned village. Her mother was insisting she come along but Evie was equally insistent it should just be the two of us. And there was no arguing with her when she wanted to have things her way. Evie was stronger now but there was still some concern over her breathing. Emily handed me the puffer, the salbutamol, that Evie needed when she was short of breath. Fearful over Evie's recovery and watching the pandemic events unfolding in the wider world, Emily had given herself over to the need for some medical intervention. Her mind was changing about many things.

Evie held my hand as we walked out into the bright sunshine and cool air. I can't say the taste of the morning air had ever been sweeter and, as it filled my lungs, I savoured every second of it. As I looked at the little girl, I believed she felt the same way. Her recovery had been slow at first and then the improvements came quickly. Soon she and her mother would return to Halifax. By the following week, I knew, I would be alone again in my house. I wasn't sure if I was looking forward to it or dreading it.

We had already donated the oxygen concentrator to the nursing home where it was in use with several residents who had contracted the illness. I had stopped listening to the news and decided to keep my contact with others as limited as possible. I was still of the belief that it was sheer stubbornness, cussedness as my mother had called it, that was keeping me alive. Whatever it was, I felt in my bones that I was not intended to die any time soon, despite all that had happened and all that was happening in the crazy world around me.

"I love this forest," Evie said. "I missed it when I was away."

"When you were at home in Halifax?"

"No, when I was sick. I felt like I was away somewhere."

"Where?"

"I don't know. I keep trying to figure it out. I have a theory but that's all it is, a theory."

"Ten-year-old kids usually don't have theories."

"I do. I have many theories."

"Okay, so spit it out, Einstein. Where were you?"

"I was there but not there. I was only slightly aware of what was going on around me, the constant whirr of the machine, you and Sheila and my mom hovering all the time. Worrying."

"We all did a fair bit of worrying."

"You didn't need to."

"It kept us busy," I said.

"Wasted energy. Most worry is just that."

"Another theory of yours?"

"More like an opinion."

"Of which you have many."

"True. But while you were all worrying, I was in this other place."

"There in my house but not there?"

"Yes. It's hard to explain."

"I'm sure it is. Try."

"I love these trees," Evie said, changing the subject. "Black spruce, white spruce, red spruce, hemlock, oak, maple, poplar."

"What's the matter, you don't know the Latin names?"

"If you like, I'll memorize them and teach you."

"You're changing the subject. Let's get back to where you were while recuperating."

"Well, it's hard to explain. But I was in a safe place. I felt that."

"Safe is good."

"I think you all did that for me. You, your house, Sheila, my mom. And there were others but I didn't recognize them. They were kind and encouraging. I needed that."

"We all need people to be kind and encouraging, even strangers."

"But they weren't strangers. They were familiar."

"Could you see their faces?"

"No faces. No, it wasn't like that. All of you were mushed together. Kind of like a cloud."

"Cumulus or cirrus or stratus?"

"Cumulus."

"And this cloud helped you get through your illness?"

"It did."

"I'm glad. I'm truly glad."

That seemed to be the end of the conversation as Evie turned her attention to naming trees and then identifying low-lying shrubs along the rocky path. Our progress up the mountain to the old village was slow but not at all painful. Somehow she knew when to stop so I could catch my breath. When we were almost there, she said we should sit and talk some more so I found us a fallen tree that a mighty wind must have taken down in a storm. It was an ancient oak with deep grooves in the bark.

"That night when I woke up screaming, who was it that walked through the house and went out the door?"

The question took me by surprise. "I think you must have been dreaming."

"It was so dark. I know the machine had stopped working and I was awake. At least I think I was awake. I ripped the mask off my face. At that moment I did not feel safe. I was scared. I screamed."

"I remember your scream."

"I heard footsteps coming from your bedroom and going across the living room to the door. It opened and I felt cold air rushing in. Then I heard the door close and I called out your name. I didn't understand why you were going outside in the middle of the night. It was stormy, I think. Windy. Very windy."

"It was that."

"And then the power came back on."

"It did."

"I was scared but my mom was right there. And then Sheila and then you. But I didn't see you come back in from outside."

I was not about to tell her I had not gone outside that night. When the power had come back on I had gotten up from bed and had felt all cramped up and my face had been wet. My T-shirt was soaked, and I felt chilled. I had gone to check on Evie. Sheila and Emily had looked at me strangely. "Night sweats," I said. "Is she okay?"

"She's okay," Emily said. "She's just scared. Funny that the power going out didn't wake her. The machine stopped. But the power came back on right after she screamed."

Sheila had checked on the oxygen machine and then began to reposition the mask back over Evie's face as she kept pushing it away. She looked confused but she was wide awake as both Sheila and Emily were fussing over her. I had slipped back into my room to change my clothes but when I returned Evie was already asleep again and her mother had fit the mask back over her face and adjusted the oxygen machine.

* * *

When we arrived at the site of the old homesteads, I felt dizzy and had to sit down again. The day had grown darker with a ceiling of low grey clouds. The trees looked even taller than they did on our last visit. Everything on the ground was covered in dew-laden moss that made the place glow. "Isn't it beautiful," I said.

I guess I must have been staring off into space. "What do you see?" Evie asked.

"I see what happens if we all just go away." I didn't have to explain further.

She nodded. "Things just go back to being like they were before we came along."

"Yes."

"Do you think that is the way it will be?"

"You mean like all of us?" I asked.

"We all might get sick and die. I've been listening to the news, you know, since I started getting better."

"I should have put that damn radio in the barn."

"You can't stop an inquiring mind," she retorted.

I smiled, still looking off into the beauty of the forest. "I know that," I said. "Especially in your case. But no, I don't think we'll all just go away. Disease, climate catastrophe, who knows what else. Some of us will still be around."

"But look at this. You told me this was a village. They're all gone. There's hardly a trace."

"You're wrong. I can still see it. The whole town. Look over there." I pointed to a swelling of the ground that I believed to be where the small church had once been. "I believe if we were to dig down right there, we'd find the stone foundation of their little chapel. Probably find some more artifacts as well. And over there. Another foundation. Maybe that one belonging to my great-great-grandfather. All under those layers of moss and fallen trees and soil."

"It's so peaceful here."

"It is. Peace is a fine ending to a place like this. I'm pleased that everyone has left it alone."

"You wouldn't want to dig down and find what is in the basement of that little church?"

"No. Not really. And I wouldn't want anyone else to either. Sometimes it's best to leave the past behind. Leave things as they are."

"But how do I know that you're not just making this up?"

"Well, I'm sitting here with you, aren't I? These houses are all gone and the ones who live here have long since gone into the ground, but I'm still here, talking to you."

"What happened to Dr. Holbrook?" she suddenly asked. "He stopped coming to see me."

"He went away. Told me to tell you goodbye. And he apologized for not saying it himself. But he knew you were better and getting stronger every day. He knew you didn't need him anymore."

"Where did he go?"

"I'm not sure." No, I wasn't prepared to tell her about Holbrook. And there was so much about that man, if he was a man, that I didn't understand and, right now, didn't want to think about.

"You won't go away, will you, John Alex?"

"Where would I go? No place I want to be but here on Cape Breton Island. Down there in my old house. Who would feed the chickens? No, I think I'll stay put."

She gave me a look that nearly melted me into the mossy stone I was sitting on. You're ninety years old, she might have said. You are going to die soon. But she didn't say it.

"Can you see them walking around?" I asked.

"Who?"

"The people who lived here." It was just a game, a diversion, not a vision.

"I think I can. They all seem worried."

"Worried? I see them all smiling."

"The children are smiling. The adults all look worried or unhappy."

"Well, it was a tough old life back then. Maybe the children don't know what they're in for yet." But as soon as I said the words, I felt a prickling on the back of my neck. I was not speaking about the past but the present. The world was not prepared for this new disease, nor was it prepared for the changes happening to the entire planet. None of this was anything I could do a damn thing about. And yes, soon, I would be gone.

"Let's go back," I said.

"Back in time?" she asked impishly.

"No, back to my house. Grilled cheese and tomato soup for lunch, okay?"

"Okay."

* * *

A few days later, Emily and Evie were gone, back to Halifax. I avoided what Evie called "big talk" in her remaining time with me. It was all small talk. Sheila offered to stay on. Once Emily and Evie were out of the house, I told her about the nighttime visits of Holbrook. She listened but did not judge. She encouraged me to get a thorough medical exam, even suggested an MRI scan.

"Brain tumour, dementia, what else?" I asked. "All of the above? What would it mean if any of that turns out to be the case? I'm not going anywhere. If it was a brain tumour or dementia that brought Eva back to me after her death, so be it. If it was also responsible for Dr. Death trying to take me out, then what of it? I'm a tough old critter, remember?" I did not come right out and say that I believed I had died twice and willed myself back to the land of the living. That might have convinced her I was ready for the institution for mad old farts. So I kept that to myself.

"Call me if you need me, John Alex. And don't turn off the ringer on your phone, okay?"

"I promise to leave the damn thing on. Waste of money as far as I'm concerned."

"You're a hard man, John Alex."

"No, I'm not," I heard myself say. "Sometimes I think I'm the weakest of the lot."

"Why would you say that?"

I didn't know. But I didn't feel strong. I felt my age, a sweeping weariness that overtook me and made me feel small, weak and vulnerable.

But I refused to show it. I gave Sheila a hug and she pecked me on the cheek. "Go write another one of your damn books and make it a good one," I said.

"I will," she said, smiling that same smile I'd seen a thousand times over the years. "And what about you? What are you going to do with yourself?"

"That's a very good question. I think I'll do nothing. Nothing at all."

"Good luck with that," Sheila said.

CHAPTER 33

I WAS FAIRLY SERIOUS ABOUT doing nothing. I'd had enough of everything lately and decided it was time to take stock of myself, go about my daily routines as if all was right in the world and spend my afternoons napping. I unplugged the radio and carried it out to the barn. I'd listened to enough of the CBC to know that Holbrook had been right about the infection now sweeping the world. I still worried about Emily and Evie back in Halifax around others who might be carrying the disease, but I reckoned Evie would have developed some immunity to it now that she'd recovered. But what did I know?

Alas, I made the mistake of forgetting to turn the ringer off on the phone. Emily called a couple of times to check on me and so did Sheila. When I asked them both why they were calling, they said they just wanted to make sure I was okay. Truth was, I didn't like that. Just because I was alone in my own home, it didn't mean that anyone should be concerned. They should well know I could take care of myself. I tried not to let on that I was annoyed by the questions but I guess it showed.

When the phone rang again, and I heard Sealy's voice on the other end of the line, I barked, "What now, goddamn it?"

"Good morning to you, too, John Alex. You didn't need to bite my head off."

"Sorry, Sealy. Just practising my grumpy old man routine, still hoping to get a role in one of those Hollywood movies."

"Well, you're doing a pretty good job of it. I'd hire you if I was directing."

"Cut the flattery, Sealy, what is it you want now?"

"Okay. Okay. Well, here's the thing. I've been worried about those two boys alone out on that island. I mean we hauled Mason out of there once and he might have died of gangrene if we hadn't. And that punk kid, Fowler, I mean, I should have arrested him and had him safely incarcerated somewhere. The thing is, I'm feeling some responsibility for them. I wake up in the middle of the night and wonder if they're out there starving or already dead."

"I can see that but, Sealy my lad, you can't watch out for every-one. You did good, so let it be."

"That doesn't seem to work for me. My wife says the same thing. But I need to know they're okay."

"Well then, go out there and check on them. Don't pester me about it."

"Yeah, I know. But there's this one other thing."

"And what would that be?"

"Chester Wilkes from over at the funeral home, he asked me to call you."

"What? That young bastard looking for more work? He was on my case five years ago about getting an order in for some fancy-ass coffin. I told him to shove it up his ass then and I'd say it again now. What the devil is he involving you for?"

"It's not about you. It's about Dr. Holbrook."

"I don't see how that concerns me."

"Well, apparently, it does."

"How's that?"

"Well, the doctor left a note. Not much to it really. No real explanation as to why he did what he did. But the thing is, he asked that his ashes be spread at sea."

"Good for him. I don't see much problem with that. Just take what's left of the bugger and head on down to the beach when the tide's going out and give it a good toss."

"But there was more to it. He specifically said he wanted you to take them out far from shore and do the deed."

"Me?"

"You. Do you have any idea why? I never thought you two were that close."

"We weren't."

The line was quiet. In my opinion, there's nothing worse than having to talk to people on the phone or worse yet, listening to the phone when no one is talking back.

"Look, John Alex, I thought we could kill two birds with one stone, pardon the expression. We could take Kern's boat. He's still down in Florida and says he's not coming back any time soon. He's got a girlfriend down there now, he says."

"I thought he was married."

"Well, not anymore."

"Kern's an idiot."

"That's neither here nor there. The point is, we can use his boat."

"We?"

"Jesus, man. Yes, *we*. Dr. Holbrook wanted you to spread his ashes at sea. Are you deaf?"

"Partially."

I was a little surprised that Sealy was getting impatient with me, but I guess I was working too hard at being the stubborn old goat I aspired to be. I cleared my throat and gave myself a full second or two for consideration.

"So you were thinking we could do a two for one. Dump the doctor's mortal remains and check up on the two lads playing survival out there?"

"That's right. We could be out and back in a morning. Bradley said he'd come along to help check on Mason and Fowler. He feels a kind of responsibility as well. He plans on buying food and some other things to take out."

"And when were you hoping to mount this expedition?"

"Tomorrow," he said.

"I'm busy tomorrow."

"Doing what?" The edge was back in his voice now.

I held the blasted phone out in front of me and scowled at it like it was some evil thing. I didn't have an honest answer. More phone line silence to rattle my nerves. "I'll meet you at the wharf at seven tomorrow," I said reluctantly.

I heard Sealy suck in his breath. "Much appreciated," he said. "See you then."

* * *

I woke up early the next day when darkness still ruled the world. It was quiet in the house as I made coffee. When I sat at the kitchen table, I had a brief instant where I was certain that Eva was back with me again. It was just a quick flash but it warmed my heart. I was convinced she was there, as real as real could be. And then she was gone. But not before I had taken down another cup, her favourite teacup that was still on the shelf, and filled it with coffee for her.

The loneliness settled over me again as I could not will her back into the room. And then an even more terrible notion. She had been gone so long that our marriage seemed like something from another life. It was as if it was someone else, not me, but another man who had married her and lived with her during those good years before she was taken away.

The first ray of morning sun from the east was streaming through the window now. I wanted to sit there for a very long time, trying to bring back the memory of those long-gone days. I wanted to sit there and remember. Sit there and do nothing. Nothing at all.

But the old rooster crowed. Jack was doing his work, what he did every blessed day of his life, ever since he arrived here. Doing what was in his nature.

Which is what I needed to do.

I picked up Eva's cup, took a long gulp from it and then set it by the sink. My feet took over and walked me to the door.

* * *

Bradley and Sealy were waiting for me on Kern's boat just as planned. The engine was already running. They both smiled broadly when they saw me drive up in my truck and then walk toward them. Once on board, Bradley untethered the boat from the dock and Sealy steered us out of the little harbour.

The water was like glass. The sun was warming the world and welcoming us to sea. "Where is he?" I asked.

Sealy pointed to a fairly ordinary wooden box sitting on the deck.

"Nothing fancy, I see."

"Nothing fancy," Sealy said. "Let me know when you want to do it."

"Later," I said.

We arrived at the island after a most pleasing cruise from Inverary on a morning that was as calm and clear as any I'd ever witnessed along these shores. The three of us took the little dory ashore with Bradley's supplies where Mason and Fowler greeted us, looking as happy and healthy as could be.

They didn't appear at all surprised at our arrival. Sealy kept asking them questions about how they were doing and they both just kept shaking their heads, saying everything was just fine. Mason showed off the living quarters that they had improved during their time here and Fowler proudly explained in great detail their diet of food mostly provided by the sea. Mussels, haddock, mackerel, sea urchins, various kinds of seaweed. Edible wild plants. "Nothing but the best ingredients," he said.

Sealy asked them if they wanted to return to the mainland for a while or even for good and they both smiled, laughed and looked like he had just said something truly ludicrous.

"We're happy here. We have most everything we need," Mason said. "We have each other. We don't need anything else."

I was baffled, and I think Sealy was too. Two young men, living together, away from the rest of the world on an island legendary for turning lightkeepers into lunatics. One a former drug addict, the other the son of a hermit. How could this be?

Bradley was shaking his head and smiling. He seemed to understand.

We unloaded the food and blankets and other supplies we had brought. Fowler and Mason hugged us and Mason said, "Thanks for coming. Everything okay back there?" He nodded toward the mainland.

I was about to speak but Sealy shot me a look that shut me up. Bradley kicked at the pebbles on the beach.

"Everything's just fine," I said. "Life as normal. Nothing's changed."

"Good," Fowler said. "That's as it should be."

On the way back, a slight breeze came up out of the west, warm air with the scent of fish and salt. "Don't forget about the wedding," Bradley said. "I haven't sent out the invitations yet but you're invited."

"I wouldn't miss it for the world," I said.

Halfway back to Inverary I asked Sealy to cut the motor. As we drifted, I breathed in the salty air, savoured the bright vision of the open sea and the sound of small waves lapping against the hull.

I lifted the wooden box, opened the lid and, I don't know why, but I touched the ashes inside. Powdery, whitish grey. Some of the ashes clung to my old wet bony fingers and I touched them to my face. How strange, I thought, that this is what we amount to when we come to the end of our days. Sealy and Bradley must have thought this was some antiquated ritual because they did the same until all three of us had a single streak of pale ash on our cheeks.

I wasn't about to speak to them about what I knew or believed about Dr. Holbrook. It was all so unclear to me as to who he really was and why he had come to Inverary. What was most unclear was why he had taken his own life.

"Here's to the death of death," I found myself saying. I'm sure it sounded strange to my two shipmates. But it felt like the right thing to say.

"To the death of death," Bradley repeated.

I stepped forward and leaned against the gunwale and, as the two of them looked on, gently dispersed the ashes into the sea. We watched as the ashes spread slowly across the surface of the water and drifted away.